THE STARTER WIFE

ROWEN CHAMBERS

The Starter Wife

By Rowen Chambers

PROLOGUE

Lauren

"Mrs. Bishop." An older man stands at the doorway of my hospital room. "I'm Detective Myles, the investigator assigned to your case. The nurse said you were up for answering a few questions?"

"Of course." I push myself up to a seated position and pull the thin white hospital blanket up to my waist as the detective walks over to my bed.

"I'd like to ask you about the pill you took," the detective says. "The one that caused you to end up here."

"I didn't take it. It was given to me."

"Yes, I understand." He takes out a small notepad and pen. "Mrs. Bishop, do you remember what happened before you passed out? Let's start from when you woke up."

"I had breakfast, watched TV. My leg was hurting and kept me up all night so around nine I took a pill to help me rest."

"What kind of pill? Do you remember?"

"Just an over-the-counter sleep aid."

"And Hannah, your home health care nurse. She's the one who gave you the pill?"

"No, I took it myself. Hannah had already left to go into

town." I run my hand over the thin, scratchy hospital blanket. Why can't they get better blankets? Ones that are soft and warm and provide comfort when you're stuck in a cold, sterile hospital bed.

"And what happened next?" Detective Myles asks.

"I woke up an hour later and heard someone in the house. I thought it was my friend Audrey. I'd asked her to stop by that morning."

The detective jots down some notes. "But it was Hannah you heard in the house. Is that correct?"

"Yes. She came into my room and asked how I was feeling. I told her I was in a lot of pain."

"And did she offer you a pill?"

"Yes. I didn't want to take it, but the pain was more than I could bear."

Detective Myles scribbles something down on his notepad, then looks up at me. "Where was your husband when all this was happening?"

"He was in Boston. He'd been there all week. He'd planned to come home Friday night but had to work late and said he'd drive back Saturday afternoon."

"Leaving you alone with Hannah."

I cock my head to the side. "Detective, what are you trying to say? That Hannah did this to me?"

"I'm not saying *anything*. I'm simply trying to gather information. But Hannah did give you the pill and was the only person there when it happened."

"Those pills have been on my nightstand for weeks, since the day I got home from the hospital after the accident. Anyone could've switched them out."

"Is that what you believe happened? That it was someone other than Hannah?"

"I hired Hannah myself. Do you really think I'd hire a woman who would try to kill me?"

Detective Myles clears his throat. "Mrs. Bishop, perhaps you didn't know, but Hannah was—"

"I'm aware of that, detective. But believe me, Hannah would never hurt anyone, at least not intentionally."

"You've only known this woman a few weeks."

"Yes, and in those few weeks, she's taken very good care of me."

"Until she gave you a pill that could've ended your life."

"Detective Myles, no offense, but you're going down the wrong path. Hannah isn't the reason I'm in this hospital bed." I glance away, then look back at the detective. "I know who did this to me. And this isn't the first time he's tried to kill me."

1

ONE MONTH AGO

LAUREN

"Are you sure you don't want me to stay?" Steven asks, looking down at me in the bed. "I feel like I shouldn't leave you alone."

"I'll be fine." I smile at him, reassuringly. "Audrey will be here in a few minutes. I can make it that long without help."

"I wish you'd let me hire that woman they sent over." Steven walks up to the mirror above the dresser and adjusts his tie. "She seemed very capable, and the agency said she had excellent references."

"She was in her seventies. She was far too old to help me if something happened. What if I slipped in the shower? She wouldn't have the strength to pick me up."

"I suppose you're right," Steven says, running his hand along his chin as he admires himself in the mirror.

"I want a nurse who's closer to my age. Someone I can talk to." I sit up in bed, cringing at the pain from my bruised ribs. "After all, she's going to be living here, spending all her time with me. I'd like to find someone I can relate to."

"Of course. I understand." Steven turns away from the mirror. He's so handsome, even more than he was on our wedding day, 12 years ago. He was handsome then, but in a boyish way. Now, at 36, his face is slimmer, his jawline more pronounced, and his dark hair is flecked with gray. The suit he's wearing fits him perfectly. Steven is very picky about his clothes. If the fit is even the slightest bit off, the item goes straight to the donation box.

"I'll let you know how the interview goes," I say.

"Will Audrey be with you?"

"No, she has a meeting at ten. It'll just be me."

"Well, I hope this woman works out." He walks to the door. "Call me if you need anything."

"I will."

He leaves the room and I hear his dress shoes clicking on the wood floor as he walks quickly out the door to his car. Steven works in Boston, an hour's drive from here, more with traffic. I told him he could stay there on nights he has to work late, but he insists on making the drive back to Maine to be with me.

After the accident, I decided I wanted to recover here, at our cottage in Maine. With its three bedrooms, three baths, and the room Steven uses as a home office, it's more of a house than a cottage. It sits on a cliff overlooking the ocean. From my bedroom window I can see the waves—large, cresting waves crashing against the sand. They seem angry, or maybe I'm just imagining that because it's how I feel as I lie here, helpless and grieving.

"Lauren?" Audrey's voice rings through the house. "Lauren, it's me."

She always announces herself like that, as if I don't know the voice of my best friend.

"There you are." She appears at my door, smiling.

I smile back. "Where else would I be? I can't exactly go anywhere." I glance down at my leg, which is in a cast that goes all the way up my thigh and has metal pins sticking out of it with a circular metal frame holding them in place. It looks like something out of a science fiction movie.

Audrey walks up to me and hands me one of the cups she's holding. It's a caramel latte from my favorite coffee shop, a little place downtown that's locally owned by a woman who also teaches yoga. I took classes from her last summer.

"How are you feeling?" Audrey sits on the chair beside my bed.

"The same. But I'm getting better at sitting up on my own. That's progress." I sip my latte. "This is amazing. Thank you for going there."

"Of course. I'd bring you one every day if I could." She checks her phone and sighs. "Five more messages from Ryan. The man is insufferable. I wish I'd never signed him as a client." She sets her coffee down and texts him back.

Audrey owns a public relations agency that mainly works with corporate executives. It's a small boutique agency which is intentional. Only taking on a few clients at a time creates exclusivity, making people want to work with her, especially wealthy people who try to buy their way to the top of her waiting list. Ryan, a rich software-company owner in Boston, was one of those people.

Audrey sets her phone down and picks up her coffee. "So is the agency sending over a new nurse today?"

"No, I've decided not to use them. I found someone else."

"Who?" she asks, her brows drawing together in concern. The way Audrey worries about me, sometimes she feels more like my mother than my best friend.

"A woman I found online." I set my coffee down.

"From what agency?"

"It wasn't an agency. I found her through her nursing school. They have an online job board where people can post jobs. I put a post up a few days ago and found Hannah. She's 24 and lives in Boston, but is willing to move here for the job."

"You can't be serious," Audrey scoffs.

"What do you mean?"

"You can't trust people you find online. This girl could be a psychopath."

"Relax. I did some checking and she is not a psychopath. She has no criminal record. She used to work at a hospital but quit and is looking to do home health care instead."

Audrey sets her cup down. "You're not really going to hire this girl?"

"I might. I have an interview with her in an hour."

"And Steven's okay with this?"

"Steven said it's my decision. After all, I'm the one who will be spending all my time with her. Steven will only see her when he's home from work."

"But isn't he concerned? To have some girl living here that hasn't been vetted by an agency? I can't see him being okay with that."

"He'd rather have me choose someone from the home health care agency in town, but the nurses they've sent over either don't want a live-in position or are much older than I'd like. I need someone young and fit who can help me get around. And she has to be willing to make my meals and keep the house picked up. There aren't a lot of people willing to do that."

"Exactly, so what's wrong with this girl? Why is she agreeing to do this?"

"Because she wants a job. And I'm sure she finds the salary appealing. It's much more than she'd make at a hospital or clinic."

Audrey shakes her head. "I don't trust her. What normal young woman wants to give up her life in the city, move to small town Maine in the middle of winter, and spend all her time here, in this house? She'll have no friends. No social life."

"She'll make friends. I'll give her time off. She won't be working every second of the day."

"Okay, so she has a night off. What's she going to do? This town shuts down at ten, or more like eight in the winter."

"Maybe she's not someone who likes to go out. I think she'll like living here. It'll be a nice break from the city. That's why Steven and I moved here. And how I convinced you to."

"For the summers. I never planned on being here in the winter."

Hearing her say that, guilt creeps over me. "Audrey, you know you don't have to—"

"Lauren, no." She grips my hand and moves to sit beside me on the bed. "I didn't mean that. You know I want to be here for you. I only said that because this was supposed to be a place we went during the summers." She sighs. "It was stupid of me to say. I wasn't thinking."

"It's fine." My eyes meet up with hers. "But you know I don't expect you to do this. You should be in Boston. You have a house there. A job. Friends."

"You're the only friend that matters right now. And I'm not leaving you when you're bedridden and about to hire some psychopath you found online who claims to be a nurse." She rolls her eyes. "I might have to move in to protect you."

I laugh, but then stop because of the pain it causes my bruised ribs. "I wish you'd reconsider. Driving to Boston every day is dangerous this time of year with all the snow and ice. I don't want to lose another friend in a car accident." I choke on my words, then clear my throat.

Audrey frowns. "I miss him too."

She does, but not like I do. She'll never understand how much I miss David, or why.

"Anyway," I say, not wanting to talk about him. "Maybe you could stay in Boston during the week and just be here on weekends."

"I can't." She gets up from my bed and returns to the chair. "I gave Barry the house."

"You *what?*" I ask, certain I must've heard her wrong. She loves that house. I can't imagine her giving it up.

"It was either the house or pay him alimony, so I gave him the house."

Audrey and her husband Barry split up a year ago but the divorce isn't final. They don't have children so the divorce should've been simple but things keep coming up to delay it being finalized.

"Barry wanted alimony?" I ask.

"His lawyer convinced him he did, which is ridiculous because if he wanted to, Barry could make three times what I do."

Barry's a doctor but he works for a non-profit clinic that doesn't pay him much. I admire him for doing it, but it always bothered Audrey that he refused to get a better paying job.

"But you love that house," I say. "Are you sure you want to give it up?"

She shrugs. "I'm sick of fighting. I just want the divorce to be done. And honestly, I hate being in that house. It's where my marriage fell apart. I don't need to be surrounded by those memories."

"So is that the real reason you moved here? Because you gave Barry the house?"

The hurt expression on her face fills me with remorse. I shouldn't have said that. I know she moved here for me, and I know it was a huge sacrifice for her. I should be grateful, not accusing her of only being here because she needed a place to live.

"How could you ask me that? You know how much I care about you. When I heard about the accident—"

"I know," I rush to say. "I shouldn't have said it."

Her phone rings, startling us both. She checks it. "It's Ryan again." She gets up from her chair. "I'm sorry, but I have to go."

"Yes. Go. Drive safe."

She leans down and gives me a gentle hug, knowing how much pain I'm in. "Call me if you need anything."

What I need, she can't give me. Nobody can. But she doesn't know that. She doesn't need to. He's gone. And never coming back.

2

LAUREN

"Mrs. Bishop?" a voice answers.

"Yes, I'm here. Just give me a minute." I click on the webpage to bring up the video. It appears and I smile when I see she looks just like her photo online. Porcelain skin, pale pink lips, soft blue eyes, silky blond hair. It's like I'm looking at a younger version of myself. The only difference is the innocence on her face and the uncertainty in her eyes. I'd been stripped of that long before my twenties. It's why I made the choices I made, ones I never imagined would lead me here.

"Hello Hannah." I smile to put her at ease. "It's nice to meet you. I wish it could've been in person, but perhaps that'll be next if things work out."

"Yes." Her lips twitch up to a smile and her eyes dart around. She seems nervous, but she shouldn't be. It's just a job interview, something she's probably done many times since finishing nursing school. "So how are you, Mrs. Bishop? I mean, how are you feeling?"

"Not great, but that's to be expected so soon after the accident. My doctors assure me the pain will subside in a week or two." I look directly at her eyes until I catch her gaze, but she quickly glances away. "So tell me about yourself."

"Um, well, I received my nursing degree a couple years ago, but I guess you already know that." She laughs a little. "After that I worked at a hospital, mainly with patients recovering from surgery."

"And you decided the hospital setting wasn't for you. Is that correct? That's why you quit?"

She shifts in her seat, turning slightly to the side. "Yes." She clears her throat. "It just wasn't for me."

"And what exactly didn't you like about it?"

"There were too many patients. I couldn't give them the attention they needed. I felt like they weren't getting the best possible care." Her voice cracked on those last few words. She's either a very sensitive girl who really cares about her patients or there's something she's not telling me.

"Are you okay?" I ask.

"Yes." She quickly smiles. "Sorry. I get emotional sometimes when I think about patients not getting the care and attention they deserve. That's why I want to work in home health care. So I can dedicate my time and care to a single patient."

"And tell me again, Hannah, why this particular job appeals to you."

She shrugs. "It's short-term, so it's a good way to test whether or not this type of job is right for me. I think it is, but you know how it goes. Sometimes you're not sure if something's right for you until you try it."

I'm always sure. I just choose to not always do what's right for me. But Hannah's someone who seems lost and uncertain about her path. She doesn't know herself well enough to know what's best for her. Perhaps she had overbearing parents who made all her decisions, leaving her insecure and open to suggestions from those who don't have her best interests at heart.

"Your job posting said the position was for two months?" she says. "Is that correct?"

"It depends on how my recovery goes. My leg was broken in multiple places. It'll take time to heal to the point I can get around on my own. Is that an issue? The uncertain time frame?"

"No, not at all," she rushes to say. "I'm happy to stay as long as you need me."

She's so eager to please. So fearful of rejection.

"Do you have any concerns about living here?" I ask. "I must warn you it's a very small town with not much to do. That's even more true now in the winter months."

"I'm actually looking forward to being in a smaller town. The city is getting to be too much for me with all the noise and the traffic."

"How would you fill your time here? On your days off?"

That's really none of my business, which is why I asked. I want to see her response.

"I like to read. Watch TV."

That's all she does? Reads and watches TV? When I was her age, I wanted to be out every night, meeting people, being seen. Steven was the same way. It's why we were such a good match.

"Mrs. Bishop, can I ask you something?" Hannah says in the hesitant, weak tone that I'm starting to realize is just her normal speaking voice.

"Of course. What is it?"

"I'm just wondering why you chose to recover there instead of your house in Boston?"

I pause a moment. "How did you know I own a house in Boston?"

"I, um, looked you up online. I hope that's okay. It's just that you can never be too careful these days and—"

"And what did you find?"

"Just some articles about your husband. They said his business is here so I just assumed you have a home here."

"We do. Our main home is in Boston. This is our summer cottage, or that's what it was intended to be. Winter's not the best time to be here, but I find it more relaxing here than in the city. It's so peaceful, looking out at the waves. It distracts me from the pain."

"I understand. I guess I was just thinking about your recovery. I don't know much about the town you're living in, but the medical care here in Boston has to be better than where you're at. Is there even a hospital nearby?"

"It's a half hour away, but I don't need a hospital. I need a place I feel comfortable that allows me to relax and recover."

"Of course," she says, sounding nervous, like she's worried her question offended me. "I totally get that. I was only asking out of concern for your health, but of course you've already considered that. I don't know what I was thinking." She laughs a little and fidgets with her hands.

"Let's move on," I say. "Tell me more about your training."

She rambles on about her schooling and her experience at the hospital. I should be listening more closely, but I find my mind drifting as she talks. To be fair, I do this with everyone. Most people bore me. Combine that with the pain meds I'm on that put me to sleep and it's a wonder I'm even aware that she's talking. My eyes flutter closed until her words suddenly wake me up.

"What was that about your mother?" I ask.

"She fell down the stairs and died," Hannah says, in the same casual tone one might use to describe what they had for lunch.

"Your mother is dead," I confirm.

"She died when I was 18." Hannah glances away before looking back at the camera. She looks directly at me for the first time since the call began. "It's why I became a nurse. I tried to help her, but I couldn't. I didn't know what to do."

"You were there when this happened?"

"I found her when I got home from school. She was in the basement. She was taking a load of laundry down when she fell. By the time I got there, she was unconscious. Just lying there on the concrete floor. I called for an ambulance but by the time they got there, it was too late."

"So you weren't able to talk to her before..."

"No." Hannah shakes her head. "It was awful. I felt like I should be doing something, but I didn't know what. That's when I decided I was going to be a nurse."

Her hands have stopped fidgeting and her eyes aren't darting around. She seems eerily calm compared to how she was just moments ago.

"How do you know she was doing laundry?" I ask.

"What do you mean?"

"You said your mother was doing laundry. How do you know that if your mother was unable to talk?"

"Because of the clothes. They were scattered all over the place. And the basket was upside down beside her."

"I see." I give her a sympathetic smile. "Well, I'm very sorry that happened. I lost my mother as well. She died of breast cancer when I was 21."

"But your father's still alive?"

"I don't know. He took off before I was born. My mother never heard from him again. What about yours? Does your father live in the area?"

"He died when I was ten."

So she has no parents. Is that why she's so unsure of herself? Because of a lack of parental guidance? It's interesting how the two extremes—overbearing parents and a lack of parents—can create a child who lacks confidence and has poor self-esteem.

"I'm surprised you didn't ask," Hannah says.

"Ask what?"

"How he died." She looks down at her hands. "People always ask. I'm surprised you didn't."

"Would you like to tell me?"

Her eyes slowly rise back to mine. "He jumped off a building. Killed himself."

"Oh God, that's terrible," I blurt out, then realize that's probably not the best thing to say. The words just came out as I imagined this man jumping to his death.

"He was schizophrenic," Hannah explains, in the same casual tone she used when telling me about her mom. "The meds they gave him didn't seem to help. My mother said his death was probably for the best. You know, to put him out of his misery."

Her mother told her it was for the best that her father committed suicide?

"I know it sounds bad," Hannah says, as if she knew what I was thinking. "But my mom only said it to protect me. She didn't want me thinking it was my fault."

"Why would you think it's your fault?"

"It's just what kids think. They assume everything's their fault."

I didn't. As a child, I never assumed blame for an adult's actions. I was very aware that adults made mistakes. While other children looked up to them and saw them as role models, I studied them, listened to their lies, watched them screw up, time and time again.

"I got us off track," Hannah says with a nervous laugh. "I only brought up that story about my mom to explain why I got into nursing. Please, Mrs. Bishop, continue with your questions."

"Actually, I'm done with the questions."

"Oh." Hannah's head drops and her shoulders slump. "I understand."

"Hannah, I'm giving you the job."

Her head jerks up, her pale blue eyes filled with excitement. "You are?"

"If you're still interested."

"Yes! Absolutely! When would you like me to start?"

"Tomorrow, if possible. Do you have much to move?"

"I was just planning to bring my clothes. I have someone wanting to sublet my apartment and I told him I'd leave the furniture. I'll call him right now and let him know he can move in."

"Why don't you wait until tomorrow? Come here in the morning. We can meet in person and kind of try things out for the day. You can see the house, maybe drive around town. Make sure this is a good fit for you."

"Yes, of course. I'll do that."

I smile at her willingness to do whatever I suggest. "It was very nice meeting you, Hannah."

"You too, Mrs. Bishop. What time should I be there tomorrow?"

"I'll text you the details later today. Goodbye, Hannah." I hit the button to turn off the camera and end the call.

I lay back in bed, pleased with myself. Hannah is lost, alone, unsure of herself, easily swayed by suggestion, and desperate for someone to notice her.

She's perfect. Exactly what I was looking for.

3

LAUREN

"I can't believe you hired this girl without meeting her," Audrey says the following morning as she brings me my coffee.

"I *did* meet her." I take a sip of the coffee. "She was very nice. She's a little shy, but I think she was just nervous."

"Meeting her online is not the same as in person." Audrey sits down on the chair by my bed. "The woman is going to be living with you. She'll be here with you all day. Sleeping in your house at night."

"You worry too much. She's not dangerous. She's just a young girl who wants to get out of the city and try something new. You know how it is at that age. You're experimenting. Trying new things."

"I wouldn't know. My carefree days were over by that age. I was working eighty hours a week and you were..." She pauses as she tries to think of a way to describe my life without insulting me.

"Being a pathetic doting wife to my workaholic husband?" I say, knowing it's what she wants to say but won't.

"I never once judged you for not working. I don't know why you would even say something like that."

"Because it's true." I set my coffee down. "Do you really

think I didn't notice how you looked at me when I married Steven and decided not to get a job?"

"I was surprised, yes, but I didn't judge you for it. If anything, I envied you." She sips her coffee.

"Why? You love working. You'd go crazy being home all day."

"I wouldn't be home. I'd go to yoga. Go out for lunch. Maybe volunteer somewhere. I could get used to not working." She rolls her eyes. "Unfortunately, I married the one doctor who insists on not making money."

"Barry makes money."

She just looks at me, like that statement doesn't deserve a response.

"Okay, yes, he doesn't make what most doctors do," I say. "But he's helping people. People who can't afford medical care. That's admirable."

"Are you seriously sticking up for the man who took my house? The dream house that was mostly paid for by me?"

"You're right," I say, apologetically. "I blame the pain meds. I don't always know what I'm saying when I'm taking them."

"The man is horrible. I can't believe I ever married him."

I'm surprised Barry wanted the house. Audrey's the one who insisted on buying it. Barry thought it was too big and extravagant. He's not the least bit materialistic. I'm guessing it was his lawyer that insisted he take the house.

I've always liked Barry. He isn't sophisticated or strikingly handsome like Steven, and he's definitely not as driven as my husband, but he has a quiet, kind soul that's easy to be around. Audrey, on the other hand, is very high strung. A true Type A, which always made her and Barry seem like an odd match.

"Going back to this girl," Audrey says, tugging down the sleeve of her creamy white cashmere sweater. "What's her name again?"

"Hannah. Hannah Reese."

"Did you ask her anything personal? Like about her family?"

"A little. Unfortunately, her parents passed away and it doesn't sound like she has any siblings."

"Her parents are dead?" Audrey asks in a suspicious tone. "How did they die?"

"I didn't ask," I say, knowing if I told her she'd be even more suspicious of Hannah. I will admit I felt a chill go through me when Hannah mentioned her father's suicide and her mother falling down the stairs. I think it was her casual tone when describing it that bothered me the most, but perhaps that's her coping mechanism. Talking about it in an unemotional way may be her way of dealing with her parents' deaths.

"There's something not right about this." Audrey gets up from her chair and goes out to the hall.

"Not right about what?" I call out. "Where are you going?"

She returns holding a plaid wool blanket, one my mother gave me years ago.

"You look cold." She drapes the blanket over my legs.

"You worry about me too much."

"I have to. You're far too trusting." She puts her hands on her hips and turns to me. "What if she's one of those mentally deranged people that comes off as normal but it's all an act? That's not as uncommon as you think. In fact, I just saw a story about it on the news."

"You need to stop watching the news. That's why you can't sleep at night. You think someone's going to break in and kill you."

She sighs. "It's worse now that I live alone. At least when Barry was there, I could sleep through noises in the house. Now I wake up every time I hear even the slightest creak."

Just then, the wind blows and we hear a door slam.

I look at Audrey. "Did you leave the door open?"

"No. Of course not."

"Did you lock it?"

"I think I did." She glances at the hall. "I'll go check."

"Be careful," I tell her as she leaves.

I'm sure the door slamming was nothing, but Audrey's making me paranoid with all her talk about crazy people.

"It was the wind," she says, coming back into my room. "The back door wasn't locked. It must not have been closed all the way and the wind blew it shut."

"That's strange."

"What's strange?" She sits down and picks up her coffee.

"We almost never go out that way, at least not in the winter. We either go out the garage or out the front door."

"Maybe Steven went out back this morning and forgot to lock it."

"Why would he go out back before work?"

She shrugs. "To check on something? Maybe he heard a noise. I wouldn't worry about it. It's locked now. So going back to this girl, please tell me you at least did a background check on her."

"Yes, of course," I lie.

In most cases I would have, but not for Hannah. She fits all my criteria. The chances of finding someone else as perfect as her are slim to none. She seems completely harmless, and it's only for a couple months, maybe less if things work out the way I hope they do.

"So when is this girl showing up?" Audrey asks, checking her phone. "I have to leave soon."

"I told her to be here at nine." I check the time. It's five after nine.

"She's late," Audrey says. "On her first day. That's not a good sign."

"She probably hit traffic. You know how it is getting out of the city."

"She should've left earlier."

The doorbell rings.

"That's her," I say as Audrey gets up. "Be nice."

She smirks. "When am I ever not nice?"

"Audrey, I mean it. Give her a chance."

As she leaves to get the door, my pulse speeds up and I notice my palms are clammy. It's almost like I'm nervous to meet Hannah.

But why would I be nervous?

4

HANNAH

This house is amazing. When the job listing described the place I'd be living in as a cottage in Maine, I was imagining a small cabin-like house. Given what the job paid, I assumed these people were rich, but not rich enough to afford a house this nice. This is just their summer home, and oceanfront homes—even small ones—cost a fortune.

When I drove down the road and saw the house, my jaw dropped. I even stopped a moment to check that I was at the right address. But it's the only house around so it had to be it. The house is two levels and massive, at least by my standards. It has a traditional New England look with gray clapboard siding and white trim. The exterior is very well kept up. The siding doesn't look worn or damaged from the harsh seaside air the way most homes along the coast do.

On my walk to the house, I suddenly realize Mrs. Bishop probably can't get to the door in her condition, which means someone else will have to answer it. Maybe her husband? What if she told him she hired me and he didn't approve? Will I have to go through another interview?

Straightening my stance, I take a deep breath and ring the bell.

Relax, I tell myself. You already have the job, or you will if you don't screw this up.

The door swings open and I see a woman who I'd guess is around 35 with long dark hair and shiny red lips, wearing black dress pants and a cream-colored sweater.

"I assume you're Hannah?" the woman asks with a slight smile as her eyes move over my gray wool peacoat down to my black rubber boots. I don't have money for clothes so most everything I have is second-hand.

"Yes, Hannah Reese," I say, drawing her eyes back to my face. "Are you a friend of Lauren's?"

"We're *best* friends," she says, emphasizing the best. "We met in college. I'm Audrey." She steps aside. "Please. Come inside."

As I come into the house, my gaze rises to the tall ceiling and the wood beams that run along it. There's a large iron light fixture hanging down from a rod that's centered over the expansive living room. The furniture is clean and modern—a brown leather sectional, dark wood tables, a fireplace framed with stacked stone. A beige throw is draped over the couch like it's strategically placed there to look nice. There are very few decorative items and the ones that I see look selectively chosen, like a professional picked them out.

"Are you done gawking?" Audrey asks.

My eyes dart back to her. "Sorry. I've just never been in such a beautiful house."

"I'm kidding." She laughs and looks out at the room. "It *is* beautiful. They did a lot of work on the house when they bought it."

"Do you live around here?" I ask.

"I live in town. Unfortunately, oceanfront property wasn't in my budget." She turns and walks off. "Come say hello to Lauren, then I'll show you around the house."

Assuming the master bedroom is upstairs, I'm surprised

when Audrey leads me down a short hallway to a bedroom on the main floor. It's large enough to be a master, with its king-size bed, two nightstands, two dressers, and an oversized chair.

Mrs. Bishop is in the bed, a blanket covering her.

"Hannah," she says. "Welcome."

"Good morning, Mrs. Bishop." I walk up to the bed. "It's nice to meet you in person."

She sits up as I reach over to shake her hand.

"Call me Lauren." She takes my hand and gives it a squeeze. "There's no need to be so formal."

Her hands are ice cold and bony. She's a very thin woman, although she might've lost weight since the accident. I think one of her emails said the car accident happened a couple weeks ago, but I can't remember the exact date. We exchanged several emails before our call, mostly with information about her injury and the treatment she's had so far.

She lets go of my hand and I take a step back, noticing the view of the ocean from the window. "You have a beautiful view."

"It's why I chose to live here while I recover. I find it peaceful."

I wonder how much a view like that cost. It had to be millions.

"You haven't asked how she's feeling," Audrey says, and when I turn back, I see her arms are crossed tightly over her chest. "Isn't that your job? To be concerned with your patient's health?"

"Audrey, stop," Lauren says under her breath.

"No, she's right," I say, turning back to Lauren. "How are you feeling today?"

"My leg is okay, but my ribcage is throbbing. It's amazing how much pain can come from bruised ribs."

"Did you take an anti-inflammatory this morning?"

"I've taken my pain medications." She points to the bottles lined up on her nightstand.

"I hate to interrupt," Audrey says to Lauren, "but I have a meeting at 10 and I need time to prepare for it."

"Go ahead and show her around," Lauren says. "I'll talk to her when you're done."

"This is why it's important to be on time," Audrey says, smiling at me. "Come with me. I'll show you your room."

My first impression of Audrey is that I don't like her. Lauren seems much nicer. How are those two best friends?

Audrey takes me up to the second floor. There's a room on each end and the hallway that connects them is open and overlooks the main living area.

"This will be your room," Audrey says, going into a bedroom that's much smaller than Lauren's but bigger than the tiny bedroom in my old apartment.

The window looks out at the ocean, drawing me to it as I gaze at the crashing waves. "What an amazing view."

"Don't get used to it," Audrey says. "You won't be here long."

I turn back to her and smile. "Well, as long as I'm here, I won't take it for granted."

"I'm sure you'll take full advantage of living here. You seem like someone who would." She smirks at me, then walks quickly to the bathroom. "Lauren has the basics stocked in here. Toilet paper. Soap. Towels. You'll need to provide everything else."

Joining her in the bathroom, I watch as she adjusts the towel on the rack. "I'll make sure to get whatever I need."

"Oh, and you'll need to keep it clean." She turns to me. "I assume Lauren went over what she expects in terms of cleaning?"

"She said I just need to keep the house picked up. She said they have a maid that does the actual cleaning."

"The maid is only here every other week. In between those times, you'll be in charge of cleaning up. Both Steven and Lauren like a very clean house. That includes the room you'll be staying in."

"I understand." I say it just to appease her. I'm not really going to clean. Lauren hired me to care for her, not scrub toilets.

"Let's continue the tour." Audrey goes past me and I follow her out of the room.

"What about down there?" I ask, pointing to the room at the end of the hall.

"That's the master bedroom. Steven's room. You don't need to see that." She hurries down the stairs.

"You mean Steven and Lauren's room," I say, following her down the stairs.

"Well, obviously," she says with an annoyed sigh. "But Lauren isn't staying there at the moment. She wanted to be on the main level so she could get to the kitchen." Audrey turns toward me. "Despite what she tells you, she's not good on the crutches yet. She's fallen twice. Steven put the crutches in the closet for now so she's not tempted to use them."

"Now that I'm here, I'll help her with them. She needs to practice using them so she's able to get around."

"She has a wheelchair."

"Yes, but it's better for her to use the crutches. They'll help build up her strength."

Audrey smirks. "I suppose you would know best in your, what... one year of nursing experience?"

Choosing not to respond to that, I glance over at the kitchen, which is open to the living room. "Is there anything you need to show me in there?"

"I think it's self-explanatory," Audrey says. "You know how to cook, right?"

"I'm not a chef, but I know how to make the basics."

"Steven will expect more than the basics. Perhaps you should read some recipes online. Watch some cooking videos."

"I'll do that," I say. "Thanks for the suggestion."

I've decided my approach with this woman is to kill her with kindness. Being rude to her would just support her belief that I'm not right for the job. She's clearly trying to convince Lauren of that, and since they're best friends, she could probably do it, especially if I say the wrong thing. So I won't. I'll choose each word carefully, talk in my sweetest tone, and keep a smile plastered on my face.

A job like this doesn't come along every day and I'm not letting this woman take it away from me.

5

HANNAH

"So that's it," Audrey says as we walk back to Lauren's room. "Oh." She stops just before we get there and points down the hall. "The powder room is on the right. You should use that rather than the bathroom in Lauren's room."

"Is there another bedroom down there?"

"That's Steven's office for when he's working from home. He keeps it locked to protect his clients' financial files. If he's home and the door is open, don't go in there. He gets very upset."

"Are you saying he has a bad temper?" I ask, realizing I know next to nothing about these people. And yet I agreed to live with them.

"I'm saying to stay out of his office." She checks her phone. "I have to get going. I need to call a client on my way to this meeting." She goes into Lauren's room and up to her bed. "I'm sorry I have to leave, but I have a million things to do today."

"Thank you for coming over." Lauren smiles at her. "You've been such a huge help through all this."

"I'd do anything for you. You know that." Audrey leans down and gives Lauren a hug. "Call if you need anything."

"I should be good now that I have Hannah here." Lauren looks at me, a slight smile on her face.

"I'll call if I get a break this afternoon," Audrey says, grabbing her black leather purse from the chair.

"You don't need to. I'm sure we'll be fine."

Audrey eyes me with suspicion. "I'll call anyway. Just to make sure everything's going well."

When she's gone, I walk up to Lauren's bed. "Can I get you anything?"

"Not right now." She points to the chair. "Have a seat."

I sit down on the cream-colored chair, noticing the stiffness of the seat cushions. It's either a new chair or no one ever sits on it. There's a dark gray throw draped over the back of it that seems more for decoration than actually use.

"So what do you think?" Lauren asks, pushing herself up to a more seated position.

"About the house? It's beautiful. The most beautiful house I've ever been in, and the views are amazing. Almost like a postcard."

"You've been here before, right? To Maine?"

"Only a few times. My dad had a brother in Freeport. We went to see him a few times when I was younger. He died on a fishing boat."

"Oh, I'm sorry to hear that."

I shrug. "I didn't really know him."

She studies my face for a moment, then says, "When I asked for your thoughts, I was referring to the job, not the house. I assume you're still interested?"

"Definitely!" I sit up straighter. "Sorry, I didn't know what you meant. But yes, I definitely want the job."

"And you're okay with making my meals?"

"Yes. I mean, I'm not a chef or anything, but I'll do my best. Audrey mentioned I'd be cooking for your husband as well."

"Only occasionally, if he's home and doesn't want to make something for himself or go out."

"Your husband cooks?"

"When he chooses to, yes. He's quite good at it. In fact, he cooked for me when we were dating. He says it's what won me over." She smiles a little. "That's not actually the reason, but I let him think that."

"What was the reason?" I ask, but then regret it and say, "Sorry, that's personal. I shouldn't have asked."

"No, it's fine. We'll be spending a lot of time together the next couple months. I expect we'll be sharing a lot about ourselves during that time." She reaches for her glass of water on the nightstand.

"I'll get it," I say, noticing her cringe from the pain her movements are causing. I hand her the glass. "Here."

"Thank you." She takes a sip, then gives me the glass. "So what was your question?"

"I was asking about your husband. About how you two got together."

"Oh, yes." She looks down at the white blanket that's over her lap and runs her hand over it. "Steven and I met in college. Audrey met him first. She had class with David, Steven's roommate. She'd go to David's room to study, which is how she got to know Steven. I didn't meet him until sophomore year. I thought he was handsome, but not really my type."

"Why?" I relax back in the chair, enthralled by her story. I love hearing how people met.

"I thought he was too serious," she says with a laugh. "He talked about stocks and investing and his plans for starting his own wealth management firm. I found it terribly boring. I'm more of a creative type."

"What was your major?"

"Marketing with a minor in graphic design. The plan was for Audrey and I to open our own marketing and PR agency.

But then I married Steven, we bought a house, and Audrey and I never got around to starting the business. She got a job at a PR agency in Boston and eventually started her own. It's a small boutique agency. She's only had the business a few years, but she's done well for herself. The only downside is that she works all the time. She rarely takes a day off."

"What about you? Where did you work after college?"

"I didn't." Lauren gives me a half-smile. "I supported Steven in his career. He worked at an investment firm downtown Boston that required a great deal of his time. It was my job to keep the house in order, run errands, and make sure dinner was made when he got home." She glances down. "I realize women today don't typically give up their career for their husband's, but Steven assured me I could get a job once he'd established himself."

"And did you?"

"No." She pauses. "I never did." She coughs a little. "Could I have the water again?"

I hand her the glass and she takes a sip. I get the feeling there's more to that story, but I don't want to ask. It's only my first day. I shouldn't be prying into her personal life, but I want to. I've never met anyone as beautiful and wealthy as Mrs. Bishop. I want to know everything about her.

"I didn't finish my story, did I?" She hands me the glass. "About how Steven and I got together."

"It's okay. We can talk about it some other time," I say, but I'm really hoping she tells me now.

"I forgot where I left off."

"You said something about him being too serious."

She nods. "Yes, he was. He was the complete opposite of David, his roommate." She smiles a little. "David was always joking around, making people laugh. The two of them couldn't have been more different, and yet they were best friends." She pauses a moment. "Anyway, I met David through Audrey and spent time with him the summer before our sophomore year. We became very good friends. When we got back to college, I went to David's room and Steven was there. I couldn't take my eyes off him. He was the most handsome man I'd ever seen."

"When did he ask you out?"

"Right after we met. I was shocked. David told me Steven didn't date much, but he called me up right after I left his room and we went out that night."

"Wow, that's fast."

"It was. Turns out he was just as interested in me as I was in him."

"And the date went well, I assume?"

"Very well. He showed up with flowers. Took me to a very expensive restaurant. He wore a nice suit. At the end of the night, he said he couldn't wait to see me again, so we went out the following night too. We dated from then on and got engaged the end of our senior year."

"That's so romantic," I say, wishing something like that would happen to me. Unfortunately, my dating life has been nothing but a string of losers, usually guys still living in their parents' basement who have no idea what they want to do with their lives.

"It seems like forever ago," Lauren says. "Almost like another lifetime."

"What happened with that other guy? Your husband's roommate? Are you two still friends with him?"

"We were." Lauren looks down. "Until just recently."

"Why? What happened?"

Her eyes lift back to mine. "My accident. David was driving the car. He died at the scene."

6

HANNAH

"Mrs. Bishop, I'm so sorry," I say. "I didn't know."

"I suppose I should've started with that. I just don't like talking as though he's gone. I still can't believe it."

Lauren's told me very little about the accident. All I know is that it happened at night and that the car slid off the road and hit a tree.

"It was just you and him in the car?" I ask.

She nods. "We were on our way to dinner. Steven called and said he had to work late and would meet me at the restaurant. I called David and asked if he'd pick me up on his way there. We were only a few miles from my house when..." She wipes her eyes and forces out a smile. "I don't mean to get so emotional."

"It's understandable." I get up and sit beside her on the bed. "It's only been a few weeks and this is someone you've been friends with a long time."

She nods and reaches for the box of tissues on the nightstand.

I hand them to her. "How's your husband dealing with it?"

"Steven's not someone who shows emotion." She dabs her nose with the tissue. "He was upset when he heard the news, but since then, he hasn't really talked about it. But I need to. It's how I process. I need to talk out my feelings to accept what happened. Thank goodness for Audrey. She's listened to me talk for hours, any time of day or night. She's the only way I'm getting through this."

"Did she stay friends with David after college?"

"Yes, we all remained friends. Then Audrey married Barry and he became part of our little group. But now that Audrey's getting divorced and David's gone, our group will become much smaller." Lauren takes another tissue and dabs her eyes. "It's sad when things change, especially when it's not a change you wanted. But you would know that as well as me, losing your parents the way you did."

I look over at the nightstand and see Lauren's pill bottles lined up on a silver tray. "Mrs. Bishop, have you taken your pills this morning?"

"Just one. I'm trying to wean myself off them."

"You really shouldn't do that yet." I walk over to the nightstand and pick up one of the pill bottles. "This one reduces inflammation. You need to take that to keep the swelling down. It'll help you heal faster and can help with the pain." I pick up another bottle. "This one prevents blood clots. You need to be taking this for another week."

"I took that one. It's the narcotics I've been weaning myself off of. They help with the pain, but I've heard they're dangerous."

"Only if you take too many." I set the pill bottle down. "How is your pain right now?"

"It's tolerable."

"Take a deep breath."

She starts to, then stops, cringing as she puts her hand over her ribs. "I can't. It hurts too much."

"I really think you should take something for the pain."

"Fine, but only one." She holds out her hand.

I pick up the bottle of oxycodone, open the cap, and pour a pill out onto my hand.

My eyes glaze over as I stare at the pill. *Do it. They'll think it's an accident. You won't be blamed. Just do it. What are you waiting for? Give him the pills.*

"Hannah?" Lauren's voice startles me and I drop the pill. I watch as it rolls over the wood floor. "Hannah, what's wrong?"

My eyes dart to hers. "Nothing. I just... I felt dizzy for a moment."

"Go sit down. I'll take the bottle."

"No, I got it." I shake out another pill and hand it to her. "I'll throw the other one away." I close the bottle and pick up the pill I dropped. "I'll be right back." I race to the bathroom and toss the pill in the waste basket, then glance at myself in the mirror, noticing the redness on my cheeks and neck. I quickly splash cold water on my face, then blot it dry with the hand towel.

"Hannah?" Lauren calls out. "Are you okay?"

"I'm fine." I hurry back to her. "Sorry about that. I didn't have breakfast this morning."

"Are you sure that's all it was?" she asks, her brows drawing together. "Your hands were trembling."

"It's because I skipped breakfast. Sometimes when I go without eating for too long, I get shaky."

"Go to the kitchen and make yourself something. I'm going to rest."

"Let me help you." I take away one of the pillows propped up behind her so she can lie down. "Do you need another blanket?"

"Not right now." She closes her eyes.

"I'll be in the kitchen if you need anything."

Leaving her room, I gently shut the door, but not all the way. I need to be able to hear her if she calls for me.

When I'm in the kitchen, I take a moment to get myself

together. I can never let Lauren see me like that again. She'll think I'm not capable of doing the job. She'll fire me and I'll have to find another job and a place to live. I lied when I told Lauren I had sublet my apartment. The truth is, my lease ended this week. If I lose this job, I'll have to live in my car until I can save up enough for a new apartment.

I'm so tired of struggling. Living here will be like a vacation from my real life. I'll get to see what it'd be like to be rich. And when I leave here, I'll have enough money saved to get a decent apartment. I'll make more in these two months than I'd make in six months at my old job. I can't screw this up.

My phone dings and I see a text from Tanner, my ex-boyfriend. He offered to help me move out of my apartment. He's letting me store my stuff in his basement for fifty bucks a month, which is way cheaper than a storage unit. For his moving help, I'm paying him in beer. I hope he doesn't expect more than that, like sex, but if it comes to that, I'll do it. I really need his help and it's not like we haven't done it before.

His text reads, *What time tomorrow?*

Can we do it tonight? I text back. *I start my job tomorrow.*

What time?

6 or 7?

Let's say 7. When we're done we'll go for a drink.

It'll be late. Let's skip the drink.

It's your last night here. Just one drink?

Yeah, okay, I text back. I don't want to argue with him and risk him changing his mind. *See you at 7.*

Setting my phone on the counter, I open the large stainless steel fridge. There's not much in it. Two shelves are devoted to protein drinks and organic juices. The bottom shelf has a package of raw chicken breasts and the shelf above it has sushi in a takeout container.

I close the fridge and check the cupboards. There's no food, just stacks of white plates and bowls. At the end of the kitchen, I notice a small door. I open it up and find a pantry hidden behind it. There's not much in it but what's there is neatly organized. Protein bars are lined up in shallow wooden boxes, and glass jars with wood lids hold oatmeal, pasta, granola, and crackers.

Taking the jar of crackers, I bring it to the living room, stuffing a few crackers in my mouth as I sit on the couch. I'm probably not supposed to eat in here but it's just crackers. A few crumbs aren't going to hurt anything.

It's so quiet I can hear myself crunching. I'm not used to all this silence. My apartment in Boston is on a busy street. I'm always hearing cars honking, trucks backing up, sirens going off. It's going to take some time to get used to how quiet it is here.

There's a TV above the fireplace. I'm tempted to turn it on but don't want to wake up Lauren. She needs her rest. She looked tired. I think it's odd she doesn't sleep with her husband at night. I understand why she'd want to be on the main level during the day, but why wouldn't she be with her husband during the night?

Getting up from the couch, I walk over to the fireplace and look at the photos on the mantel. There's a wedding photo of Steven and Lauren taken in front of a cathedral. I've seen that place before. It's one of the historic cathedrals in Boston that tourists like to go to. I've walked past it but never been inside. My mother wasn't religious. I've never once been to church.

Picking up the photo, I look closer at Steven. He's very good-looking, but this was probably taken 10 years ago. I wonder what he looks like now. Lauren's gazing at him in the photo, a huge smile on her face. Steven's looking at the camera. His eyes are captivating. They're a really bright blue. My eyes are blue too but it's a pale blue that I've never liked.

My mother said my light skin and eyes were a sign of pureness, like an angel in human form. If she only knew what

I'd done. What would she say? If she were still alive, would she scold me or praise me for what I've done?

A scream pierces through the silent room, startling me so much I drop the wedding picture.

"Help!" Lauren screams. "Help me!"

7

HANNAH

"Mrs. Bishop!" I race into her room and over to her bed. She's lying down, her eyes wide and a horrified look on her face, like she just saw a ghost. "What's wrong? What happened?"

She blinks a few times, then notices me beside her. "Who are you?"

"Hannah. Your nurse. You hired me, remember?"

She pauses a moment, then says, "Yes. Of course. I'm not fully awake yet. How long did I sleep?"

"Not long. Maybe 20 minutes?"

"Why did you wake me?" she asks in an angry tone. "You know I need my rest."

"I, um... I didn't wake you up. You had a nightmare. You were screaming."

She stares at me a moment, then glances out the window. "Did I say anything?"

"You were calling for help."

She nods. "Yes. I've done it before. Steven said it's happened a few times since I got home from the hospital." Her gaze moves from the window back to me. "What's odd is I apparently never did this when I was in the hospital. It's only happened here, in this house."

"Can I get you something? Some water? Tea? Something to eat?"

"No. Stay here with me. I always feel uneasy after it happens." She shudders.

"You look cold." I pull the blanket over her, which somehow ended up at the end of the bed.

"Thank you," she says with a drawn-out sigh. "I'm sorry I accused you of waking me up."

"Don't worry about it. It's normal to be confused when you wake up from a deep sleep."

"It's those pills. I don't like what they do to me. It's why I don't want to take them." Her gaze drops to my body. "Why are you still wearing those clothes?"

"What do you mean?"

"You were wearing those clothes yesterday. Don't you have anything else to wear?"

"Mrs. Bishop, I wasn't here yesterday. I got here this morning. I've only been here a couple hours."

"Oh." She looks down, then laughs a little. "You must think I'm crazy. I don't know what I'm saying."

"Actually, I'm worried. I think I should take you to a doctor."

"Why?" Her eyes dart to mine. "Do you really think I'm crazy?"

"I'm worried you might have swelling around your brain. You said you had a concussion after the accident, right?"

"Yes, but only a mild one. The doctors weren't concerned."

"Still, I'd feel better if you got checked out. Memory loss, even temporary, can be a sign of something serious."

"I'm fine. It's those pain pills. I've never reacted well to pills, even just basic aspirin."

"How do you feel now?"

"Tired. Like I'm not quite awake."

"I'll let you rest." I turn to leave.

44

"No!" she yells. "Don't go!"

I turn back and see the desperate look in her eyes, begging me to stay.

"Okay." I sit down on the chair.

"I don't mean to be dramatic. It's just after I have those nightmares, I feel very uptight. Almost frightened, but I don't know why. I know what I saw isn't real."

"What did you see?"

She swallows. "David. After the accident. He's in the car, bleeding." She pauses. "His neck is severed by the seatbelt."

An image of that appears in my head. "Is that... is that what really happened?"

She shakes her head. "They said the impact of the crash killed him. I didn't want to know all the details. He was a very close friend and..." Her voice trails off as her gaze moves back to the window.

"Do you remember anything from the accident?"

"No. The doctors say I was probably knocked unconscious when we hit the tree. But..."

"But what?"

Her gaze remains on the window. "I feel like I talked to him. Or he talked to me. Before... before he was gone."

"What do you think he said?"

"I can't remember. I don't even know if it's true. I might have just dreamed that it happened." She looks over at me. "Let's talk about something else. Something more pleasant."

"Like what?"

"Tell me about you." She smiles. "Do you have someone special back in Boston? A boyfriend?"

"No," I say with a laugh. "I don't have the best luck with guys. The ones my age are so immature. Most of them don't even want to work. They just want to sit around all day and play video games or watch TV."

"I felt the same way about boys when I was your age. But

45

Steven was different. He was far more mature than the boys I'd dated in the past. It's one of the reasons I found him so appealing. He was planning for the future, which made me feel safe and secure."

As she says it, I remember the picture I dropped when I heard her scream. I broke the frame—a really nice silver frame that had their wedding date engraved at the bottom.

"Mrs. Bishop, I have to tell you something." I say, wringing my hands together.

"What is it?"

"I, um, I broke your picture. I didn't mean to. I was looking at it when you screamed and I got startled and dropped it."

"What picture?"

"Your wedding picture. The one on the mantel. I'm really sorry. If you tell me where you got it, I'll replace it. Or you could take money from my check and use it to buy a new one."

She cocks her head. "Why were you holding it?"

Think fast. You can't tell her you were checking out her husband.

"I wanted to get a closer look at the church," I blurt out. "The one you and your husband were standing in front of. It looked familiar. I was trying to see it better."

"That's the Old South Church. Being from Boston, I'm sure you've been there or at least walked past it. Steven loves history so he insisted we get married there."

"Well, it's a beautiful photo, and as I said, I didn't mean to break the frame. I'll try to replace it or pay you for it."

"That won't be necessary. I'll just replace it with something else. I'll ask Audrey for ideas. She's wonderful at picking out home decor."

"Are you sure? It's your wedding photo. Don't you want to display it?"

"After 12 years of marriage, I really don't see a need to." She

46

laughs a little. "It's just a reminder of how much older we look now."

"I don't think you look old. You almost look the same as you did in that photo."

"You're very sweet," she says with a slight smile. "Enough about me. Tell me more about you. So you're not currently seeing anyone, but are you looking? Because I feel like I should warn you, there aren't many single men your age in this town."

"That won't be a problem. I'm taking a break from dating. I want to focus on my career, save up some money."

"What about friends? If you'd like to invite them up here, I'd be fine with it, as long as you let me know beforehand."

"I won't be inviting anyone. It's only a couple months. I'll see them when I move back."

"Really, Hannah, I don't mind. I'd hate for you to feel lonely living here. It can be hard being away from your friends. There's a cute little cafe downtown that's perfect for a girl's lunch and then you and your friends could go through all the local shops."

"The truth is, Mrs. Bishop." I hesitate, wondering if I should say this, but if I don't, she'll keep pestering me about it. "I don't have a lot of friends. I never have. I kind of keep to myself."

"Oh, well, the offer still stands. If there's someone you'd like to invite over, just let me know." Her phone rings and she picks it up. "Hello, Steven." She listens. "Yes, I think Hannah and I will get along quite well. I'd love for you to meet her before she leaves tonight." She looks over at me. "Steven will be home at six. Can you stay that late?"

"Yes, of course," I say, although I was hoping to leave earlier than that. I'll have to tell Tanner I can't meet him until later.

"She'll be here," Lauren says to her husband. "Maybe you could bring home dinner." She smiles. "Yes, that would be fine.

I'll see you tonight." She ends the call and says to me, "Steven's bringing home food from our favorite Thai restaurant. I hope you like Thai."

"I don't think I'll be able to stay for dinner. I have to pack up my things."

"That won't take long. It's just some clothes, right?"

"Actually, I'm moving my furniture into storage. The guy subletting my place decided he wanted to bring his own furniture so I need to get mine out of there."

"I wish you'd told me that. I wouldn't have asked you to stay. But Steven would really like to meet you. He wasn't too pleased that I did this on my own. He wanted to be involved in the hiring process, and since he wasn't, I'd really like him to meet you before you officially start."

"I'll stay long enough to meet him, but then I really do need to go."

"Well, we'll be sure to save you some leftovers."

"Speaking of food, I noticed there isn't much in the fridge. Should I go to the store tomorrow?"

"Yes. Steven hasn't had time to get groceries. And while you're there, pick out whatever you'd like for yourself. I'll give you my credit card."

"What about lunch today? Would you like me to order something?"

Her phone dings with a text alert. "It's Audrey. She says she's stopping by later with lunch. That's nice of her."

Lauren and I talk some more, then watch TV until just before noon, when the doorbell rings.

"That must be Audrey," Lauren says. "Could you see if she needs help bringing lunch in?"

I get up and hurry to the door, dreading having to see this woman again. I bet she's only here to check on me. I don't know what I did, but she really doesn't like me. I need to find a way to win her over before she convinces Lauren to fire me.

"Hi, Audrey," I say, greeting her at the door with a big smile.

She doesn't smile back, but just shoves the sack of food at me. "Put this in the kitchen."

"I'd be happy to!" I head to the kitchen while Audrey takes off her coat.

"What happened?" she says.

I turn back and see her racing up to the fireplace, staring down at the broken frame on the floor. I should've cleaned that up, but I didn't have time.

"Did you do this?" Audrey asks, pointing at the frame.

"It was an accident." I set the sack of food on the counter. "Mrs. Bishop needed me and I—"

"Don't bother trying to explain it." She stalks over to me. "I know what you're doing, but you won't get away with it. Lauren is my closest friend. She may not see you for what you are, but I do."

"I... I don't know what you're talking about," I say, my heart beating faster. "I didn't mean to drop the picture. It was an accident."

"Do you really think I'm that stupid? That was their wedding picture. And you destroyed it! Out of all the things in the house you could've broken, you chose that?" She steps closer to me, her eyes on mine. "I'm watching you, Hannah. And whatever you're planning? I won't let you get away with it."

8

LAUREN

"How's the patient?" Audrey asks, coming into my room.

"Good, but you didn't need to bring me lunch. I know how swamped you are with work."

"Work can wait. I couldn't let you starve. You need to eat to get better."

"Hannah would've made me something."

Audrey sits beside me on the bed. "I don't like that girl. There's something not right about her."

"You don't even know her. If you did, you'd see she's a very nice girl, and very accommodating. I can tell she'll be a hard worker."

"Do you know what she did?" Audrey glances back at the door. "To your wedding picture?"

"Yes, she told me. And it wasn't her fault. It was mine. I was having one of my nightmares and scared her."

"Yeah, right," Audrey huffs. "I'm sure that's all it was."

"What exactly do you think she's up to?" I ask, hearing plates clink together in the kitchen as Hannah gets lunch ready.

"I don't know, but I don't trust her." Audrey lowers her voice. "Why would a young, beautiful girl want to be secluded in this house for two months? Doesn't she have friends? A boyfriend?"

"Apparently not. I asked her that this morning and she said she's not seeing anyone and has never had many friends."

"Well, there you go," Audrey says. "She's a loner with no family and no friends. That's the characteristics of a psychopath."

"You're being ridiculous. Hannah is not a—" I stop when I notice Hannah at the door.

"Sorry to interrupt," she says, "but what would you like to drink?"

"Water is fine," I tell her. "If you could just refill my glass."

"I'd be happy to," she says, coming over to get it. "And what would you like to drink, Audrey?"

"I'll get my own, thank you," she says.

Hannah smiles at her, then leaves.

"You see how polite she is?" I whisper to Audrey. "You just need to give her a chance."

"It's all an act. How can you not see that?"

"Because it's not an act. That's just how she is."

"What if she goes after Steven?"

"She hasn't even met Steven, and he's 12 years older than her."

"Yeah? So? Girls like her love older men. They're sophisticated. They have money. And Steven is very good-looking and very charming. I could easily see Hannah being led to believe he's interested in her when he's not. You know how girls that age tend to fantasize about things like that."

"Like when you thought your boss was interested in you?" I smile at her, remembering the story.

Audrey was 25 and had just been promoted at the PR agency she'd been working at since graduating college. She had a new boss and he was always complimenting her and smiling at her. She took that to mean he was interested in more than a professional relationship, so one night when they were working late, she went into his office and tried to kiss him. He told her he had a fiancé and ordered her to leave. The next day, he fired her. She convinced him to change his mind, but immediately began looking for another job.

"I told you to stop talking about that," Audrey snaps.

"C'mon, it was a long time ago. I think enough time has passed that you can laugh about it now."

"How could I laugh about it?" She gets up, her voice rising. "It was humiliating! And I had to beg to get my job back after he fired me." She walks away, then turns back. "Honestly, Lauren, you, of all people, should not be making comments about this."

"Audrey, I didn't mean to—"

"You've never had to work. You have no idea how difficult it is, especially as a woman. The stress. The long hours. Dealing with horrible people who don't respect what I do or how hard I work."

"I know how hard you work," I say, surprised at how upset she's getting. "I'm sorry I brought it up. I really thought you'd moved past it by now."

"I have, but that doesn't mean I need to keep reliving it."

"Should I come back later?" Hannah asks, noticing the tension in the room as she stands at the door with my lunch tray.

"Come on in," I tell her. "I see you found my tray."

"Yes." She brings it to me, gently setting it over my lap. "I wasn't sure what you wanted so I gave you a little of everything."

On the plate is a small amount of chicken salad, fruit salad, crackers, and a whole grain roll. I take a bite of the chicken salad and immediately know it's from one of my favorite lunch spots in Boston.

I look over at Audrey. "Ellie's Bistro. My favorite."

"I know you miss going there." She smiles, the kind of smile that says our fight is over. I didn't mean to fight with her. I didn't think she'd get that upset over that story.

"Do you want me to make you up a plate?" Hannah asks Audrey.

"I'll do it." Audrey leaves my room and goes to the kitchen.

"Is everything okay?" Hannah asks. "I thought I heard fighting."

"We just disagreed about something." I pick up my napkin and set it over my lap.

"Was it about me?" Hannah asks.

I look up at her. "Why would it be about you?"

"I can tell Audrey doesn't like me. I thought maybe she was telling you to find someone else."

"That's not Audrey's decision. It's mine. After all, I'm the one who needs care, not her. I told Steven the same thing."

"Are you saying your husband didn't want you to hire me?"

"He was worried you lacked experience, but I assured him you were more than capable of doing the job."

"I appreciate that."

I look into her pale blue eyes. "We all need to be given a chance to grow and learn. Otherwise, we remain stuck and unfulfilled, and what kind of life would that be?"

Hannah looks back at the door. "I'll get out of here so you can have lunch with your friend."

"I hope she brought enough for you as well."

"There was only enough for two, but it's okay. I'll find something else to eat." She hurries out just as Audrey's coming back.

"Why is she always racing around like that?" Audrey says. "It's dangerous. She could knock someone over."

"She only walks that fast when you're here. I think you make her nervous."

"Good. I want her to be afraid of me." Audrey sits down on the chair with her plate of salad.

"Did you really only bring enough for the two of us?" I ask, tearing apart the roll.

"Yes. Why would I buy lunch for the help?"

"To be nice. There's nothing here for her to eat."

"She can have one of Steven's protein drinks. He's got like 30 of them in the fridge."

"Those are for me. I'm supposed to get more protein. The doctor said it'll help me heal faster."

The sound of a glass breaking comes from the kitchen.

"Sorry!" Hannah yells.

"Don't worry about it," I yell back.

Audrey rolls her eyes. "She's a disaster. Seriously, fire this girl before she does even more damage."

"Let's talk about something else," I say, buttering my roll with the knife. "So why were you in Boston this morning? I thought your meeting was over the phone."

"It was supposed to be, but the guy changed his mind. I drove all the way there for a ten-minute meeting."

"That's it? Ten minutes?"

"It was scheduled for an hour but he was late." She sighs. "Sometimes I really hate this job. I thought having my own company would be better than working for someone else, but it's not turning out that way." She sets her plate down on the nightstand and picks up her bottle of water. "I wish we'd followed through on our plan to start an agency together. With your design skills and my sales and marketing talent, we would've made the perfect team."

"Maybe we still—" I stop before I say too much. I've been thinking about going back to work, but I'm not sure being in business with Audrey would be a good thing. I love her, but she's very controlling.

"Still what?"

54

"Nothing." I shake my head. "Never mind."

"Lauren, are you thinking of getting a job?"

"No. I mean, not right now. But maybe in the future."

"Why? Steven's making a fortune and he got all that money from his inheritance. You don't need to work."

"Maybe I want to. Sitting around all day is getting old."

"You never sat at home all day. Before the accident, you went to yoga class, went shopping, met friends for lunch. Most people would dream of having that life."

"It's not as great as it sounds."

"I'd take that any day over what I'm doing," she says as her phone rings. She grits her teeth as she picks it up, then takes a breath and answers the call. "Yes, Andy, do you need something?" She listens, shaking her head as he talks. "I understand why you're upset. That woman was clearly out to get you." She stands up and paces the floor. "I'll get a press release out to you by five. I realize we may not need it, but just in case, we need to be prepared." She stops pacing. "Just between you and me, did anything actually happen?" She listens. "Okay, I'll take care of it and be at your office tomorrow at eight." She ends the call and holds up the phone. "This is why I hate my job."

"What happened?"

"He had inappropriate relations with an intern and now I have to do damage control. Luckily, it's his word against hers, so if she tried to prove it, there'd be nothing there."

"How old is the intern?"

"Twenty-four." Audrey glances at the door, then comes over to me. "Same age as your new nurse. And Andy is 36, same age as Steven. I'm telling you, Lauren, you can't trust her around him."

"What are you trying to say?"

"You know I love Steven, but he's a man, and men have needs. Right now, you're unable to fulfill those needs. You invite a pretty young girl to move in with you? You're just asking for trouble."

"I'm not worried," I say, and I'm not.

In fact, Audrey has no idea that the scenario she described is exactly what I'm hoping for.

9

HANNAH

After Audrey left, I was finally able to relax. That woman makes me nervous. She's definitely trying to get me fired, but Lauren seems determined not to listen to her. I'm not sure why Lauren's standing up for me when she barely knows me and has been friends with Audrey forever, but I'm not going to ask. I'm just going to leave it alone and hope Lauren's able to convince Audrey I'm not as bad as she thinks.

Lauren stirs in the bed and her eyes flutter open. "How long was I asleep?"

"A few hours." I set my phone down and get up from the chair where I've been sitting the whole time Lauren slept. I didn't want to risk walking around the house and breaking something. I don't know what my problem is, but I haven't even been here a day and I've already broken a glass, a plate, and that picture frame.

While Audrey was having lunch with Lauren, I picked up the frame and swept up the broken glass on the floor. I carefully removed the photo and left it on the kitchen counter, then tossed out the frame. I feel bad that I broke it, but I'm relieved Lauren didn't fire me for it. I guess I don't officially have the job yet. Today was supposed to be a tryout, for both of us, to see if we're a good fit. I still want the job and Lauren seems to want me here, but if her husband doesn't like me, there's a chance I won't be back tomorrow.

"What time is it?" Lauren asks, slowly sitting up.

"Almost five." I walk around to the side of her bed that has her pills. "Do you want something for the pain?"

"No." She shudders. "I don't want to have that nightmare again."

"It might not have been caused by the pill. It could just be memories from the accident coming back."

"I don't want to risk it."

"You could take something to calm your nerves. There are plenty of drugs that could help you relax."

"They all have side effects." She rests back on her pillows. "I'd rather just deal with it. Could you hand me my phone?"

I give it to her. "I need to use the restroom. I'll be right back." I head to the door.

"You can use the one in here," Lauren says.

"Audrey told me not to."

"Audrey isn't your boss." Lauren gives me a curious look. "What else did Audrey tell you?"

"To keep the house picked up when the maid's not here. And to stay out of your husband's office. And his bedroom."

Her brows rise. "Why would you go into Steven's bedroom?"

I find it odd she said 'Steven's' instead of 'ours'. Did they not share the same room before her accident?

"I wouldn't. I don't know why she told me that."

Lauren smiles. "Audrey's suspicious of everyone she meets. She's been that way forever. I think it's because she's always watching the news."

I glance down the hall. "I'll just use the bathroom out here."

When I reach the powder room, I shut the door and lean against it, taking long, deep breaths to calm my pounding heart.

Audrey's suspicious of me. But why? What does she know? And how did she find out?

She doesn't know. It was an accident. If Lauren finds out, that's what you'll tell her. The hospital would back you up. They ruled it an accident. Case closed. So stop acting guilty! Only you know what you did.

The voice in my head calms me down. I use the bathroom, then look at myself in the mirror, fixing my hair and plastering a smile on my face. When I've finally composed myself, I return to Lauren's room.

"Steven texted me," she says. "He left work early. He'll be here soon."

As she says it, I hear a door open and the sound of someone walking in.

"That must be him," Lauren says. "Steven, we're in here!"

Moments later, he appears at her door, a wide smile on his handsome face. He's even better-looking than his wedding photo. He was much younger then, but he's improved with age.

"Steven, this is Hannah," Lauren says.

I walk up to him and shake his hand. "It's nice to meet you."

As I start to pull my hand away, he keeps hold of it and leans down to me, his eyes on mine. "I trust you're taking good care of my wife?"

"Of course," I say, hearing the shakiness in my voice. I'm nervous, but not like I was with Audrey. This is different. It's the type of nervous you feel when you're around a very attractive man. His eyes are truly intoxicating. They're such a vibrant shade of blue. His hair is dark and longer on top, with a few strands hanging over his forehead in a deliciously sexy way.

When he releases my hand, the flutter in my chest remains. I need to get control of myself. I've been around handsome men before. I shouldn't be reacting this way. But there's something about Steven. When he walked in the room, the energy changed. He's one of those people who commands a room from his mere presence. I see now why he's so successful.

He walks past me to Lauren. "How are you feeling, sweetheart?"

"Tired. I just got up. I slept most of the afternoon."

"Did you take your pills?" he asks, sitting on her bed.

"Not the pain pills. I'm trying not to take them."

"Lauren, don't put yourself through this." He lovingly holds her hand. "There's no need to be in pain. Just take the pills."

"I can't. I think that's what's causing the nightmares."

"You had another one?" he asks with concern.

Lauren glances at me, like she's signaling me to leave.

"I'll be in the kitchen," I say, then hurry out of the room.

"Was it about the accident?" I hear Steven say.

Remaining just outside the door, I listen in, knowing I shouldn't, but then again, maybe I should. I'm Lauren's nurse, and if she thinks the nightmares are somehow related to her meds, I should hear this.

"There was blood everywhere," Lauren says in a shaky voice. "David's head was... I can't even say it." I hear Lauren crying. "It was awful."

"That's not what happened," Steven says. "You know that, right?"

"Yes, but it seemed so real. I woke up screaming. Hannah heard me and rushed right in." Lauren's voice gets softer. "She broke our wedding frame. It was an accident. Don't say anything to her about it. I've already talked to her."

60

"How did she break it? It was sitting on the mantel."

"She picked it up to look at it and dropped it."

"Do you want me to get a new frame?"

"No. Just leave it. I'll deal with it later."

"So how is she working out?" Steven asks.

"Great! She's easy to talk to and I enjoy having her here. She's a much better choice than the woman who was here the other day."

"And you feel confident in her skills? You think she's experienced enough to care for you?"

"For what I need? Yes. She's more than capable and a hard worker."

"Then I guess we're hiring her."

"Yes, she'll officially start tomorrow morning, although I'm paying her for today. It wouldn't be fair not to."

"I'll work up a contract. Maybe I could even get it done tonight."

"We don't need that, do we?"

"Of course we do. She's our employee and she'll be living in our house. We have to take precautions."

"For what? What are you concerned about?"

"Well, for one, we have significant assets, which puts us at risk for a lawsuit. And then there's the issue of your care. If she did something to harm you, she needs to be held responsible. Don't worry about it. I'll figure it out and have her sign it tomorrow."

"Don't make it more than it needs to be. Keep it simple. I don't want her thinking we're accusing her of things she hasn't done."

"You can't be so trusting, Lauren. We don't even know this girl. We need to protect ourselves."

"Let's not talk about this now. I don't want her hearing us." There's a pause and then, "Hannah? Could you come in here, please?"

I wait a few seconds before going to her door. "Did you need something?"

"Yes." Lauren smiles at me. "Would you mind helping Steven with dinner? I'd like to eat soon. I don't think I'll be awake much longer."

"I'd be happy to," I say.

Steven leans over and kisses Lauren's forehead. "Let us know if you need anything."

She nods and looks at the window, but there's nothing to see. I've already drawn the drapes since it's dark out now.

"Shall we go?" Steven asks, coming up beside me. I feel that flutter again, but ignore it. Feeling something for a good-looking man is completely normal, especially when I haven't been with a guy for almost a year.

I follow Steven to the kitchen. "Where's the food?"

"Oh." He stops suddenly. "I left it in the car. I'll go get it."

"I can do it."

"If you wouldn't mind. I need to check in with the office. My car's in the garage. Right through there." He points toward the laundry room, which must lead to the garage.

He gets his phone out as I head to the car. "Yes, I left early to check on Lauren," I hear him say to whoever he called.

He's such a concerned husband and so sweet to Lauren. I felt a pang of jealousy just watching them together. Why can't I find a guy like that?

Going out to the garage, I find a black Mercedes sedan and a white Lexus SUV. Just one of those vehicles probably cost more than the house I grew up in.

Walking over to the Mercedes, I open the door but don't see any food. Maybe it's in the trunk. I sit in the driver's seat and search for the button that opens the trunk. I find it and pop open the trunk, but remain in the seat. The leather is buttery soft and still warm from the heated seats. I inhale the car's scent, a mix of leather and men's cologne, the expensive kind, not the cheap drugstore stuff my ex used to wear.

I would love to have a car like this instead of the rusty piece of crap I'm driving now. It's always breaking down and the defrost doesn't work, so when it's cold and the windows freeze up, I have to keep stopping to clean them off.

"Did you find it?" Steven says.

He's standing at the door to the garage, probably wondering why I'm sitting in his car.

"Um, no." I quickly get out of the car.

"It's in the trunk. I'll get it."

"No, I got it." I hurry back there but Steven beats me to it. He picks up the sacks and shuts the trunk.

"Sorry I sat in your car," I say, as we walk back to the house. "I was looking for the thing that opens the trunk."

"And you apparently found it," he says with a smile.

He caught me. He knows I was sitting in his car like a weirdo.

My cheeks flush and I nervously laugh. "It's just that I've never been in a car that nice. I wanted to know how it felt."

He opens the door and steps aside. "After you."

I go past him into the house, through the laundry room to the kitchen.

"I could take you for a drive sometime," he says, setting the sacks on the counter.

"Oh, no, that's okay."

"We wouldn't go far. I could just drive you around town, show you the area. Lauren said you've never been here before."

"I've been to Maine, just not this town."

"Then we'll plan on it." He flashes that smile at me, the one that causes that fluttery feeling. "Maybe this weekend, while Lauren's taking a nap."

"Um, yeah, okay." I smile back at him, then watch as he opens the cupboard behind him and takes out some plates.

Maybe I should turn down his offer to drive me around. I don't want to upset Lauren. But why would she be upset? It's not like anything's going to happen. Steven clearly loves her and I'd never do anything to get in the way of that.

10

HANNAH

Steven and I had dinner with Lauren in her room. She kept telling us we didn't need to, but Steven insisted. He brought in another chair and a folding table so we wouldn't have to balance our plates on our laps. He's so considerate. Lauren's a very lucky lady.

Just before six, I headed back to Boston. With traffic, I didn't get to my apartment until 7:30. I was expecting Tanner to be there waiting for me, but of course, he forgot. I texted him and he said he was at a friend's house across town.

"It's almost nine," I say when he calls. "You said you'd be here a half hour ago."

"I'm downstairs. God, Hannah, stop yelling at me. You should be grateful I'm even doing this for you."

I sigh. "Come on up. I'll leave the door open." I go over and open it and see Tanner coming down the hall.

"Hey." He smiles, showing off the dimple in his cheek. He's cute, but in a boyish way. He's 25, but could pass for a college freshman.

"We have a lot to get done. We're going to be up late."

"Relax," he says, coming into my apartment. "We've got plenty of time."

I shut the door. "You want to start in the bedroom?"

"We could do that." He comes up to me and takes me in his arms. "I've missed you, babe."

I roll my eyes. "I meant should we start moving stuff out of the bedroom?"

"Or we could do something else first." He kisses me softly on the lips.

He was always a good kisser, which is one of the reasons I stayed with him longer than I should have.

"Tanner, come on." I pull away but he keeps his arms around me. "We don't have much time."

"We'll make it quick." He kisses my neck, in the spot by my ear that he knows turns me on.

Maybe I should do it. It's been a long time and I'm really stressed about starting the new job. This might help me relax.

"Let's go."

Tanner looks at me. "Wait, are you saying we're—"

I press my lips to his, which is all the answer he needs.

We go in the bedroom, which has boxes stacked everywhere and garbage bags full of clothes. It's not the least bit romantic. There aren't even sheets on the bed. But this isn't about romance. It's fulfilling a need, and will hopefully make the thoughts I had earlier go away. I didn't mean to think about Steven that way, but I did, and I need it to stop.

"Relax," Tanner whispers in my ear as we lie on the bare mattress. "You're so tense."

It's because I keep thinking about Steven, imagining it's him whispering in my ear and his body on top of mine.

Why am I thinking about Steven this way? What is wrong with me? He's married. I've never once been with a married man. I wouldn't even consider it.

"That was good, babe," Tanner says, getting up to put on his jeans.

The whole thing couldn't have lasted more than five

minutes and I got nothing out of it. That's the problem with guys Tanner's age. It's all about them. Their own satisfaction. They don't care if their partner enjoyed it.

"You had fun, right?" Tanner asks.

Okay, so maybe he does care, but then why didn't he wait for me to finish?

"Yeah." I get up from the bed. "Just what I needed."

It's what I needed to remind myself why I don't date. Maybe I need to date men who are older and more mature. Men like Steven, but that aren't married.

Tanner looks around the room. "So the bed and dresser? What else needs to go in the truck?"

"The couch in the living room. The coffee table is broken. We could toss it in the dumpster. Oh, and I'll need you to store the boxes."

"Where are you sleeping tonight? You won't have a mattress."

"I'll just sleep on the floor."

"You could stay with me," he says, giving me a smile that makes it clear we wouldn't be doing much sleeping.

"I'll be fine on the floor." I go over to one of the boxes and close the flaps on the top. "Are you sure you have room for all this?"

"I got a whole basement with nothing in it."

Tanner's renting a house from his parents. His grandma used to live there, but she died a few months ago. Instead of selling the house, Tanner's parents told him he could live there if he paid rent. They're only charging him three hundred a month. They just wanted him out of their house.

"Let's start with the mattress," he says, lifting it on its side.

Just before midnight, we've got everything loaded in the truck. I follow Tanner to his house and help him unload. By the time we're done, it's one in the morning.

"You really want to do this?" Tanner asks, as he walks me to my car.

"Do what?"

"Move in with some lady and her husband. You don't even know these people."

"I know them. I spent all day with them. They're nice."

"You can't tell what people are like after a day. Anyone can pretend to be normal for a few hours."

"What do you think is going to happen? The wife is stuck in bed and her husband is at work all day."

"Yeah, well, at night you better lock your door."

"You're being paranoid. They're not going to kill me in my sleep."

"They could do other things." Tanner leans against my car. "What's the husband like?"

I shrug. "I don't know. I didn't talk to him much. But he was really sweet with his wife. I can tell how much he cares about her."

"Or he just wants her to think that."

"What's that supposed to mean?"

"He's playing her. Making her think she's the only woman he wants so she doesn't suspect anything."

"About what?"

"Him fooling around. You said they're rich, right?"

"Yeah, but that doesn't mean he cheats."

"Almost all rich guys cheat."

"You don't know that. You're basing that on movies, which isn't real life."

"Trust me, it happens more than you think. And now this guy's got some hot young girl moving in? You really think he isn't going to try something?"

"He's not like that. He's devoted to his wife, and he's like 12 years older than me. He doesn't see me that way."

Tanner laughs. "Yeah, okay." He puts his hand on my shoulder and leans down to me. "You know you're hot, right?"

"I'm not hot. I'm average."

"You're hot." His gaze moves down my body. "I don't know what this guy's wife looks like, but she's got competition with you living there."

"Nothing's going to happen." I get in the car. "I need to go. Thanks for helping me move."

He hangs onto my door. "Give me a call this week. Let me know how it's going."

"I won't have time. And why do you care? We're not dating."

"We're still friends, and I don't feel good about this. There's something not right about it. I mean, no offense, but you've only been a nurse for like a year. Why would some rich lady hire you to take care of her? Why didn't she pick someone with more experience?"

"Not many people would be willing to move to that town and take a job that's only for two months."

"Yeah, I guess. Just be careful, okay?" He leans down to me in the car and gives me a kiss. "I'll see you in a couple months."

Tanner's not a bad guy. He's just immature, and I'm tired of immature guys.

As I drive back to my apartment, I think about what Tanner said about the Bishops. It's true I don't really know them, but I'm not worried about living there. Audrey's the only person I'm concerned about, but it's not because of my safety. I'm worried she'll get me fired.

Everything's going to be fine. Better than fine. I'll be living in a beautiful house on the coast of Maine while saving up money to get back on my feet. It's exactly what I need right now.

11

LAUREN

"What time will you be home?" I call out to Steven as I hear him running down the stairs.

He appears at the door to my room, dressed for work in his dark suit and the tie I gave him on our last anniversary. "I'm not sure yet. I've got a meeting that might run late. Hey, do you think now that Hannah's here I might be able to stay at the house a few nights a week?"

He's referring to our house in Boston that's been sitting empty since we came to live here a few weeks ago.

"I'd feel better if you were here."

"It's just such a long drive after working all day, and it's not good having the house just sitting there not being used. At the very least, I need to go there and check on it. Run the faucets. Flush the toilets. Make sure the pipes don't freeze."

"We could hire someone to housesit for us. Audrey did that when she and Barry went to Italy."

"We don't need a housesitter." He sighs. "If you don't want me staying there, I'll see if I can stop by during lunch and check on it."

"I didn't say you couldn't stay there. I'd just rather it not be every night. I don't like being here alone."

"You'll be with Hannah."

"Yes, but I'd feel better if you were here too."

His brows draw together. "Do you have concerns about her?"

"Hannah? No, not at all. But I doubt she could fight off an intruder if she and I were alone here at night."

"It's a very safe area. And very secluded." He gives me a slight smile as he adjusts his tie. "I don't think we need to worry about intruders."

The doorbell rings.

"That must be Hannah," I say. "Do you have a key to give her?"

"It's on the kitchen counter. I'll go get the door." Moments later, I hear him talking to Hannah. "Welcome back. First day. Are you nervous?"

"Should I be?" she says with a laugh.

"I'm just kidding. Take off your coat and join me in the kitchen. I need to go over some things."

"Can I check on Mrs. Bishop first?"

"Of course. Go ahead."

I told Hannah several times yesterday that she could call me Lauren, but she insists on calling me Mrs. Bishop.

Hannah appears at my door. "Hi, Mrs. Bishop. How are you doing today?"

"Good, but I'd like to shower soon and get dressed. Audrey might stop by."

"Oh," Hannah says, biting her lip.

"Is something wrong? You seem nervous."

Hannah comes into my room and stands by my bed. "Audrey just makes me uncomfortable, but I'm sure I'll get used to it."

"Don't take it personally. She's very protective of me."

"Hannah, I need to be going soon," Steven calls out from the kitchen.

"Go ahead," I tell her. "We'll talk later."

She goes to the kitchen and I hear Steven talking.

"Please don't think this has anything to do with us not trusting you," he says, "or thinking of you in any negative light. This is standard for anyone we'd hire to work for us."

"What is this?" Hannah asks.

"It's an employment agreement. It outlines how long you'll be here, what we're paying you, and other standard terms of your employment. As I said, this has nothing to do with you personally. It's strictly a necessary part of doing business."

"What's this part about liability?"

"It basically says you won't sue us if you're injured while working here, or living here."

"Why would I get injured?"

"You might slip on some ice in the driveway or trip going down the stairs. It's just standard legal language meant to clear up any misunderstandings should something happen. Hannah, I'm sorry to rush you, but I really need to get to the office. I've got a full morning of meetings."

"Um, okay."

She must've signed the contract because I hear Steven say, "Thanks, and again, this has nothing to do with you. It's just a standard employment agreement."

"I understand."

"I'll let you get back to Lauren. Have a good day."

"You too, Mr. Bishop."

I hear them walking around, then Steven comes into my room with Hannah following behind.

"I couldn't leave without saying goodbye." He walks over to me and leans down to give me a kiss. "Bye, sweetheart. I love you."

"I love you too." I glance at Hannah and see her watching us with envy in her eyes.

If she only knew. But when I was her age, I, too, believed it was real. I thought I had the dream. It wasn't until years later that I finally did. But not with the man I married.

"I'll see you tonight." Steven turns to leave, passing Hannah on his way out the door.

Her gaze follows him, like she can't take her eyes off him. I'm not surprised. Most women have that reaction to him, and Steven encourages the attention by smiling at them and turning on the charm. That should've concerned me when we were dating, and yet it was just another quality of his that I chose to look past.

"He really loves you," Hannah says, coming up to my bed. "That's rare these days."

I smile a little. "I don't know about that. I think it's more about finding the right person."

"Well, you definitely found that with Mr. Bishop. The way he looks at you? It's obvious how much he loves you."

Looks can be deceiving. And words are just letters put together and assigned a meaning. I learned long ago that 'I love you' is nothing more than words. It doesn't have to mean anything. The first guy I dated said he loved me, then used my body and tossed me aside. From then on, I learned not to trust those words.

"So Steven spoke to you about the employment contract?" I say, sitting up.

"Yes, and I signed it."

"I hope you're not upset about that. I didn't think it was necessary, but Steven likes everything to be in writing."

"I'm not upset. I just wasn't expecting it."

"Please don't take it personally. Steven's just being cautious in the event that something would happen during your employment here, not that it would, of course." I smile at her. "So how was last night? Did you get everything moved?"

"Yes, but Tanner was late getting to my place so we didn't finish until one in the morning."

"Is this boy someone you used to date?"

"Yes, but we haven't dated for almost a year. We're just friends now."

"It's very generous of him to help you out like that. Most boys that age wouldn't unless they got something in return."

"I bought him a case of beer. He's a nice guy. He just needs to grow up. I'm tired of dating immature guys. Anyway, I'll go get the shower ready."

While Hannah goes to prepare the shower, I think about what she said, about wanting to be with a mature man. I saw her looking at Steven, but I can't yet tell if she'd let it go beyond looking.

Steven can be very charming. Very alluring. And very persuasive. If the opportunity were there, would Hannah take it?

12

LAUREN

"Well, look at you," Audrey says, handing me the coffee she got me. "All dressed up and ready for the day."

"I'd hardly call this dressed up," I say, smiling at her.

"You're wearing a nice sweater. Your hair's done. Makeup's on." She sits next to me, her brows raised. "Is Steven planning something for tonight? A romantic dinner?"

I laugh. "No. Have you forgotten what married life's like? Romantic dinners ended years ago."

"I could see your husband planning a nice dinner," Hannah pipes in as she puts away my laundry. "He seems like the romantic type."

"How would *you* know?" Audrey scoffs.

"I've seen how he is with Mrs. Bishop," Hannah says. "He clearly loves her and would do anything for her."

"Maybe you should leave and let me talk to my friend."

"Audrey," I say, urging her to be nice.

"I'm just saying she doesn't need to be in here when we're talking."

Hannah picks up the laundry basket. "I'll go do this somewhere else."

She leaves and I look over at Audrey. "Stop being that way with her."

"What way?"

"Treating her like the enemy. She's here to help me and she's doing a very good job. She did my hair and makeup this morning and picked out this sweater. She's the reason I look so good today."

"You can't do your own makeup?"

"Do you know what it feels like to lift your arms with bruised ribs?"

"No idea."

"It's extremely painful. That's why I haven't done my hair or makeup, not that I need to when I'm just sitting around all day. But I have to admit, it does make me feel better to not look so plain. Now that I'm all made up, I wish I had somewhere to go."

"But you can't, right? You can't leave the house yet?"

"I could, but it'd be difficult. I'd have to use the wheelchair, and I'd be in a lot of pain trying to get in and out of the car."

"What about next week? Do you think you might be able to get out of the house by then?"

"I doubt it. Why do you ask?"

Audrey sets her coffee down and moves to the end of her chair. "I need to tell you something."

"What is it? The way you said that, you're worrying me."

"It's about David."

My heart thumps harder. "What about him?"

"His parents have decided to do a celebration of life event. They felt like the funeral wasn't what David would've wanted. It was so serious and sad, and as you know, that wasn't David. He was always so happy and full of—"

"Yes, I know," I say, interrupting her. I'm not ready to talk about David. Just hearing his name, I'm tearing up.

"They're having it here, at the town hall. Even though his

parents live in Florida now, they've remained friends with a lot of people in town. And of course, David was friends with pretty much everyone."

David grew up here. He loved this town. He moved to Boston after college and did marketing for a fitness apparel company. Then, about three years ago, he decided he'd had enough of city life and moved back here. A few months later, I found this house and convinced Steven to let us buy it. I told him it'd be our summer home, but I knew I'd be the one living in it while Steven remained in Boston. He's not good at relaxing. After a day or two here, he'd get bored and restless and end up going back to the city.

Steven didn't understand why I'd want to spend the entire summer in Maine, especially when my best friend was living in Boston, so I talked Audrey into getting a place here too. It was probably wrong of me to use her like that, but I had to. And it's not like I was making her do something she didn't want to. She'd been looking for a place to go during the summer that wasn't too far from the city.

"When's the celebration of life?" I ask. "Do they have a date?"

"It's next week. Tuesday night."

"That's David's birthday," I mutter, feeling a lump in my throat. "Or it would've been."

"Yes, that's why they picked that day. His parents are coming to town this weekend to help get everything ready."

"What are they planning? Do you know?"

She nods. "The band David liked has volunteered to play and people in town signed up to provide the food. I'm not bringing anything, but I plan to donate money and maybe bid on something, if there's anything worth bidding on."

"This is a fundraiser?"

"Yes, there's a silent auction. They'll also be taking donations. The money they raise will go to the library. You know how much David loved that old library. He was determined to restore it. If they raise enough money next week, it might actually happen."

"When was all this planned? It had to have been within the past few days. Steven doesn't even know."

She hesitates, then says, "He knows. He found out a week ago."

"I don't understand. Why didn't he tell me?"

"I think he should be the one to talk to you about that."

"Why? What's going on?"

She shakes her head.

"Audrey, what is it? What are you not telling me?"

"Just wait for Steven to get home. I don't want to get in the middle of this."

"You already are. How do you know all this and I don't know? Did Steven talk to you?"

She nods. "I called Steven when I got the invite. I wanted to know if he'd told you. I didn't want to mention it and then have you be surprised."

"And? What did he say?"

"Lauren, I really think this is something you should ask him."

"No. I want to hear it from you. Steven will just tell me what he thinks I want to hear. You'll tell me the truth."

She takes a drink of her coffee, then sets it down. "He wasn't invited."

"To the celebration of life?" I pause. "That doesn't make sense. Steven and David were best friends."

"They *were*," she says, implying that had changed.

"What are you saying? Did something happen?"

"They had a fight. About a week before the accident."

"A fight? No. Steven would've told me."

"I'm sure he will when you talk to him. When I called him about the invite, he told me he didn't get one, then explained why. He said he hadn't told you about it because he thought it was too soon to bring up David. Because of the accident. And the nightmares you've been having."

"But this has nothing to do with the accident. You said they were fighting a week before it happened."

"I can't speak for Steven. All I know is what he told me, which was that he didn't want to upset you."

"So he's really not going to the celebration of life?"

"He spoke with David's parents last night and they agreed to let him come. He called me this morning and asked if I would tell you about it. He thought it might be better coming from me than from him. You know how uncomfortable he gets with these types of things."

"No, I don't. This is the first time we've lost a good friend. I'm disappointed Steven wouldn't tell me this himself. This is something we should've talked about."

"And you will. Tonight." She picks up her coffee and leans back in the chair. "Whatever their fight was about was probably something trivial and Steven was just embarrassed to bring it up."

"If it was trivial, David's parents would've invited Steven to the celebration of life."

"It doesn't matter. They worked it out and Steven plans to be there. You really don't think you could make it?"

"Like this?" I point to my broken leg and the bruises that remain on my arms and neck. They've faded since the accident but are still visible. "Even if I was able to, David's parents wouldn't want me there. It would just remind them of what happened."

Hannah walks in, then stops suddenly when she sees the serious look on my face. I'm sure my eyes are red too from fighting back tears.

"I'm sorry, did I interrupt something?" she asks.

"Yes, you did," Audrey says in a scolding tone. She stands

up. "But I need to get going." She leans down to me and gives my shoulder a gentle squeeze. "Don't be upset with Steven. I'm sure he'll talk to you tonight and you two will work this out."

I nod. "Thanks for stopping by."

She grabs her coffee cup, then leaves, not even glancing at Hannah as she passes by her.

Hannah comes up to me. "Is something wrong?"

"No. Audrey was just telling me about an event being held for David, the man who was killed in the accident, and it upset me."

"I'm sorry. Is there anything I can do?"

"I'd just like some time alone."

She nods, then walks out of the room.

Why didn't Steven tell me he'd been fighting with David? The two of them rarely argued, and if they did, it was in a joking way. It wasn't serious.

What could they have argued about that was bad enough that David's parents didn't want Steven at the celebration of life? And why didn't Steven tell me?

13

LAUREN

"What time would you like dinner?" Hannah asks as she hands me a glass of water.

It's after six and I've spent the whole day thinking about Steven and David, trying to figure out what they might have been fighting about. It couldn't have involved me. David would've told me.

"Dinner will have to be later," I say. "I need to talk to Steven. Would you mind going up to your room when he gets home?"

"Um, sure. Did I do something wrong?"

"No, not at all. I just don't want us being interrupted." I hear the garage door opening. "That's him."

"I'll be up in my room," Hannah says, hurrying off.

Moments later, I hear Steven in the kitchen, his keys clanking as he drops them on the counter.

"Steven?" I call out.

"I'll be there in a minute." I hear him walking down to his office.

What is so important in his office that it can't wait? When we bought this house, we argued about him having an office here. This was supposed to be our place to relax and spend time together. But Steven insisted he needed an office in case something came up with one of his clients and he had to access their files. I told him he could do that with his laptop. He doesn't need an entire office.

I obviously didn't win that argument, or the one about not locking the door. Steven won't even give me a key. He says he has client files in there and giving me access to that room would be breaking client confidentiality. What does he think I'm going to do? Log into his clients' investment accounts and move money around? I wouldn't even know how. I'm clueless when it comes to the stock market. That's Steven's specialty. He has a talent for knowing which investments will make money and which ones won't.

The door to the office closes and I hear the lock turning, then Steven's footsteps as he walks to my room.

"Sorry, sweetheart," he says, coming over to me in the bed. "I just had to put something away." He looks around. "Where's Hannah?"

"Upstairs in her room. I asked her to wait up there so we could be alone. I need to talk to you."

He lets out a heavy sigh as he sits down on the bed. "Audrey talked to you."

"Steven, why didn't you tell me you'd been fighting with David?"

"Because I didn't think you needed to know. It was just a disagreement."

"If that's all it was, his parents would've invited you to the celebration of life."

"That was a misunderstanding. David clearly made the argument sound worse than it was, but I spoke with his parents and straightened it all out."

"What were you and David fighting about?"

"I wanted more for him. Moving here, raising money for the town, planning those ridiculous events, he was wasting his

82

potential. He could have easily had an executive level job at a large company, but instead he was wasting his time in this town."

"He liked it here. He didn't want a corporate job. He did that for years and hated it."

"He was at the wrong company. He needed to find a place that was a better fit."

"Working at the chamber of commerce was a better fit. It's what David wanted to do, and he loved it."

"He was being sentimental. He grew up here so it's only natural he'd feel a connection to this place and want to return to it, especially after his parents moved to Florida."

"So what are you saying? That you were fighting because you wanted him to get a different job?"

"I have a client in Tampa. A very wealthy man who owns a company that makes custom yachts for high-end customers. Their head of marketing recently left and my client asked if I knew of anyone who might be right for the job. I immediately thought of David. He would've been perfect for the job and he would've been close to his parents."

Why didn't David tell me this? I knew something was bothering him in the weeks leading up to the accident, but when I asked, he said everything was fine. But it wasn't fine. My husband was trying to get him a job and convince him to move away. But why? Was Steven trying to get David away from me? He'd only do that if he knew about us, and he didn't. He couldn't have.

"David didn't want to leave here," I say. "You know that, Steven. He always said he'd never leave New England."

"Which was short-sighted and completely irrational. I understand his connection to this area, but it's not like he couldn't come back and visit. This job would've changed his life, and I'm not just talking about the money, but the connections he would've made. When you get an opportunity like that, you don't just pass it up."

"When you told him about it, did he consider it at all?"

"No. He was adamantly opposed to the idea. He wouldn't even participate in the call I set up for him with my client. It was only to discuss the opportunity, not commit to it, but he refused."

"Why did you set up a call before talking to him?"

"Because I was certain he would do it." Steven gets up from the bed. "Why wouldn't he? It was a half million a year base salary plus bonus. He'd get to travel the world at the company's expense. Meet powerful people. An opportunity like that doesn't come along every day."

"But those things didn't matter to him. You know that, Steven. David's never cared about money or possessions the way other people do. That's why he gave up his job in Boston."

"Yes, and because of that, he was living in a small condo, driving a 10-year-old car, and making what he made his first year out of college." He huffs. "And he wonders why he never found a wife."

"What does a wife have to do with this?"

"What woman wants to live that way?" He motions to me. "You certainly didn't."

"What are you saying?" My hands fist as rage builds inside me, but my voice remains calm. "That I married you for your money?"

"That, and my earning potential." He smirks at me. "Don't try to deny it, Lauren. We both knew what this marriage was."

And yet it's the first time he's brought it up. In 12 years, we've managed to keep that to ourselves, pretending it wasn't true and that we married for love.

"If I married you for money," I say, "I wouldn't have signed the prenup."

"You only signed it because of the clause you made me add.

You assumed I'd be unfaithful." He leans down to me and whispers in my ear. "But you know I'd never be with someone else." He smooths my hair and kisses my cheek, then looks into my eyes. "You're mine, Lauren. Why would I want anyone else?"

Because he doesn't love me. He never has. He wanted me because of how I looked. I fit the image of what he imagined for his future. He'd live in a large house, drive an expensive car, wear designer clothes, and have a wife who was taller than average, very thin, with blond hair, blue eyes, and porcelain skin. The moment he saw me all those years ago, I could see it in his eyes that he wanted me. Back then, I thought it was love at first sight, that his heart was what made him look at me that way. It wasn't until after we said our vows that I realized I was just a box he was checking off. A stepping stone to the future he'd imagined.

But what he said about our marriage isn't true, not entirely. When I accepted his proposal, part of me did love him. It wasn't just about the money. That was more about a promise I made to my mother. Before she died, she told me to marry wisely. She said if I had feelings for more than one man, to choose the one with the most money.

I did as she said. I had feelings for two men, but chose the one with the most money and the greatest potential to make more. I kept my promise. Only to regret it later.

14

HANNAH

"What about the event next week?" I hear Lauren say as I come down the stairs. "Are you going?"

"Of course I'm going," Steven says. "I was his best friend."

I pause at the bottom of the stairs. Lauren told me to stay in my room, but I'm really hungry and wanted a snack. I thought Steven and Lauren would be done talking by now, but it sounds like they're not.

"There's nothing more to say," Steven says. "I've told you everything."

"I doubt that," Lauren says.

"I'm not going to keep explaining myself," Steven says. "I resolved the issue and will be going to the event next week." I hear him leaving the room and hurry back up the stairs.

"Hannah?" Steven says.

Damn. He caught me.

I turn back and see Steven at the bottom of the stairs. "Hi, Mr. Bishop. I was just going to grab a snack from the kitchen."

He gives me a playful smile. "Then why are you running up the stairs?"

"I, um, heard you talking to Mrs. Bishop and didn't want to interrupt."

"Lauren and I are done now. You're free to go where you wish."

"Oh. Okay." I smile and continue down the stairs, brushing Steven's arm as I pass him.

"When will dinner be ready?" he asks, following me to the kitchen.

"Probably an hour," I say, taking a pan from the drawer. "We're having chicken. I took it from the freezer and it's still kind of frozen. I didn't get a chance to go to the store today."

He loosens his tie as he walks up to me. "Why don't we go out?"

"You and me?" I ask, confused, because I'm not sure why he'd want to go to dinner with the hired help.

"That chicken's been in the freezer for over a year. I think it's past being edible, and I'd like to get out of the house."

Why? Because of the argument he had with Lauren? I'm assuming they were arguing. They both sounded angry, but it's possible I misread their conversation.

"Hannah?" Lauren calls out. "Can you come in here, please?"

"I'm coming." I hurry to her room, stopping next to her bed. "What do you need?"

"I told you to stay upstairs," she says in a cold, angry tone, her eyes narrowed at me.

"I was hungry. I was just going to run down and get a snack, then go back upstairs."

"You couldn't wait?" she snaps. "You're not a child, Hannah. You don't need to be fed the second you feel hungry."

Why is she getting so angry about this? She didn't get mad when I broke her wedding frame and that seems way worse than me overhearing her conversation.

"Yes, you're right," I say. "I shouldn't have done it. I should've stayed in my room."

"Did you hear anything?"

"No. I just heard you talking and went—"

"Don't lie to me, Hannah. If you're going to work for me, I need to be able to trust you, and I can't trust you if you lie to me."

"Yes," I say with a sigh. "I heard you two talking, but I didn't hear much."

"What did you hear?"

"Just something about an event next week. It sounded like you two were arguing so I decided to go back upstairs." My heart's pounding, but I'm trying really hard to keep my breath steady and act like this isn't a big deal, even though I think there's a very good chance she's going to fire me.

If she does, where will I live? My apartment's gone and I don't have money to get another one. If she kicks me out, I'll have to sleep in my car tonight, in the freezing cold, with snow coming down.

"Thank you for being honest with me," Lauren says in a calm voice, her anger suddenly gone. She takes my hand in both of hers. "I appreciate honesty, even if it upsets me. The truth hurts, as they say, but I'd still rather have the truth. Wouldn't you?"

I nod. "Yes, definitely."

"I'm glad we worked this out." She releases my hand and rests back on the pillows. "Now go ahead and get dinner started."

"Um, about that. Mr. Bishop wants to go out."

Lauren's eyes were closed, but they blink open and she looks at me with surprise. "You and Steven? Just the two of you?"

"I guess. Unless you want to go, but you're always saying you're not ready to leave the house. But if you are, I'd be happy to help you get—"

"No." She smiles. "I think it's a good idea. You've been here

88

all day. It'll be good to get out. And you can get to know Steven."

"Did I hear my name?" he says.

When I glance back at the door, I see him standing there. He's still wearing his suit pants, but his dress shirt and tie have been replaced with a fitted black sweater that clings to his chest and the muscles that line his arms.

He is definitely the most handsome man I've ever seen.

"Hannah tells me you're taking her to dinner," Lauren says, smiling at her husband.

"It's either that or try to choke down that chicken that's been in the freezer since who knows when."

"Yes, we should throw that out," Lauren says. "Hannah, tomorrow if you have time, would you mind tossing out whatever's in the freezer?"

"Yes, I'll do it while you're resting," I say. "And I'll be sure to make it to the store tomorrow."

"Use my car when you go. It has more room than yours and it's safer on the icy roads."

"We should get going," Steven says to me.

I walk to the door as Steven goes over to Lauren. He leans down and kisses her forehead. "I love you, sweetheart. Call if you need anything."

He's back to being a caring and sweet husband. It's good he doesn't stay angry at Lauren. When my mom and her boyfriend used to fight, they'd stay angry for days, sometimes weeks. I don't want that kind of relationship.

"Will you bring me something back?" Lauren asks.

"Whatever you like." Steven picks up her hand and gives it a gentle squeeze. "How about I get you one of those cheeseburgers you love so much?"

"That sounds wonderful." Lauren looks over at me. "Have a good time. And don't worry about me. I'll just relax and watch some TV."

"We'll make it quick," I say.

"No rush," Lauren says, picking up the TV remote.

Steven passes me as he leaves her room. "I'll go pull the car out."

"Oh. I was going to change."

He glances at my body. "What's wrong with what you have on?"

"It's just that you're kind of dressed up and I'm in jeans and a sweatshirt. I could change really fast."

"Go ahead. I'll be in the car. Come out when you're ready."

I race upstairs to my room and dump out one of the garbage bags I filled with clothes. My entire wardrobe fit in four garbage bags. You'd probably need a hundred bags for Lauren's clothes. Her walk-in closet downstairs is filled to capacity and I'm guessing she has more clothes in the master bedroom and at her house in Boston.

"This will have to do," I say to myself, throwing on a red sweater I got for Christmas a few years ago. It was a gift from a guy I was dating, but he had his mom pick it out. He told me that after I opened it, which kind of ruined the moment, but his mom has good taste. It's a really nice sweater that fits me well. For pants, all I have are jeans, sweats, and my scrubs. I find my nicest pair of jeans and put them on, then race into the bathroom and add more mascara to my lashes and swipe some blush over my cheeks.

I feel like I'm getting ready for a date, which is silly. It's just dinner with my employer. I shouldn't even care what I look like. The only reason I'm going is because I'm hungry and need to eat.

It's not a date. It is absolutely, one hundred percent, not a date.

15

HANNAH

Steven takes me to a diner downtown. It's cute, like a diner you see on TV, with red swivel stools lined up by the counter and red booths along the window. There's even a jukebox, although it doesn't look like it works.

The place isn't busy, other than a foursome of old people in one of the booths and some middle-aged men sitting at the counter.

"Hope this is okay," Steven says, handing me a laminated menu from the metal stand that's on the table. "Lauren loves this place." He laughs a little. "She calls it kitschy, whatever that means."

"I feel like we're overdressed," I say, noticing the guys at the counter wearing sweatshirts and jeans.

"You dress how you want to feel," Steven says as he peruses the menu. "I like to feel successful and stylish. I wear clothes that reflect that. I don't care whether or not it fits my surroundings."

"That's an interesting way to look at it." I flip the menu to the other side. "So what's good here?"

"Nothing. But our options are limited. It was either this or the Mexican place down the street. I had an unfortunate reaction to the last meal I had there and haven't been back."

"That's all there are for restaurants? Two?"

"There are a few others, but they close early on weeknights. Most close at eight during the winter."

"Wow, that's early. It must be a small town thing."

Steven sets his menu back in the metal holder. "Have you made a decision?"

"I'll probably get a burger. Honestly, I'd eat most anything right now. I'm starving. I didn't have time to eat lunch."

"Lauren's keeping you that busy?"

"No, but I stayed with her for most of the day."

"You know you don't have to. When she needs you, then yes, but she's perfectly fine being alone in her room."

"She told me that, but she keeps having those dreams and I worry she might try to get out of bed and end up hurting herself."

His brows draw together. "Are the dreams about her accident?"

"Yes. She wakes up screaming and reaching her arms out. This morning she tried to turn on her side to get out of bed. She would've fallen if I hadn't been there."

"Does she say anything during these dreams?"

"Sometimes she'll say that guy's name. The one who died?"

"David." Steven nods. "He was a close friend of mine. We'd been friends since college."

An older woman with gray hair pulled back in a tight bun stops at our table. She's wearing a light blue dress with a white apron tied around the waist, like one of those old-fashioned waitress uniforms.

"Haven't seen *you* for a while," the woman says to Steven, taking out her order pad. She doesn't seem pleased to see him. She's glaring at him from behind her glasses.

"Hello, Doreen." He gives her that alluring smile of his, but it does nothing to change the scowl on her face.

"You want the usual?" she asks.

"No, I believe I'll be adventurous tonight and have a cheeseburger." He says it like he's making a joke, but she doesn't even crack a smile.

She turns to me. "And for you?"

"I'll have the same," I tell her.

"Doreen, this is Hannah," Steven says. "She's Lauren's new nurse. She'll be staying with us until Lauren's able to care for herself."

"You look just like her," the old lady says.

"I do?" I ask, surprised by her comment.

"Pale skin. Blond hair. Skinny. You could pass for her sister. In fact, I thought you were when I saw you come in with him." She glances at Steven.

"I guess I don't see the resemblance," I say.

"Where you from?" the lady asks.

"Boston."

"Doreen, I'd really like to get our order in," Steven says. "I don't want to leave Lauren for too long."

She laughs. "Now THAT'S funny."

I don't get it. What does she mean?

"You two want drinks?" she asks.

"I'll have a soda," I say.

"Water for me," Steven says. "Oh, and I'll need an extra cheeseburger to go. I'm bringing one home for Lauren."

The old lady jots it down on her order pad, then takes off.

"She seems kind of cranky," I say, keeping my voice down.

"She's always like that. It's how people end up when they limit themselves. Bitter. Angry. Envious of those who have success."

I set my menu in the holder. "What do you mean by limit themselves?"

"Not going after what they want. Doreen's a smart woman. She went to college. Manages the bookkeeping for this place. Handles the taxes. She could've got a job at an accounting firm or a large company, but instead she limited herself to living in this town, working at this diner."

"Maybe that makes her happy."

"Does she seem happy?"

"No. Not really."

"Exactly. Her life's almost over and she never did anything. Never achieved her goals or took risks. She sees someone like me, and instead of admiring me for my success, she hates me for it because it reminds her of what she could've had."

I look over at Doreen behind the counter as she fills a glass at the soda machine. One of the men at the counter is talking to her. She's smiling at whatever he's saying and nodding her head. Seeing her now, she looks happy and not the least bit grumpy. Steven might have the wrong idea about her.

She returns to our table and sets down our drinks, then turns toward Steven, her hands on her hips. "So how's she doing? Any better?"

"She's coming along," Steven says, taking a sip of his water. "She isn't yet able to get around on her own, but that's to be expected. The doctors warned us it'd be a slow recovery."

"Bet you're happy about that," Doreen mutters.

Steven clears his throat. "If you'll excuse us, I'd like to talk to Hannah."

"Be my guest," Doreen says, rolling her eyes as she walks away.

"What did you want to talk about?" I ask Steven.

"Nothing in particular," he says, taking a napkin from the metal dispenser and putting it over his lap. "I just wanted her to go away." He leans back in the booth and smiles at me. "So tell me about yourself, Hannah."

That nervous flutter I feel whenever I'm around him was

finally starting to settle down, but now it's back, because of his question. I don't like talking about myself, especially to someone as smart and successful as Steven.

"I grew up in Boston," I say, which he already knows, but I'm struggling with what to tell him. "I'm an only child. My parents are gone."

"Yes. Lauren told me. That's a shame. Unfortunately, the same is true for Lauren and me."

"Oh. She didn't tell me your parents had passed."

He nods. "I was eight when it happened. They were hit by a car on their way home one night."

"That's terrible. You were so young. Who took care of you after that?"

"My uncle. He lived in Manhattan. Worked on Wall Street. He's the one who taught me how to invest." Steven picks up his glass of water and takes a drink. "I wouldn't be where I'm at now if it weren't for him."

"Is he still alive?"

"Yes, he's living in France now. I suppose you could say he's retired, although he'd never admit that. He believes you should work until you die. He still studies the market daily and manages his investments, which could be considered working, I suppose."

"Is he married?"

"He was, but it didn't last. And he never had children. Just the ones he inherited when my parents died."

"So you have siblings."

"A sister. She lives in Switzerland."

"What does she do there?"

"I really don't know. She and I aren't close. We haven't spoken in years."

That's sad. I wonder why they don't talk. Did they have a fight or just grow apart? I'd like to ask but it's probably too personal. I decide to keep quiet and take a drink of my soda.

"What does your boyfriend think about you moving here?" Steven asks.

"Oh, I don't have a boyfriend."

"You don't? I thought Lauren said something about a young man helping you move."

"That's Tanner. He's not a boyfriend. We're just friends. We dated last year, but it didn't work out. He's kind of immature."

"And you prefer a mature man?" he says with a slight smile.

"If I can find one, then yes."

"I would think a beautiful young woman like yourself would have no problem finding a suitable man."

Was that a compliment or was he flirting with me?

I'm sure he wasn't flirting. He's married. He loves Lauren and is devoted to her.

"Two cheeseburgers," Doreen says, appearing at our table with two plates topped with burgers and a huge mound of fries. She sets the plates down. "Need anything else?"

"Just the order for Lauren," Steven says.

"The cook's got it under the warmer. I'll pack it up when you're ready for the check. Say, are you going to the fundraiser this week?" Doreen asks Steven.

"You mean the celebration of life?"

"I guess that's what they're calling it. It's for David. His parents are putting it on. I assumed you'd be there since you two were friends."

"Yes, I'll be there," Steven says. "Why do you ask?"

"I'm wondering if she could help." Doreen motions to me. "You give her time off, right?"

"Help with what?" I ask.

"The event this week," Doreen says. "We're raising money to restore the library. David always loved that building and wanted to fix it up, but the town didn't have the money. We're

96

hoping this event will raise enough to at least fix part of the building."

"Hannah didn't even know David," Steven says. "And she has no connection to this town. You shouldn't be asking her to volunteer."

"Actually," I say to Steven, "if it's okay with you, I wouldn't mind helping. It'd be a good way to meet people. And it's for a good cause."

"Great!" Doreen reaches in her pocket and pulls out a piece of paper with a phone number written on it. "That's Kathy's number. She's in charge of the food. Give her a call and let her know you'll be there to help serve."

"I'm serving the food?"

"It's easy. You just dish it up as people go through the line. And she'll probably want your help setting up."

"You don't have to do this," Steven says to me.

"I don't mind," I say. "But I'll need the time off."

"We'll talk to Lauren, but I'm sure she'll be fine with it."

I hope she lets me go. If I'm going to be living here for two months, I should meet some of the people in town. I'm curious what the locals think of Steven and Lauren. Doreen clearly doesn't like Steven, but she seems like someone who doesn't like people in general.

I'm sure Steven is well-liked in town. How could he not be? He's charming, polite, and nice to look at.

If only I could find a man like him. He's exactly what I'm looking for.

16

HANNAH

The next morning, after I get Lauren ready for the day, she tells me to go to the grocery store. But every time I try to leave, she adds more to the list. I finally told her to just text me what she wants because I'll never remember.

"Oh, and get some strawberries," Lauren says. "Fresh ones. Make sure they're organic."

I walk back to her room and stand at the door, my coat and hat on, Lauren's car keys in my hand. "Strawberries. Got it. Anything else?"

She pauses to think. "I'd love some Brie, but the store in town doesn't carry it."

"Maybe they could order it. I could ask the manager."

"Don't bother. I can always ask Steven to pick some up when he's in the city."

"Isn't he there now? You could text him."

"He doesn't like it when I text or call during work hours."

"But you're his wife. I'm sure he wouldn't mind."

"It's fine," she says with an uncomfortable smile. "I don't need it. If you have any questions while you're at the store, just give me a call."

"I thought you were going to sleep."

"I'm not tired. I think I'll just watch TV."

"Okay. I'll be back soon."

Lauren's been acting off ever since she had that argument with Steven. They haven't fought since then, so I don't know what's bothering her. I want to ask, but I don't think I should.

When I get into her SUV, I savor the feel of the soft leather seats. The interior is immaculate. There aren't any empty cups tossed on the floor, nothing in the cupholders, no charging cords dangling from the center console. The back seat is just as clean.

Pushing the button to start the engine, I let it warm up as I adjust the mirrors. The garage door is already open and from the rearview mirror, I notice snowflakes beginning to fall. I don't like driving in the snow, but at least I'm in a large SUV that probably has a million safety features. My car's so old, the only safety feature it has is a seatbelt, which always gets stuck when I try to put it on.

Once everything's adjusted, I slowly and carefully pull out of the garage. I've never driven something this nice. I'm worried I'm going to run into something and damage it. I stop in the driveway and press the button to shut the garage door, then punch the grocery store name into my phone. I could use the car's navigation system but it seems complicated and I don't want to waste time trying to figure it out.

The store is 10 miles away but the navigation app says it'll take me 20 minutes to get there. It's not a big town, but the Bishop house is in a remote location. It takes forever to get anywhere because you have to drive really slow on a small winding road before reaching the main road into town.

As I'm driving, I hear a low murmuring sound. I think it's the radio. Turning up the volume, I hear a man talking at a slow, steady pace.

"He put the rope around her neck and tightened it until her body went limp."

"What the hell?" I mutter, turning up the volume another notch.

"A hiker found her body in the woods a day after her husband reported her missing. Her ankles and wrists were bound with duct tape and the rope was still around her neck."

What am I listening to? Glancing at the screen on the dash, I see the words 'true crime drama' and a station number. The car must have satellite radio, but why would Lauren listen to this? The narrator's voice is creepy and the story he just told is even creepier. I never in a million years would've imagined Lauren liking something like this.

"After this short break," the man says, "we'll continue with... murder in a small town, a husband's revenge."

I search for a way to turn it off but can't figure it out, so I hit the down arrow for the volume until the man's voice goes away.

The snow is falling harder now and the windows are icing up. I search for the defrost button and feel the tires sliding off the road. I quickly look up and grip the steering wheel until all four tires are back where they should be. The road is narrow and there's no shoulder. I need to pay attention.

The main road is just up ahead. I go slow until I reach it, then stop at the intersection and wait for the defrost to clear the windshield. The wipers are going, but they smeared the ice and left frozen patches blocking my view.

As I'm waiting, a car turns off the main road and pulls up beside me. Red lights start flashing. It's a cop. What did I do? I'm just sitting here. Is that a crime?

The cop comes over and knocks on my windshield. I go to crank the window down, then remember this isn't my car. I search for the button that lowers the window and hear the guy talking to me.

"Miss, can you please lower your window?"

"I'm trying," I tell him. I find the button and press it. Snow flies in the car, hitting my face and sending a chill through me. Or maybe the chill is caused by my fear of cops. I'm always worried they'll find out what I did and arrest me.

I look up at the officer, who doesn't look much older than me. "Is something wrong?"

"I was going to ask *you* that. Are you having car issues?"

"No. I was just waiting for my windshield to clear."

The officer takes a step back and looks at the SUV. "This is Lauren Bishop's vehicle. Is there a reason you're driving it?"

How did he know this was Lauren's? It's a small town, but not small enough to know what everyone drives.

"I'm Lauren's nurse," I say. "I'm staying at her house until she recovers."

He leans down to see my face. "You look kind of young to be a nurse."

"I'm 24."

"You from around here?"

"I'm from Boston," I say, forcing a smile on my face to hide how nervous I am. "I'm on my way to the store to get groceries. I can't be gone long so if you don't mind—"

"How's Lauren doing?" he asks. "She getting better?"

"Yes, but it'll take awhile for her leg to heal."

"Damn shame what happened," he says. "Wasn't even bad weather that night."

Snow's whipping around him, collecting on his hat and coat, yet he doesn't seem to notice. Meanwhile, I'm panicking that the wet snow that's now dusting the seats is going to damage the leather.

"You know they're having a service for him this week," the officer says. "The man who was with her? I assume she told you about him. They're doing a fundraiser in his honor. Raising money for the library restoration."

"Yeah, I volunteered to help serve the food."

He gives me a smile. "Then I guess I'll see you there." His smile drops and he taps his hand on the door. "You be careful."

"I will." I glance at the cleared off windshield. "At least I can see out the window now."

He pauses, his eyes on mine. "I wasn't talking about the road." He turns and walks back to his squad car.

What's that supposed to mean? What do I need to be careful about?

I don't have time to worry about it. I need to get to the store.

17

HANNAH

With the icy roads, it takes me 40 minutes to get into town. I'll have to text Lauren and let her know I'll be home later than I thought.

Seeing the sign for Drexel's Market, I pull into the snow-covered parking lot and find a spot near the door. Lauren said Drexel's is locally owned and the only grocery store in town. I was expecting it to be really small, but it looks as big as the one I used to go to in Boston.

When I go into the store, I'm greeted by a guy wearing a white shirt and green apron with the store name embroidered on it.

"Can I help you?" he asks.

"Um, no, I don't need help," I say, getting a cart.

"You're new here," he says, like it's a given. "I'm Dan." He points to the name tag pinned to his apron. "Dan Drexel."

"You own the place?" I ask.

"My grandfather does. I just work here." He grins. "So what brings you to town?"

"I'm working for Lauren Bishop. I'm her nurse."

"Oh, yeah?" He folds his arms over his chest. "My aunt's a nurse. She works in Boston."

"That's where I'm from. I'm just here for a couple months."

"Welcome." He stares at me, that big smile still on his face. I hope he's not thinking of asking me out. He looks close to my age, and in a town this size, he's probably already dated all the local eligible girls.

"I should get going," I say, pushing the cart.

"Hey, why don't I show you around?"

"I don't need you to. I'll just go down each aisle."

He laughs. "I didn't mean show you around the store. I meant show you around town. Maybe we could go to dinner. Are you free tonight?"

Just as I expected, he's asking me out. I had a feeling he would from the eager look on his face the moment he saw me. It's probably rare for someone my age who's single to move here.

"Sorry, but I don't have time," I say. "I need to take care of Lauren."

"She doesn't give you a night off?"

"She does, but..." I should just end this now, before I have to keep coming up with excuses for why I can't date him. I'll be coming to this store on a regular basis. I don't want him asking me out every time I come here to shop. "The thing is, I don't want to get involved with anyone right now. I just got out of a relationship and I'm only here for a couple months so..."

"Yeah, I get it," he says with a nervous laugh as he stuffs his hands in his apron pockets. "But hey, if you just want to go out as friends, I'm open to that."

I'm not. Friends to a guy means you're not dating yet, but will be soon. Guys see friendship with a girl as a possibility for more. It's never just friendship.

"Well, it was nice meeting you," I say, pushing my cart past him. "I'm going to do my shopping now."

"Hey! It's fresh meat Friday!"

I look back at him. "What?"

"Fresh meat Friday. Any meat from the meat counter is ten percent off on Fridays."

"Um, okay. I'll check it out."

The produce section is just up ahead so I start there. Getting out my phone, I check the list Lauren texted me. She kept adding to it so I have to scroll to see the whole list. She's very specific about what she wants. Instead of lettuce, she wrote 'butter lettuce, organic, make sure it's wrapped, not loose, and check that all the leaves are fresh'. With that level of detailed instructions, this is going to take forever.

After the produce section, I head to the meat counter. There's a big sign on top of it advertising the ten percent off.

"What can I get you?" the man behind the counter asks.

"I need a minute," I say, scanning the items behind the glass.

"You here visiting? I don't remember seeing you before."

"I'm only here for a couple months." I look up at him. "I'm a nurse. I'm taking care of a woman in her home."

"Lauren Bishop?" he asks, rubbing his hand over his scruffy jaw.

How does he know that? Does everyone in town keep tabs on everyone else's business? I'm not used to this. In Boston, nobody even notices me, but here, people want to know everything about me.

"Yes," I say. "I'm her nurse."

"How's she doing?"

"She's getting better," I say, wondering if I should be commenting on her health. Lauren should've warned me how nosy these people are and told me what to say if they asked questions about her.

"Tell her I said hi. I'm Cameron, by the way." The guy reaches across the counter to shake my hand. "People just call me Cam."

"Are you friends with the Bishops?" I ask, thinking he looks close to their age, although I can't imagine Steven being friends with a guy who works at a meat counter. He seems like someone who would have friends more like him—rich, successful men who wear suits every day. But maybe I'm wrong. He ate at that diner last night, which surprised me. I would've thought he'd only eat at fancy places.

"I'm friends with Lauren," Cam says. "Well, kind of. I knew her through David. He introduced us. He and I have been friends since kindergarten. We grew up together."

"I'm sorry about what happened to him."

"Yeah, me too. I know they say it was an accident but..." He shakes his head.

"But what?" I ask, sensing he wants to say more.

"Nothing. Forget it." He points to the meat case. "So what are you thinking? Steak? Chicken? A lot of people like to get the rump roast this time of year."

"I have a list." I check my phone. "I need boneless, skinless chicken breast."

"Over here," he says, walking to the end of the counter. "How many?"

"Are they organic?"

"No, the organic ones are in the case." He points to it a few feet away. "But you'd save a lot getting it here with the meat special we've got going on. Those organic ones are frozen. They're not part of the deal."

"I don't think Lauren's worried about the price."

He nods. "Yeah, you're right. She's got more money than she knows what to do with." His eyes pause on mine. "You and her getting along?"

"Yeah. Why?"

He shrugs. "Just wondered."

I feel like he's implying Lauren's hard to be around, but I haven't found that to be true. We've been together several days now and she's been really nice. The only time she wasn't was when she thought I was listening in when she and Steven were arguing. But she didn't stay mad at me.

"I need grass fed steaks," I say. "Do you have those?"

"Not here. They're in the case. All that organic, grass-fed, free-range shit is in the case. We don't sell enough of it to keep it at the meat counter."

"Okay, well, I guess I'll keep moving then."

"Good luck with everything," he says as I head to the meat case.

Good luck. Be careful. Why do I get the feeling people are concerned about me being with the Bishops? Do these townspeople know something I don't?

My phone rings when I'm going down the rice and pasta aisle. It's Lauren calling.

"Hey, Mrs. Bishop, I'm still at the store."

"What's taking so long?" she asks, sounding annoyed. "You were supposed to be home by now."

"Sorry. It took a long time to drive here. The snow's really coming down and then this cop stopped me and—"

"You were pulled over by the police? Why? What did you do?"

"Nothing. I stopped at an intersection because the windows iced up and I was waiting for them to clear. The cop just wanted to know why I was sitting there. He thought I had car trouble."

"Who was it? Officer Trumble?"

"I don't know. I didn't get his name."

"That's just wonderful," she huffs. "Now this will be all over town. I assume you told him you're living with us?"

"Yeah. Why? Was I not supposed to?"

"No, it's fine. People will find out eventually. I just don't want them making up some ridiculous story and spreading it around town. As much as I love this area, I hate how the locals gossip."

I'm not sure what kind of story they'd make up. I'm Lauren's nurse. That's it. That's the whole story.

"Did you say you're still at the store?" she asks.

"Yes. I'm only halfway through the list."

"What in the world is taking so long? That store isn't very big. You should be done by now."

"I've never been here. I have to find where stuff is, and then people keep talking to me."

"What people?" she asks. "Who did you talk to?"

"The owner's grandson. I can't remember his name. And the meat counter guy."

"Cameron?"

"Yeah. He asked how you're doing, but I wasn't sure what you wanted me to say."

"Just tell him, and anyone else who asks, that my recovery is going well. That's all people need to know."

"Okay, well, I better finish up this list."

"Don't forget the strawberries."

"Yeah, got it." I'm glad she reminded me because I did forget the strawberries. She told me to get them, but they weren't on the list.

I finish going through all the aisles, avoiding eye contact so no one tries to talk to me. In the bread aisle, an older lady came toward me to say something, but I pretended not to notice her and raced past her with my cart.

Now I'm back in the produce section, searching for the strawberries. It's not a big area and I've looked twice now and still can't find them. I spot Dan rolling a cart of boxes to the stack of bananas. I don't want to talk to him again, but if anyone knows about the strawberries, it'd be him. Maybe he has some in the back.

"Dan." I walk up to him.

He sees me and smiles. "You're still here."

"It took me awhile to find everything."

"I would've been happy to help."

"Actually, that's why I'm here. I can't find the strawberries."

"We don't get those in this time of year. We used to, but they're really expensive and had no flavor. People didn't buy them so we stopped ordering them in the winter."

"Is there somewhere else I could get them? Lauren really wants strawberries."

"Sorry, but we're the only store in town that has fresh produce. You'd have to drive to the city to get them, but you may not find them. A lot of stores don't carry them this time of year."

"Oh. Okay. I'll tell her."

"You could always get frozen. They're in aisle six."

"Thanks, but she really wants fresh. I'll see you later." I take off before he asks me out again. I don't think he would, but you never know. He seems persistent.

18

HANNAH

"It's getting really bad out there," I say to Lauren as I go into her room. "They haven't put anything down on the roads."

"They usually don't," she says, "unless we're expecting an ice storm or a foot of snow."

"I'm glad I was driving your SUV. I felt a lot safer in that than in my car." I pick up her glass of water, which is almost empty. "I'll go fill this up. Do you need anything else?"

"Yes, I need to use the bathroom."

"Okay, I'll do this later." I set the glass down and bring her wheelchair around to the side of the bed.

"I've had to go for almost an hour," she says as I move the covers off her. "I don't know why you took so long."

"I'm really sorry. I went as fast as I could." I lean down and wait for her to get her arm around me. "Ready?"

As I go to lift her up, her arm slips off me. I catch her before she falls, straining my back and feeling a sharp pinch on the side of my hip.

"You idiot!" Lauren yells. "What is wrong with you? I nearly fell to the floor!"

"I've got you," I say, struggling to lift her. "Just put your arm around me."

She does, and I'm finally able to transfer her to the chair.

She blows out a breath. "The reason I hired someone your age was because I assumed you'd have the strength to lift me. But I guess I was wrong."

I'm able to lift her, but I need her help. All she had to do was put her arm around me, and it was, but then she let go. Did she do it on purpose? It seemed like it, but why would she do that? Why would she risk falling and hurting herself even more?

After she's done in the bathroom, I get her back into bed, then go fill her glass with water. I need to put away the groceries, but I have to attend to Lauren first. She's in a bad mood today, or maybe this is how she really is and the past few days were all an act to get me to commit to staying here.

"Hannah?" Lauren says as I'm cleaning up her bathroom. She tried to do her own makeup this morning and made a mess of the counter.

"Yes?" I stand at the door of the bathroom, holding the bottle of organic cleaner in my hand.

"Did you get the strawberries?"

"I couldn't. They didn't have any."

"I need strawberries. I told you that."

"Yes, but I asked the guy at the store and he said they don't order them in the winter."

She sighs. "I'll have Audrey get them. She's working in Boston today. The stores there will have them." She swipes through her phone.

"Maybe your husband could bring some home."

"He's staying in the city tonight."

"On a Friday?"

Her eyes dart to mine. "What are you implying?"

"Nothing. I just... I'll finish cleaning the bathroom." I go in there and scrub the sink, then the counter where Lauren spilled her foundation. It's one of those expensive brands I could never afford. A small bottle probably costs more than I make in a day.

"Audrey, it's Lauren," I hear her say. "Would you do me a huge favor and get me some fresh strawberries on your way home?" She's quiet, then says, "Yes, I understand. Tell Sandy I said hello. You two have fun."

I finish up in the bathroom and return to the bedroom. Lauren's gazing at her phone, then touches the screen and whispers something.

"Mrs. Bishop?" I say.

She startles and drops her phone on the bed. "You scared me! You can't sneak up on people like that."

"I wasn't. I was just standing here." I glance down at her phone and see a photo of a man. "Who's that?"

"No one." She grabs her phone and shuts it off. "Are you done in the bathroom?"

"Yes. I was going to go unload the groceries now."

"You haven't done that yet? Hannah, the food could be spoiled by now!"

"It's only been a half hour. I'm sure it's fine."

"Go do it right now."

I hurry out of there and go to the kitchen. Lauren's in a really bad mood today. It could be her pain making her cranky. She keeps refusing the pain meds, saying she doesn't like taking pills, but she needs the meds to feel better.

As I unload the groceries, I regret not asking for more money. When Lauren told me what the job paid, it sounded like a lot, even with the added work of having to make her meals. But after being here a few days, I'm finding the job is way more work than I'd planned on. By the time I go up to my room at night, which usually isn't until after ten, I'm exhausted.

Tomorrow I get the night off, but I don't know what I'm going to do. I don't know anyone here and Steven made it sound like everything closes early. I could hang out in my room but it doesn't have a TV. Maybe I could drive to Boston tomorrow and get my TV from Tanner's basement. But if it snows again, I'll be stuck here. My car would never make it on these snow-covered roads.

Just after six, I'm with Lauren in her room watching one of the housewife reality shows she likes when I hear the garage door open.

I look at Lauren. "I thought Mr. Bishop wasn't coming home tonight."

"I thought so too." She picks up her phone. "I don't have a text from him."

"Maybe it's Audrey."

"No, her sister's in Boston this weekend so Audrey isn't coming back here until Monday."

"I'm home," Steven calls out, sounding more upbeat than usual. He appears at the door to Lauren's room. "How is my lovely wife this evening?"

"Steven, why didn't you tell me you were coming home? You scared us nearly to death."

"I didn't mean to." He walks over to her and leans down to kiss her. "I was hoping this would be a nice surprise." He glances at me. "Hello, Hannah."

"Hi, Mr. Bishop. How were the roads?"

"Slick, but I managed to get home without hitting anything."

Lauren clears her throat.

Steven quickly looks back at her. "I'm sorry, dear. I wasn't thinking."

It takes me a moment to figure out why Lauren's upset, but then I get it. Steven made it home without hitting anything. Like a tree. The tree that killed his friend and could've killed his wife.

"I brought us dinner," he says to her. "I stopped at that Italian restaurant you like. The one by my office?"

She nods. "That was very thoughtful, but I'm not hungry. I might just go to bed."

"This early? It's not even seven."

Lauren looks at me. "Hannah, would you help me get ready?"

"Of course." I go to the dresser and get one of Lauren's long, silky pajama shirts. She has two drawers full of them, all in beautiful patterns. I'm sure they cost a fortune.

"Well, Hannah, I guess it's just you and me tonight," Steven says, watching me walk over to Lauren's bed.

"You can eat without me," I say. "This will take about 20 minutes."

"I can wait. I need to do a few things in my office. Come get me when you're ready." He leaves the room.

"I hope you don't mind," Lauren says.

"Don't mind what?"

"Having dinner with him. He likes the company."

She sits up more as I help her take off her cashmere hoodie. Yes, her hoodie is cashmere. I didn't even know that was a thing. I can't imagine what it must've cost, and she's wearing it to just sit around in bed all day.

"We could eat in here," I suggest.

"I'd prefer to rest. I've been really tired today."

I get her pajama shirt on, then help her into the wheelchair. This time she holds on. I wheel her to the bathroom and wait for her to take off her makeup and brush her teeth.

When she's back in bed, her eyes fall shut. I hope she's okay. She shouldn't be this tired. Maybe she didn't sleep well last night.

I shut off the lights and leave her room, softly closing the door but leaving it open just a crack so I can hear her if she needs something.

"Did you get her tucked in?" Steven asks.

Looking down the hall, I see him closing the door to his office and locking it. That's really odd. Why does he need to lock the door? I wouldn't go in there, and Lauren's stuck in bed.

"She's not asleep yet," I say as he walks toward me. "But she will be soon."

"Let's go have dinner. I'm starving."

We go to the kitchen and I open the takeout sacks. As I'm setting the containers on the counter, Steven comes up beside me and places his hand on my lower back.

"What do you think?" he says in his deep, alluring voice. "See anything you like?" he asks, referring to the food.

I suck in a breath, my heart pounding at the feel of his hand on my back. He's standing so close our bodies are nearly touching.

"Hannah?" He turns to me and his hand moves to my shoulder. "Is everything okay?"

"Yes." I turn to face him. "I'm just tired. It's been a long day."

He lightly massages my shoulder, which feels incredibly good. "How about some wine to help you relax?"

"I don't need any," I say, knowing the alcohol might make me do something I shouldn't. I doubt anything would happen, but just to be safe, I shouldn't drink.

"C'mon." Steven smiles and massages my shoulder again. "It's Friday night. Just one glass?"

I hesitate, knowing this is a bad decision. But I tend to make a lot of those.

"Okay," I say. "One glass."

19

HANNAH

It's after ten and I'm sitting on the couch, just inches away from Steven. He's got the fireplace going, and the second bottle of wine he opened is half gone.

When I said I tend to make bad decisions, I wasn't exaggerating. And when I've been drinking, my decisions get even worse. I really did try to stop after one glass of wine, but Steven insisted I have another glass, which led to another, and another after that.

On the bright side, the wine helped get rid of the stress I was feeling. I'm completely relaxed now, my body warm and my mind free of any distracting thoughts.

Steven reaches over and places his hand on my knee. "How are you feeling?"

"Relaxed," I say, a drunk smile sliding up my face.

"Good." He rubs my leg, up and down the top of my thigh, sending warm, tingly sensations through me.

"I should go to bed," I say, knowing if I don't, I'll make even more bad decisions. Like just now, I should've moved away from Steven when he touched my leg, but I didn't, because I liked it, and wanted more.

"It's early," he says. "And I just added more wood to the

fire. How about some more wine?" He reaches for the bottle and pours some in my glass.

As he gives it to me, our hands touch and I feel that tingling sensation again.

"It's really good," I say, taking a sip.

"I'm glad you like it."

I reach up to set the glass on the table and feel that pinch in my back, the one I felt when I lifted up Lauren so she wouldn't fall.

"Ouch," I say, rubbing my lower back.

"Did you hurt yourself?" Steven asks with concern.

I nod. "It happened when I was moving Lauren to the wheelchair."

"Maybe I can help."

Before I know what's happening, Steven turns me so my back's to him and his big strong hands start massaging my shoulders.

"You're all knotted up," he says. "Have you been worrying about something?"

Yeah, my lack of money, having no place to live when I leave here, not knowing what I'll do for a job. I don't want to work in a hospital again, not after what I did. I could maybe work at a nursing home or get another home health care job, but those don't pay much and living in Boston is really expensive.

"My shoulders are always tight," I say, not wanting to tell him all my problems.

Steven's hands massage their way down my back. It feels so good that I don't even notice my shirt lifting up until I feel Steven's hands on my skin. He's rubbing the area just above my waistband, kneading it with his thumbs.

"Is that the spot?" he asks.

"No, it's lower, but what you're doing feels good."

"Would you let me go lower? I think I could help."

I unbutton my jeans and pull down the zipper. Bad decision number five for the night. Actually, I'm probably way past that. I lost count when we opened the second bottle of wine.

Steven rolls down the top of my jeans. I feel his warm hands on my skin, his fingers spreading out over my lower back as his thumbs knead the muscles that surround my spine.

"How's that feel?" he asks.

"Amazing," I say, my eyes falling shut.

He keeps it up, that slow gentle massage. It's so relaxing I can barely keep my eyes open.

"Hannah," I hear him say.

"Yeah?"

"You're falling asleep. You should probably get to bed. Unless you want to sleep here by the fire."

"Maybe I will." I turn and face him. "Thanks for the massage. It helped."

"I'm glad." His eyes lock on mine. I try to look away, but can't. He's so incredibly handsome, and the flickering light of the fire makes him look even better. He tucks a strand of my hair behind my ear. "You're a very beautiful woman, Hannah."

He's still looking into my eyes. I find myself leaning toward him.

He wraps his hand around the side of my face.

I should back away. Get up. Go to my room. But that would be a good decision and I seem unable to make those tonight.

Steven presses his lips to mine, just once, then looks at me. I slide closer to him and a slight smile appears on his handsome face. He kisses me again, longer this time.

The kiss is just like I imagined, but better. I knew he'd be good at this. He's mature, experienced, and not in a rush like guys are when they're younger.

A loud popping sound fills the room and I jump back, my eyes darting around.

"Relax," Steven says with a gentle laugh. "It was just the fire."

I face him on the couch, pulling my legs up and hugging my knees. That sudden interruption from the fire woke me from the fantasy I was living out and I'm now very aware of what Steven and I were doing.

"Hannah, what's wrong?" Steven asks, moving closer to me.

"What we were doing." I glance at the fire. "We shouldn't have done it."

"And why is that?"

At first I think I heard him wrong. How could he not know the answer to that? He knows what we were doing wasn't right. He's married, and I'm caring for his wife.

"Lauren is right there," I whisper, pointing to her room.

"Would you like to go upstairs?" he casually asks.

I pause a moment to consider that. Wait, what am I thinking? I can't do this. I shouldn't even be considering it.

"Mr. Bishop, we can't do this. You're married."

"To a wife who doesn't love me."

"What?" I shake my head. "No. You're wrong. Lauren loves you. I can tell when I watch you two together."

"It's all an act. One we're quite good at." He picks up his glass of wine and finishes what's left of it before setting it down.

"I don't understand. Are you saying you don't love her?"

"I did at first. But things changed after we got married. Lauren changed. She wasn't the girl I fell for back in college. That girl was never her. She was just pretending it was. It was all a performance."

Is he making this up? He has to be. It's probably the wine talking. People say strange things when they're drunk.

"You should get some sleep," I tell him, getting up from the couch. "You'll feel better in the morning."

I lean down to pick up the wine glasses, but Steven stops me. He takes hold of my hand and brings me back beside him on the couch.

"Lauren married me for my money. It's as simple as that. It had nothing to do with love."

"But she already had money. Didn't she?"

"No. She was raised by a single mother who struggled to pay the bills. Her father took off before she was born."

Lauren told me she was raised by her mom, but for some reason I imagined her growing up with money.

"Then how did she afford college?" I ask.

"She got a scholarship. A needs-based scholarship. She tried to hide that from me, thinking I wouldn't marry her if I knew. She was aware I had money. A lot of it."

"When did you find out she was poor?"

"Soon after I met her. She drove a rusty old car that was always breaking down. She said it had been her grandfather's and she was keeping it for sentimental reasons. I knew she was lying, but I didn't want to call her out on it and embarrass her. The thing is, I didn't care that she didn't grow up with money. I loved her. I wanted to be with her. I just wish she'd been honest with me."

I'm having a hard time believing this. I can't imagine Lauren hiding her past from the guy she was marrying. That's a lot of work and would require some great acting skills.

"Hannah, I need you to keep this between us," Steven says, giving my hand a squeeze. "I'm only telling you about my marriage because you're living here and I'm tired of having to pretend. Lauren and I are the perfect couple out in public, but it's hard to maintain that when we're home. I asked Lauren to tell you the truth, but she wanted to give it more time. And I would have, but after what happened between us just now, I didn't want you feeling guilty, or as though you'd betrayed Lauren."

"I *do* feel that way, even after you said all that."

"There's no need to. Lauren and I are more roommates than anything else. We don't even sleep in the same bed."

"Then why are you still married?"

"It's complicated," he says with a sigh. "I considered divorcing her soon after we were married, but I was still in love with her then. I didn't want to let her go. And honestly, she was an excellent wife. She still is. She plays the role better than anyone I know. But that's all it is. A role she's performing. There's nothing beyond that. No love."

"But are you guys still... you know, intimate?"

"We were before her accident. But you can be intimate with someone without loving them." He runs his hand down the side of my face. "I understand if you don't want to do anything tonight, but if you do, there's no reason to feel guilty about it. We won't tell Lauren."

I should go up to my room. Go to bed. Pretend tonight never happened.

But instead, I make yet another bad decision.

Steven leans in to kiss me. And I let him.

He undresses me. And I let him.

He lays me down on the couch. And I let him.

Then I do what I said I'd never do with him.

20

HANNAH

"Good morning, Audrey," I say, greeting her at the door.

She goes past me into the house, holding a cup of coffee for Lauren and one for herself. She never brings me one.

But after what I did with Steven, I don't deserve coffee. I deserve to be fired and kicked out of this house, left to live on the streets.

Friday night was a mistake. A big, huge, horrible mistake. What was I thinking sleeping with Steven? I wasn't. I got wrapped up in the fantasy of what it'd be like to have a man like him. I got swept away by his words. Fell apart at his touch. Surrendered to his kiss. A kiss that led to more.

We didn't even make it upstairs. We did it right there in the living room, with Lauren just a few feet away.

I'm a terrible person. I should just confess and end this. How can I keep working for Lauren knowing what I did?

The only thing keeping me from feeling even worse is knowing I was drunk. It's not a good excuse, but it's true. I haven't drank that much in a really long time. After the first glass of wine, I could feel myself relaxing. It felt good. It was just what I needed after working hard all week. But then Steven poured me another glass, and another, and I started to lose track of what was real and what I was imagining. At one point, I honestly thought I was having a dream. I'd had dreams about Steven before—dreams of doing what we did—but I never intended to act on them.

"Hannah?" Lauren says from her room. "Can you come in here?"

I'm standing in the living room, staring at the white fur rug in front of the fireplace where I did the horrible thing that I never should've done. I don't want to go into Lauren's room. One, because I avoid going in there when Audrey comes over, and two, because I can't bear to be around Lauren, knowing what I did.

But I'm her nurse and this is my job, so I take a calming breath and go into her room.

"I'm here." I go up to her bed. "Did you want another blanket?"

"No. It's my leg. It's itching like crazy. I need something to scratch it with, something that will fit under the cast."

"You can't do that. It's not sanitary. You could get an infection."

"Why don't you call your doctor?" Audrey glances at me. "I wouldn't trust the opinion of someone who just graduated from school."

I ignore her insult and talk to Lauren. "You could take an antihistamine. That can help reduce the itchy feeling."

"I don't know if I have any."

"I'll go check. If not, I can run to the store and get some."

"If you think it'll work, I'll try it. I can't take this itching." She reaches down and rubs her leg while I go to her bathroom to check the drawers.

"Is Steven coming home tonight?" Audrey asks.

I listen in, wanting to hear what Lauren says, hoping the answer is no. I'm not ready to see Steven yet, or talk to him. I haven't seen him since Friday night. When I woke up Saturday, he was gone. Lauren said there was an emergency at their house in Boston, something about roof damage from the snow. Apparently, their neighbor texted Steven early Saturday morning and told him to get there right away.

"Steven doesn't know when he'll be back," Lauren says. "He's waiting to see what the roof guy says. If he can repair it today, Steven will go there after work, pay the guy, and drive back here."

"How much damage was there?" Audrey asks. "Did he say?"

"It wasn't that bad. Some water got into the attic, but Steven said it's already dried up."

"You were lucky."

"Yes. I kind of wish Steven had stayed there Friday night instead of coming here. He would've heard the water seeping through the roof and could've called someone that night."

If Steven had stayed in Boston, Friday night never would've happened. I wouldn't be feeling guilty and nervous and sick to my stomach.

"Hannah, did you find anything?" Lauren yells. "I can't take another second of this itching."

"There's nothing here," I yell back. "I'll have to go to the store." I grab the hair dryer and walk back out to Lauren. "Try this for now."

"A hair dryer?" Audrey scoffs. "Lauren, please just call the doctor. She clearly lacks the skills to deal with this."

"Blowing air on it can help stop the itching," I say to Lauren. "It'll give you at least a little relief until you can take an antihistamine."

"Check upstairs," she says. "I remember Steven buying some when his allergies were bad."

"Where would they be?"

"In the bedroom. Check the top drawer, the one between the sinks."

"Okay, I'll be right back."

"You're letting her in the bedroom?" I hear Audrey say as I go upstairs. I pause to listen.

"It's fine," Lauren says. "And stop being so mean to her. She's a very hard worker and a good person. I'm lucky to have found her."

I feel like I'm going to be sick. She thinks I'm a good person? If she only knew what I did. And what her husband did.

I keep having to remind myself that it wasn't just me. Steven had a part in this too. He had to have known what he was doing when he kept refilling my wine glass. Did he do it on purpose? Was he trying to get me drunk?

He told me his marriage was a sham and that he and Lauren put on a show when they're in public, pretending they're a loving couple. But when he's home with her, he's always touching her and kissing her and saying he loves her. Why would he do that when nobody's there to see it?

He said Lauren didn't love him, and that she only married him for his money. Is that really true? Or was he just trying to relieve my guilt so I'd sleep with him?

I don't want to believe Steven would do that. I want to believe he's a good man who drank too much and said things he didn't mean. I want to believe he desperately misses being with his wife and his male urges took over before he could stop them. He just made a mistake, and so did I, and it'll never happen again.

I'm upstairs now, standing outside the master bedroom. The door is shut so I slowly open it, thinking for a moment that Steven's in there. He's not, of course, but I still don't feel right going into his room. It's a huge bedroom with a king-size bed, two nightstands, two dressers, and two matching chairs and ottomans facing a window that looks out at the ocean. There's a fireplace across from the bed that reminds me of the one downstairs.

Now I'm thinking about what I did in front of that fireplace and feeling sick again. I haven't been able to eat much since Friday night. I haven't eaten anything today and yesterday all I had was toast. I haven't slept much either. I've had maybe five hours of sleep total the past couple nights.

I go into the bathroom and see the two sinks Lauren mentioned and the drawers between them. I open the top drawer and see a box of antihistamines. I check inside and see there are eight left. That's enough to give Lauren some relief from the itching until I'm able to get to the store.

I'm tempted to check what's in the other drawers but stop myself before I do. It'd be wrong, and I don't need to be doing more wrong things in this house.

As I'm leaving the bathroom, I stop when I see something under the bed. Steven's such a neat freak that I'm surprised he didn't pick it up. Maybe he didn't see it.

Walking over to the bed, I reach under it and pull out a silky red scarf. Why is Lauren's scarf under the bed? She said she hasn't slept in this room since before the accident. Steven said they sleep in separate rooms. I don't know who I believe, but either way, I don't know why Lauren's scarf would be under the bed. How could Steven not notice it? I noticed it just walking out of the bathroom.

Why am I analyzing this? Who cares why it was there? I need to stay out of it. I don't need to be getting myself into even more trouble.

With the scarf in my hand, I walk through the bathroom to the large walk-in closet. It's full of Steven's clothes, but I don't see any for Lauren. I assumed most of the closet would be hers, but it's not. Does that mean Steven was telling the truth and Lauren never stayed up here, even before the accident?

What if their marriage really is a sham? They're married on paper, but if they don't love each other, maybe what Steven and I did Friday night wasn't so bad. Or maybe I'm just telling myself that so I feel better.

I hold out the scarf, looking at the red shimmery fabric. It doesn't seem like something Lauren would wear, but what do I know? I've only known her a week.

I shake out the scarf, then fold it in half and in half again. I assume you fold scarves, but maybe you hang them. I don't really know.

"What are you doing in here?" someone says from behind me.

I whip around and see Audrey standing there.

21

HANNAH

"You're supposed to be checking for antihistamines," Audrey says. "Not snooping around in the closet. I'm telling Lauren about this." She turns to leave.

"No, wait!"

Audrey turns back to me, folding her arms over her chest. "Let's hear it. What lie have you come up with to explain this?"

"It's not a lie. I came in here to put this away." I hold up the scarf.

She narrows her eyes at me. "Where did you get that?"

"It was under the bed. I know Steven likes a clean house, so when I saw it, I picked it up and came in here to put it away."

Audrey yanks the scarf from my hands. "I gave this to Lauren a few years ago for her birthday. It was one of her favorites. She wore it all the time."

"Why do you think it was under the bed?"

Audrey shoots me an angry look. "That is a very inappropriate question. Steven is your boss and what he does in his private space is none of your business. Didn't your parents teach you any manners?"

"My mom wasn't big on manners and my dad killed himself."

I'm thinking that last part might shock her enough that she'll stop yelling at me and let me leave. But instead, she steps closer to me, her eyes on mine.

"Steven has been very distraught since Lauren's accident. He misses her terribly. And sometimes, when you miss someone you love, you take items of theirs and keep them close, like in your bed, so it feels like the person you so desperately miss is there with you. Does that make sense, Hannah?"

I nod. "Yes."

"Good. Now get out of here and go care for Lauren. Your hair dryer advice has done nothing to relieve her itching."

"I'll give her some pills." I leave the closet, and when I'm walking through the bedroom, I hear Audrey behind me.

"You touch her things again, I'll tell Lauren."

I turn to face Audrey. "So you're not going to tell her about this?"

"I'll give you a pass this time, but only because Lauren really wants this little arrangement of yours to work out. For some reason, she likes you and thinks you're doing a good job."

"Thanks. For not telling her."

"It'll be our little secret." She smiles, but it's the type of smile that says she's on to me, like I'm doing something deceitful and trying to get away with it.

I get out of there and race down the stairs to Lauren's room. "Found some!" I hold up the box of antihistamines.

"Oh, thank goodness," she says with a sigh. "I'm going crazy with this itching."

I hand her a pill and her glass of water. "This should help."

"You're an angel," she says, popping the pill in her mouth and gulping down what's left of her water.

She called me an angel, which I am definitely not. I'm getting that sick feeling again.

"Lauren, I need to head out," Audrey yells.

"Okay!" Lauren yells back. "Thanks for stopping by!"

Audrey appears at the bedroom door. "Do you need anything before I go?"

"If I do, Hannah will get it for me."

Audrey glares at me. "Of course she will."

"Oh, I forgot to ask," Lauren says. "Did you find someone to take to the celebration of life?"

"No, and I'm not going to. It's a service for my dead friend. That's not something you bring a date to."

"It's not a funeral. It's called a celebration for a reason. It's a party to celebrate his life. David wouldn't want you going alone."

She shrugs. "Steven will be there. I'll hang out with him."

"Steven will be on his phone all night. You know how he is. These town events make him uncomfortable. He'll hide out in the corner and pretend to be doing business. Hey, I know who could go with you."

Audrey rolls her eyes. "Do I even want to ask?"

"Mark Evert," Lauren says, her voice rising.

"I don't know him."

"Sure you do. He's the agent who sold us this house."

"That guy?" She scrunches up her nose. "Have you seen how he dresses? And he drives a beat-up Toyota from like three decades ago."

"No, he got a new car. Well, it's used, but only a few years old."

"Yeah, I'll pass."

"Audrey, come on, just give him a chance. He's a really nice guy."

"I married a nice guy. They're not as great as you think."

"Let me just call him and see if he's going."

"Lauren, I don't want to go with Mark. And I don't need a date."

"He could meet you there. You don't have to call it a date."

She sighs. "If he's there, I'll talk to him, but I am not going out with him." She checks her phone. "I'm late. I have to go."

She takes off. Lauren picks up the remote and turns on the TV. She flips through some channels, not stopping on any of them. She turns off the TV and tosses the remote aside.

"I'm going insane with boredom," she says, staring up at the ceiling. "I'm tired of watching TV, tired of reading books, tired of lying in bed."

"We could play a game," I suggest. "Do you have any cards?"

"No. Steven hates games. He says they're for children."

The mention of children makes me wonder why she doesn't have any. Audrey would say this is another example of an inappropriate question, but I ask it anyway.

"Why don't you and Mr. Bishop have any kids?"

Lauren's eyes remain on the ceiling. "Steven didn't want any. He said he didn't have time to devote to them given all the hours he works."

"What about you? Did you ever want them?"

"Of course." Her eyes dart from the ceiling back to me. "What woman doesn't?"

"A lot of women don't. I used to think I did, but now I'm not sure."

"And why is that?"

I shrug. "I just don't think I'd make a good mom. My own mom wasn't great at it. Maybe I'd be the same as her." I pause, then ask another inappropriate question, at least according to Audrey's standards. "What was your mom like?"

Lauren smiles slightly. "She was very smart and very ambitious. Sometimes I wish I was more like her."

"What do you mean?"

"If she saw an opportunity, she took it and didn't look back. She never regretted a thing, even getting involved with my father. She said he was an awful excuse for a man, but being with him resulted in me, something she never regretted."

"Was it hard for her, being a single mom?" I ask, wanting to know if what Steven told me is true, about Lauren growing up poor.

"I suppose it was, although I didn't know it at the time. We always had a nice place to live and food on the table. And when my mother got paid, she'd take me shopping and buy me an outfit, something that cost more than we could probably afford. It was usually a dress or a pair of expensive shoes. She was very focused on appearances. She'd say you should dress how you wanted to be treated. If you dress like trash, you'll be treated like trash. Dress like you have money, and people will treat you with respect."

"Huh. I guess I never thought of that."

"You should," she says, her gaze dropping to my faded blue scrubs and worn out sneakers.

From what she said, it doesn't sound like she grew up poor, or not the kind of poor Steven described. But maybe his definition of poor is different than the rest of us.

"You know, you really don't need to wear those," Lauren says, looking at my scrubs.

I wear them because I don't have many clothes and I don't want the clothes I have getting worn out. Around five, I usually change into jeans and a sweatshirt. It makes me feel like my work day is done, even though it's not.

"I don't mind the scrubs," I say. "They're comfortable and easy to clean."

"Yes, but they make me feel like I'm in a hospital, which is not what I want. I'm trying to create a calm atmosphere to help with my recovery. Being reminded of my time in the hospital is not at all calming."

"What do you want me to wear?"

"What else do you have?"

"Jeans and some sweatshirts. Is that okay?"

"You don't have anything nicer than that?"

"No. I lived in scrubs when I was working at the hospital. I didn't need to buy nice clothes."

And I had no money, which is the main reason I didn't buy clothes.

"Go in my closet." She points to it. "See if you can find something that'll fit."

"You want me to wear your clothes?"

"I've been meaning to clean them out anyway. In fact, once I'm recovered, I think I'm going to start fresh with an all new wardrobe."

"You're getting rid of all your clothes?"

"Maybe not all of them. I'll keep a few favorites and donate the rest." She pauses. "Unless you would like them."

"Um, yeah. I mean, if you don't mind. But I wouldn't feel right just taking them."

"Why not?"

"Because they're really nice and really expensive."

And because it feels wrong taking your clothes after I slept with your husband.

"Come sit for a moment," she says, patting the area beside her on the bed.

I sit down and wait for her to continue.

"I'm going to tell you the advice my mother gave me. The same advice that allowed her to give herself and me a better life than we would've had if she hadn't followed this advice."

"What did she say?"

"When an opportunity is presented to you, don't question it. Don't tell yourself you don't deserve it or you're not good enough or that you can't take something you didn't earn. Those are all lies that keep you from having what you really want." She puts her hand on mine. "You have the opportunity to look as though you have the lifestyle of someone who has much more than you, which will bring you more opportunities. Ones that could lead you to actually having the money to buy those clothes yourself. Do you understand what I'm saying?"

"That I should take the clothes and not question it."

"Yes, but it's more than that. I'm not just talking about clothes. I'm talking about any opportunity that comes your way. You can't sit back and wait for things to happen. If you really want something, look for opportunities and snatch them up, without question or guilt."

Guilt. It's all I've felt since Friday night. I wanted to be with Steven, got the opportunity, and took it. And now I feel guilty. But I doubt that's the kind of opportunity Lauren is talking about.

22

HANNAH

"Go try something on," Lauren says with excitement in her voice. "This will be fun! Like a fashion show."

I go into her walk-in closet and take out a pink sweater and a pair of skinny jeans. I'm not sure the jeans will fit. I'm thin, but not as thin as Lauren, although maybe she wasn't as skinny before the accident.

"What about this?" I walk over to Lauren, holding up the jeans and sweater.

"Try it on," she says. I head to the bathroom. "Just do it here. It's just us girls. Steven won't be home for hours."

It wouldn't matter if Steven was here. He's already seen me naked.

I shake that thought away, remembering Lauren's advice about opportunities. It feels wrong to take her clothes, but if I don't, I'm passing up an opportunity that I doubt will ever come along again. These clothes could help my future, maybe even help me find higher-quality men to date. And besides, if I don't take the clothes, Lauren's just going to donate them, so why not take them for myself?

When I put the sweater on, I instantly notice how much better the quality is compared to a sweater I would buy. The fabric is soft, not scratchy, and the fit is good. It's not hanging off my shoulders or billowing out around my waist. I put the jeans on and they're a perfect fit, like they were made for me. They're comfortable too. They have some stretch in the fabric so I can easily move around in them.

"Those look wonderful on you," Lauren says, smiling at me. "I already feel better seeing you in that rather than those sad, depressing scrubs."

"I could probably wear the jeans, but not the sweater."

"Why wouldn't you wear the sweater?"

"It's too nice. What if I get it dirty?"

"Doing what?" she says with a laugh. "You're not cleaning out the fireplace."

Hearing her mention the fireplace reminds me of what I did in front of it with her husband. He's coming home tonight. What am I going to say to him? How are we going to act around each other? What if Lauren sees us together and senses something happened?

"Hannah?" Lauren says, bringing my attention back to her.

I look at the sweater. "You really think I should wear this?"

"Definitely. It looks great on you. Go try something else on."

"But it's time for your exercise."

It's not really exercise. I just have her do some basic movements to improve her circulation, which will speed up healing. I have her lift and lower her arms, sit up in bed, and lift and lower her good leg. She hates it and constantly complains about how much it hurts, but she still does it, both in the morning and at night.

"We'll do that later," she says. "This is far more enjoyable than your torture exercises."

I smile. "They're not meant to torture you. They're meant to help you."

"Yes, well, this is still more enjoyable. Go put on something else."

For the next hour, I try on clothes, setting a pile aside to take upstairs to my room. I'm getting a whole new wardrobe for free. It still feels wrong, but I keep reminding myself that Lauren didn't want this stuff anyway. I'm doing her a favor taking it off her hands, and she's the one who insisted I stop wearing scrubs. If she wants me to dress nicer, I need nice clothes, and I can't afford to go buy them.

"I like this one," I say, showing Lauren a beige v-neck sweater that feels like cashmere. "But I don't like wearing this color. I worry about staining it."

"I'll keep that one," she says. "Audrey gave it to me last year for Christmas. She'd have a fit if I gave it away. I like it, but it's kind of plain and blends in with my skin this time of year."

"You could wear a scarf with it."

"I don't wear scarves. I don't like the feel of them around my neck. I don't like turtlenecks either."

"You don't wear scarves? Like ever?"

"No. Why?"

I shake my head. "No reason. I just thought you might wear them. A lot of women do."

"Steven likes them. He bought me one a few years ago. I tried wearing it, but didn't like how it felt." She glances at the clothes piled up on the chair. "That's probably enough for now."

I'm confused. Audrey made it sound like Lauren loved scarves, or at least the one she supposedly gave her. But Lauren said only Steven had given her a scarf and that she hadn't worn it for years. So why was it under the bed?

"Hannah?" Lauren says, getting my attention.

I smile at her. "Thank you for the clothes." I hurry over to the chair. "I'll bring them upstairs."

"Before you go, let's find you a dress to wear to the celebration of life."

"A dress? I thought it was casual."

"I'm sure some people will show up in jeans, but out of respect for David and his memory, it'd be nice if you wore a dress. And as I said earlier, clothes affect what people think about you and how they treat you. You don't want the people in town forming a bad impression of you the first time they meet you."

I really don't care what the locals think of me. I'm only living here for a few weeks. And I'm serving food that night. Nobody will even notice me. But it's not worth arguing about.

"I'll go pick one out." I return to her closet. "Do you have any suggestions?"

"How about the red one? It's at the very end. It's several years old. I haven't worn it in years. It's one I was going to donate, but if you like it, it's yours."

Red is not a color I usually wear. It draws too much attention. I prefer to fade into the background, not stand out.

"Did you find it?" Lauren asks.

"I think so." I pull it out and bring it to the bedroom. It's long sleeve with a low-cut neckline and made from a clingy, sweater-like fabric. "Is this it?"

"Yes! It'd be darling on you. Try it on!"

I wouldn't call it darling, more like sexy. My cleavage is showing and the bottom hem ends a few inches above my knee. Is Lauren trying to get me a date? Because this would do it. Grocery store Dan would be following me around all night if I wore this.

"I think I should find something else," I say, looking at myself in the mirror wearing the dress and the black heels Lauren insisted I put on.

"Why don't you like it? It fits you perfectly and you look absolutely gorgeous in it."

"I like it, but don't you think it's too fancy? The lady I talked to on the phone said the event's being held at town hall. That doesn't sound like a fancy place."

"They'll have it decorated. I've been to events there before and they always do a lovely job fixing it up. They even have weddings there."

"I'm serving food," I say, looking down at the dress. "What if it gets stained?"

"You worry too much. If the dress gets ruined, just throw it out. It's not like you're paying for it. I really want you to wear it. It looks great on you, even better than when I wore it."

"Okay, I'll wear it." I go to the pile of clothes and gather them up. "I'll bring these to my room and change." I glance back at her. "And then we're doing your exercises."

She lets out a sigh. "If we must."

The day goes by quickly but only because I force myself to keep busy. When I'm not helping Lauren, I'm either picking up the house, cleaning the kitchen, or in my room, organizing my clothes. I'm doing anything I can to keep my mind off of Steven and the possibility of him coming home tonight.

At six, I go into Lauren's room. She's reading a magazine. Classical music is playing from the wireless speaker by her bed.

"Dinner is done," I tell her. "It's in the oven on warm. I already ate so I'm just going to go up to my room, if that's okay."

She checks the clock. "Why are you going up there so early? Are you not feeling well?"

"I'm just tired."

"There's really nothing to do up there, is there?"

"It's fine. I don't mind."

"We should get you a TV. I didn't even think about that until now. You must be terribly bored when you're up there."

"A little, but I usually just sleep when I'm in my room."

"I'll talk to Steven. Maybe he could pick up a TV for you. Or perhaps you two could go shopping together."

"Oh, no, we don't need to do that. I'm not here for very long. I don't need a TV."

"Nonsense. They don't cost much and I know you would like one."

I hear the garage door opening. Steven's home.

"Well, anyway," I say. "I'll be upstairs. Just text me if you need me."

"Hannah, wait. Let's talk to Steven together about the TV. See what he thinks."

Forget the TV. I want to go upstairs. I can't see Steven. Not yet. I'm not ready.

"Honey, I'm home!" he calls out from the kitchen.

"We're in here," Lauren yells back.

I hurry over to Lauren's bathroom and pretend to be cleaning up.

"Hello, sweetheart," I hear Steven say as he comes into the bedroom. "How was your day?"

"Exhausting," she says, dramatically. "Hannah made me exercise three times. She's worse than my personal trainer," she says with a laugh. "Hannah, come out here. Tell Steven how hard you worked me today."

I plaster on a fake smile and slowly walk out to the bedroom, avoiding looking at Steven, my eyes on Lauren.

"It wasn't that bad," I say to her. "And it's helping. You're getting stronger every day."

"She's right," Steven says, leaning down to kiss Lauren. "The exercises are helping you. You're stronger now than you were a week ago."

"I suppose you're right," she says. "But I still don't like doing them. Oh, Steven, I was just telling Hannah that we should get a TV for her room."

"There's not one already in there?" he asks.

"No. We talked about getting one, but nobody ever stayed in that room so we decided against it."

"We'll have to fix that," Steven says, turning to me and smiling. "We'll get you one this week."

"You don't have to. I'm—"

"I think she should go with you, Steven," Lauren says. "So she can pick it out."

"That's a good idea," he says. "I'll check my schedule and see what night will work." His gaze lowers to my body, to my new skinny jeans and pink sweater. "No scrubs today, Hannah?"

"I asked her not to wear them anymore," Lauren says. "I find them depressing. It makes me feel like I'm back at the hospital. I gave her some of the clothes I was planning to donate."

"It's fortunate you two are the same size." Steven turns back to Lauren and sits beside her on the bed. "I'm sorry I wasn't able to be with you last weekend."

"You don't need to apologize. You were taking care of the house. Speaking of that, are the repairs done?"

"Yes. Everything's back to how it was. Even the attic is dry."

"I'll be up in my room," I say, walking to the door.

Neither of them hear me, or they do, but keep talking.

"I brought you something," I hear Steven say as I'm going up the stairs.

"Oh, Steven, they're gorgeous!" Lauren gushes. "But what's the occasion?"

"There isn't one. I just thought some nice earrings might make you feel better."

"They do! They absolutely do! There's nothing like diamonds to cheer me up!"

"I love you, sweetheart," he says.

She doesn't say it back. Maybe she didn't hear him. She's probably too focused on her new diamond earrings.

I don't know what's going on here. Did Friday night even happen or did I imagine it? Steven barely looked at me just now and didn't seem at all uncomfortable around me. He was back to acting like a doting husband who loves his wife.

Last Friday, he told me he didn't love Lauren. He told me their marriage was all for show. But he doesn't need to put on a show when he's alone with her. So why did he give her diamond earrings and tell her he loves her?

The longer I'm here, the more confused I get. I'm not sure what's real and what's not, or who to believe. Just when I think I've got Steven and Lauren figured out, something happens and I'm back to wondering who these people really are and what they're hiding from me.

23

HANNAH

It's Tuesday night and Steven and I are leaving soon to go to the celebration of life. Lauren talked to David's parents on the phone yesterday and they told her the night will begin with people telling stories about David, then the band will play and the food will be served. David's favorite cocktail, the Rob Roy, will be available at the bar.

Last week I was looking forward to this. I'd get out of the house, meet some people, maybe dance a little. It sounded like a fun night. But now I'm dreading it, especially the ride there. I didn't want to go with Steven. I told him I'd drive my own car, but he insisted on taking me, saying it didn't make sense to drive separately.

"Ready to go?" he asks as I put on my coat.

I just nod and finish buttoning my coat.

"Honey, we're leaving!" Steven yells to Lauren as we head to the garage.

"Okay, bye!" she yells back.

Steven and I haven't talked since he got back last night. He was gone when I woke up this morning, and when he got home tonight, he went straight to his room to change from his black suit into his gray one. He looks handsome as usual, but I'm trying not to pay attention to that. I'm trying to go back to seeing him as my employer and nothing else.

We get in his Mercedes and he pulls out of the garage.

"So how have you been?" he asks as he drives down the deserted road that leads away from the house. He could easily kill me out here and nobody would ever know. Nobody would even notice I'm gone. I have no family and almost no friends. The few I had haven't kept in touch, so they wouldn't think to look for me. Tanner's the only one who might check on me, but it'd be months from now when he wants my stuff out of his basement.

"Hannah, did you hear me?" Steven asks.

No. I was too busy thinking how easy it'd be for you to kill me if I ever told Lauren what we did. I don't know why I'm thinking about that. Steven isn't a killer. But he's definitely a cheater, and he won't admit it, which is starting to make me angry.

"Sorry," I say. "My mind wandered. What was your question?"

"I asked how you've been."

"Fine," I say, even though I've been the exact opposite of fine.

"What exactly is your job tonight?" he asks, messing with the heat settings on the dash.

"I'm just serving the food. It'll be easy."

"Why are you doing this?" He glances at me. "You didn't even know David."

"I just thought I'd help out. It gets me out of the house and it's a way to meet people."

"Are you referring to a man?" he asks, his eyes on the road.

"Not necessarily," I say, curious why he said that.

"Meaning you're open to the idea?" He brings his hand to his tie and loosens it just a little.

"Maybe." I glance at him. "I mean, I'm single, so why not look? See what's out there?"

He doesn't say anything, but I notice him gripping the steering wheel tighter.

"A guy at the grocery store asked me out," I say, just to see how Steven will react. "He'll be there tonight."

"Who was it?" Steven's jaw tightens. "What was his name?"

"Dan. His family owns the store."

"Dan Drexel?" Steven huffs. "You wouldn't seriously consider him, would you?"

"I don't know. Maybe. Why? What's wrong with him?"

"He works at a grocery store," Steven says, like that's enough of a reason.

"But his grandfather owns it, which means he'll eventually own it."

"And how lucrative do you think it is to own a grocery store in a town this size? The margins on grocery items are ridiculously small. You have to move a lot of inventory just to cover your costs, let alone make a profit."

He speeds around a tight curve and I tense up, worried we're going to crash into a tree. We don't, and my muscles slowly relax.

"I would advise you to not pursue a relationship with Dan Drexel. You could do far better than him."

"Like who? Do you know anyone?"

He glances at me. "Why are you asking? Why would you pursue someone who lives here? You'll be moving back to Boston in a couple months."

"It doesn't have to last. I didn't say I'm looking for a husband."

Another curve is just up ahead, but this time Steven slows down. "Are you saying you don't want to get married?"

"No, but I'm not in a hurry to. I want to wait for the right guy. And who knows? Maybe I'll meet him tonight."

Steven clears his throat as he increases his speed. He's going way too fast on these roads, especially when they're covered in snow. When we get to the main road, he turns the radio on to a classical station. I'm taking that to mean he doesn't want to talk, but just as I'm thinking that, he lowers the volume so that it's barely audible.

"The people who will be there tonight will ask you questions. You're new in town and the locals feed off that. They'll try to get information from you, and the more you tell them, the more they'll ask. I'd advise you to keep your answers short and not tell them anything of a personal nature. And if they ask about Lauren or me, tell them it's not your place to talk about us. Say it would be unprofessional given that we're your employers."

I'm not sure he has the right to tell me what I can and can't say, although it might've been in that document he made me sign. If it was, I don't remember seeing it, not that I read it that closely.

"I doubt I'll have time to talk to people," I say. "After I serve the food, I have to help clean up."

He doesn't say anything.

"So how did you meet David?" I ask. "Or do you not want to talk about it? I know Lauren has a hard time talking about him."

"David was my roommate in college, both freshman and sophomore year." Steven smiles a little. "He was so different than me. I'd never met anyone like him."

"How was he different?"

"He was very free, very uninhibited. He did what he wanted, when he wanted. He didn't care what others thought of him. Didn't care if he was broke. He didn't even know what he wanted to do with his life. He just took one day at a time."

"And what were you like back then?"

"I had everything planned out. I knew exactly what I

146

wanted my life to look like. I'd known since I was 12. I was living with my uncle then and saw that he had all that he could ever want. He told me it was because he planned for it. He imagined what he wanted for his life when he was just a young boy. He never even considered it not happening. He wouldn't let himself. He was determined to get what he wanted. And he did."

Steven turns into a parking lot. I see the town hall sign next to an all-brick building with columns in front and a big steeple at the top with a clock on it. It reminds me of a building you'd see on a college campus.

"I'm supposed to go in the back," I say to Steven as we get out of the car. "That's where the kitchen is."

He nods. "I need to go speak to David's parents."

We go our separate ways, acting as if we're just employee and employer and not two people who shared a night together. Is this how it's going to be? We're just going to forget Friday night ever happened? I suppose that's for the best, but it makes me angry. I'd at least like Steven to acknowledge it, even if it's just to admit it was a mistake.

"You must be Hannah," a lady says as I walk through the door to the kitchen.

"Yes. I'm here to see Kathy?"

"That's me!" She shakes my hand. "It's so nice of you to help out. Let me take your coat."

I take it off and hand it to her. "So where do I start?"

"Right over here." I follow her through the kitchen.

Kathy sounded young on the phone but she looks like she's close to sixty. She has dark shoulder-length hair that's curled up at the bottom and bangs covering her forehead. She's wearing a pink-and-gray plaid flannel shirt that's tucked into a pair of black pants. It makes my red dress look completely out of place. I knew wearing this was a bad idea.

"I need the rolls put into bowls so they're easier to serve," she says, stopping next to a stainless steel table. Packages of dinner rolls are stacked on it.

"Where are the bowls?" I ask.

"Right over there." She points to them on a metal rack, then looks me up and down. "You're going to need an apron. You don't want to ruin that beautiful dress. Let me go see if I can find one."

She takes off. While she's gone, two other women come into the kitchen. They're talking but stop when they see me. They're older than Kathy by maybe 10 years. One has bright red hair that matches her lipstick. The other one has gray hair and big glasses with purple frames.

"Are you helping out tonight?" the red-haired lady asks, walking up to me.

"I am. I'm Hannah."

"Hannah." The old lady looks back at her friend. "Why does that sound familiar?"

"She works at the Bishop house," the lady says. "She's that nurse they hired."

I've never met these women. How do they know about me?

"I'm Mary," the gray-haired lady says, coming up beside her friend. "And that's Joyce."

"Hope they're paying you well," Joyce says to me.

"They are." I smile. "They've been very generous."

"In what way?" Mary asks in a suspicious tone.

"I mean, letting me live there in addition to paying me well. It's very generous of them."

Mary gives Joyce a look. I'm not sure what it means, but it makes a chill go through me.

"Is something wrong?" I ask.

"I don't care what they're paying you," Joyce says, a scowl on her wrinkly face. "If I were you I'd—"

"Get her own place," Mary says, interrupting her. She laughs a little. "Joyce likes living alone. We went to

Pennsylvania last year and she made me get my own hotel room for the week."

Joyce looks at Mary. "Because you snore louder than a freight train." She looks back at me. "All I'm saying is, you might think of staying somewhere else. Somewhere in town where there's people around."

"Thanks, but I'm good staying with the Bishops."

Joyce and Mary give each other that look again. What does it mean? What do they know that I don't?

24

HANNAH

"Did Kathy give you any instructions?" Mary asks.

"Yes, I'm just waiting for an apron."

"Found one!" Kathy says, returning with a white apron. "Anyone else want one?"

"Nah, this can get dirty," Joyce says, pointing to her long-sleeve black shirt that has cardinals embroidered on it. Her pants are black too. Mary has on jeans and a purple sweatshirt.

I feel so overdressed. What was Lauren thinking when she suggested I wear this to serve food in?

Kathy takes Joyce and Mary over by the ovens and they get to work preparing the hot food. I finish up with the rolls, then Kathy has me wrap the silverware up in napkins. I get the feeling she's assigning me duties that don't involve messy food that might ruin my dress. She's probably regretting having me as a volunteer. I'm not much help if I can't get the food ready.

An hour later, we've got everything set up and we're standing behind the serving line at the back of a large ballroom. Round tables have been set up and covered with white tablecloths. Jars of candy in all different colors sit at the center of each table. I'm guessing David had a sweet tooth. Every place setting has a box of playing cards for people to take home. That must be another David thing. There are photos of him put on poster boards that are propped up on easels around the room, but I can't get a good look at them from here.

Everyone's seated now and David's dad is talking, telling a story from when David was a kid. I'm only partially listening as I scan the room, looking for Steven. I spot him at a table up front. Audrey is across from him with a man on each side of her. I wonder if one of them is Mark, the guy Lauren was trying to set Audrey up with.

Audrey's wearing a black dress and heels and so is the woman at the table next to hers. Looking around, I'd say about a third of the people dressed up, which makes me feel less out of place wearing this dress, although I still wish I'd worn something more casual.

The stories continue from David's family, then his friends, but not Steven. If he was best friends with David, why isn't he getting up to speak? Maybe David's parents are still upset with him. I can't believe they almost didn't invite him. There's got to be more to that story than Steven's version of it.

"We're on," Kathy says as people head over to the food line. She looks at Joyce. "Now remember, no chatting people up when they're coming through the line. You can do that later."

"Yes, ma'am," Joyce says, rolling her eyes. "I won't say a word."

"Don't be that way," Kathy says to her. "I only said it so we keep the line moving. We have a lot of people to get through and if you chat with all of them, we'll be here all night."

"Good evening, ladies," an older man says as he enters the line. He has a shiny bald head and a thick gray mustache.

"Good evening, Mayor Thompson," Kathy says as she serves him a piece of chicken. "How did you like the program?"

"Hey!" Joyce snaps, her eyes darting to Kathy. "No chatting."

Kathy ignores her and smiles at the mayor. "We can talk later. Would you like potatoes?"

"I'd like some of everything," he says as Mary adds mashed potatoes to his plate. He continues down the line, ending at the desserts, which is what I've been assigned to.

"I don't believe I know you," Mayor Thompson says, smiling at me.

"I'm Hannah Reese. I'm working for the Bishops for a couple months. I'm Lauren's nurse."

His smile immediately drops and concern crosses his plump face. "How do you like it?"

"So far, it's been great."

He nods. "Good. Very good." He pauses a beat. "Well, good luck!"

Good luck with what? Working for Lauren? The people in this town clearly don't like Steven and Lauren, but I've heard that's typical for small towns. The locals never like outsiders, especially if they're city people. That has to be why I keep getting these strange reactions when I tell people I'm working for them.

The line moves slowly because Joyce keeps talking to people, probably just to annoy Kathy. It takes almost an hour to get everyone through. Kathy tells me they don't need my help cleaning up, which either means she thinks I'd do a bad job or she's worried about my dress.

Now that I'm done volunteering, what am I going to do for the next hour or however long Steven decides to stay? After a stop at the bathroom to check my hair and makeup, I go to the ballroom. There's no one at the bar so I head over there.

"I'll have one of those Rob Roys everyone's talking about," I say to the man tending the bar.

He smiles at me as he picks up a glass. "You ever have one?"

"No. Are they good?"

"They are if you like whiskey. I happen to love it myself." He pours the alcohol into the shaker. "I'm the one who got David started on these. I'm his uncle. I live in Vermont. I'm just here for the event tonight. It looks like the auction items are doing well. Got some high bids already."

The auction items are up front by the band. I haven't been over there yet.

The man puts the top on the shaker and mixes the drink. "How do you know David?"

"I don't. I just came to help with the food. I'm new to town. I'm working for Lauren Bishop. I'm her nurse."

He stops shaking the drink and looks at me.

I shouldn't have mentioned Lauren. I wasn't even thinking. She was in the accident with David, something I'm sure everyone here is trying to forget. This is supposed to be a celebration of life. People don't want to be reminded of the accident.

"Yes, I know Lauren," the man says. "I've known her for years. Steven too. They were both good friends with David."

I nod. "I've heard them talking about him, saying how much they miss him."

The man pours the drink into the glass. "They tell you about that night? The night of the accident?"

"No. They don't talk about it. Why do you ask?"

"Just curious. A lot of us can't believe David would run into a tree. He was always a good driver. Never had an accident before then. The roads were clear. Weather was good." He shrugs. "Doesn't make sense that he'd lose control like that and drive off the road." He hands me the drink. "Have a taste. Let me know what you think."

I take a sip. "It's good, but strong."

He winks at me. "I go heavy on the whiskey. It's better that way."

A couple comes up to the bar. "We'll have one too," the man says, pointing to my drink.

Walking away from the bar, I head toward the front of the room where some people are dancing. The auction tables are to the right of the dance area. I notice Audrey there, bidding on something.

"What are you hoping to win?" I ask, walking up beside her as she sets the pen down.

She turns around and smiles, but then shuts it down when she sees it's me. "I thought you were supposed to be in the kitchen."

"I was, but they didn't need any more help so Kathy said I could go."

"Then what are you still doing here?" she asks in a snide tone.

"Waiting for Steven. He's my ride."

"Perhaps you haven't heard, but there's this thing now where you can arrange for a car to come pick you up."

"Why pay for a car when I could just wait here?"

She narrows her eyes at me. "This event is for David's friends and family. It's not for outsiders."

"I didn't know him, but he sounded like a nice guy. I think he'd be okay with me being here."

"You know nothing about him. I was friends with him since college, and I can assure you he wouldn't want someone like you attending what is supposed to be an evening in his honor."

"Someone like me? What's that supposed to mean?"

She steps closer to me. "You may have fooled Lauren and Steven, but I see through your little sweet and innocent act. You're nothing but a deceitful, calculating fraudster who is the absolute last person who should be caring for my closest friend."

"I'm not a fraudster. I don't know what you're talking about." I glance at some people going past us, then look back at Audrey. "What is your problem? Why do you hate me so much?"

"I just told you why." She leans down to me, lowering her voice. "You're a lying little bitch who managed to fool my best friend into thinking you're someone you're not." She smiles a little. "You think I don't know why you left the hospital?"

My muscles immediately stiffen and my heart slams against my chest. She has to be lying. There's no way she could know. It's not possible.

25

HANNAH

"I left because it wasn't a good fit for me," I say, trying to maintain my composure.

If I show even the slightest hint of fear, Audrey will know that what she's accusing me of is true, assuming we're talking about the same thing. She could never prove I did it, but that doesn't mean she won't tell Lauren. I can't believe she hasn't already. What is she waiting for? That's the one thing that could actually get me fired.

"You can deny it all you want," she says. "But I know what someone like you is capable of. You're a sick, deranged young woman who needs to be locked away."

I'm tired of this woman threatening me and threatening my job. I know I've done bad things, but I'm trying to move past that and have a better future. I'm not letting Audrey take that away from me.

"Believe what you want," I say. "I'm done trying to change your mind about me. I've tried being nice to you, Audrey, but what's the point? You hated me before you even met me. Nothing I could do or say will change that." I stand up straighter. "So I'm done trying. And really, it doesn't matter what you think of me. I don't work for you."

"Lauren trusts me. She respects my opinion and if I tell her to—"

"Get rid of me? You already have. Several times." I smirk. "And yet here I am." I narrow my eyes at her. "And I'm not leaving. So get used to me, Audrey. I'm not going anywhere."

She laughs a little. "You think you're so clever, putting on this charade. But let me tell you, Hannah, your time is coming. So watch your back."

"Audrey!" someone yells over the music. I look over and see Steven motioning her to the table. "I want you to meet someone."

"I'm coming!" she yells back, smiling at him. Her eyes dart back to mine, her smile gone. "Don't think I haven't seen how you look at him. But you're wasting your time. Steven would never see you that way. He only has eyes for Lauren. It's been that way since college. So you can give up trying to steal him away."

Audrey storms off, slowing her pace as she approaches Steven. Her smile is back as she shakes hands with the man standing next to him. The man nods toward the dance floor and Audrey follows him over there. Steven must be trying to set her up with that guy.

"You bidding or not?" someone says.

I look over and see an older lady with a cane slowly making her way to the auction table.

"I'm just standing here," I tell her as I move out of the way.

She stops in front of me. "You look familiar. What's your name?"

"Hannah," I say, realizing how I know her. "I saw you at the grocery store last week. We were in line together."

"You new in town?" she asks, her head tilted as she gazes up at me. She's very short, probably less than five feet.

"I'm only here for a couple months. I'm working for Lauren Bishop. I'm her nurse."

The woman scowls, which deepens the wrinkles around her eyes. "Why would you ever work for a woman like her?"

"I don't know what you mean. Lauren's been great."

"She's a whore," the woman scoffs. She leans closer to me. "If you ask me, she got what she deserved."

"Hannah." I hear Steven's voice, then feel his hand on my back, on my skin, since the dress is cut low in the back. His touch arouses a heat in me, but I try to ignore it. "I was thinking of heading out." He notices the old lady and smiles at her. "Good evening, Mrs. Hanson."

Her eyes bounce between Steven and me, then she mutters something and hobbles off with her cane.

"She's not well," Steven says, watching her leave. "I've heard they'll be moving her to a nursing home soon."

"Why? Because she can't care for herself?"

"That, and because her dementia is getting worse. She imagines things that aren't real, like last week she thought the mailman was the devil." He laughs a little. "I shouldn't make light of it. She's clearly suffering."

So that's why she said that stuff about Lauren. Now it makes sense.

I turn to Steven. "Are you sure you want to leave? It's not even ten."

"I've had enough *fun* for tonight." He says fun like this party is the exact opposite of that. "Let's go get our coats."

As we're walking out of the ballroom, Dan from the grocery store steps in front of me.

"You're not leaving, are you?" He gives me a big, friendly smile. "I was hoping to get a dance."

"I'll have to pass," I tell him. "We're heading out." I point to Steven.

"I can give you a ride home," Dan offers.

"She's going with me," Steven says in a harsh tone. "She needs to get back and check on Lauren."

Dan glances at Steven, then looks back at me. "Maybe we could do something next week, on your night off."

"She won't have time," Steven says. "She cares for my wife in the evenings."

Why is Steven answering for me? Is he just trying to save me from having to go out with Dan? Or is it some other reason?

"I'll see you later," I say to Dan as Steven takes my arm and leads me away.

"Hopefully, he'll stop bothering you now," Steven says, answering my question about why he was speaking for me.

"He's not a bad guy. He's just not my type."

We stop at the coat rack and Steven takes my coat and helps me put it on. "I'm sorry if I overstepped my boundaries, but you have to be very clear with men like him or they keep pestering you."

"I could've gotten rid of him, but I appreciate you helping me out," I say, buttoning up my coat.

Steven puts his coat on and we walk out of the building to the car. The parking lot is completely full. I think we're the first people to leave. I thought we'd be staying longer, but given how Steven feels about the locals, I guess it makes sense he'd want to get out of there.

"What did you think?" I ask on the drive home. "Is it what your friend would've wanted?"

"Yes. Absolutely. He always said he never wanted a funeral, but his parents felt it was necessary. Tonight's event honored his wishes. He wanted a party and he got it."

"Did you get over whatever disagreement you had with his parents?"

He glances at me. "Who told you we had a disagreement?"

"I think Audrey mentioned it," I say, remembering the morning she came over and told Lauren about it. I was walking by Lauren's room and overheard them talking. Audrey probably wouldn't want Steven knowing she was talking about him, but if I get Audrey in trouble, all the better. I'm done being nice to her.

"Audrey shouldn't be talking about issues that don't pertain to her." He turns onto the road that goes to the house. It's really dark. There are no street lights and the trees lining the road make it seem even darker. "David's parents believed something that wasn't true. It was just a misunderstanding. We're fine now." But he says it with a hint of anger in his voice, like it's not really true.

We ride in silence the rest of the way home. I was going to talk more, but Steven seemed lost in his thoughts so I left him alone.

We're home just after ten. I go into the house and straight to Lauren's room to check on her. She's sound asleep, but the light by her bed is on so I turn it off and quietly leave her room.

"She's asleep," I tell Steven, going up to him. He's in the kitchen, pouring himself some scotch.

"Would you like any?" he asks, holding up the bottle.

"I think I'll just go to bed." I turn to leave.

"You looked beautiful tonight."

I turn back and see Steven looking at me, the drink in his hand.

"Thanks." I catch his eye and feel the heat between us, the unspoken desire that I keep trying to pretend isn't there.

He sets his drink on the counter and walks up to me. He puts his hand on my arm. That small, simple touch arouses even more desire in me. I wonder if he's feeling it too.

"Hannah, I know you want me to address what happened last Friday."

"It's okay. We can just—"

"I'm sorry I didn't address it sooner. I just haven't been able to between dealing with the repairs to the house in

Boston and work consuming my time." He looks down a moment, then back at me. "I think it's fair to say we both had too much to drink that night."

I nod. "Yes. Definitely."

"But I can't say for sure it wouldn't have happened if I hadn't been drinking." His eyes lock on mine. "There's something about you, Hannah. Something that feels so right, like you were meant to show up here. Now. When my marriage is falling apart."

"What are you saying?" I ask, my heart swelling with hope that what I feel for him isn't one-sided.

"I'm saying if things were different, if Lauren hadn't been injured and we'd decided to end our marriage, I could see you and I being together."

Is this a dream? Because in my dreams, this exact scene played out. Steven told me he wanted to be with me. We lived in this house. We shared a bedroom. We had dinner together every night. We drank wine and made love in front of the fire. It was my dream life, but it was just that. A dream. I never thought it would come true. And it won't. Not as long as Steven is married, and he's not going to divorce Lauren when she's injured.

His hand cups my face, his eyes still locked on mine. "You have no idea how hard it is to see you every day and not act on how I feel. The thoughts I have about you..." He pauses. "I know it's wrong, but I can't seem to stop myself. You consume my thoughts, Hannah. I lie awake thinking of you just down the hall from me. You're so close, and yet I can't be with you."

"What if you could?" I ask, my voice breathy and weak. I place my hand on his chest. "What if we..." I wait for him to finish my thought.

He leans down to my ear. "It would have to be a secret. You could never tell. If anyone asked, I'd deny it. I'd have no choice. As much as I want you, Hannah, I can't risk losing everything I've worked for. I hope you understand that."

I nod, but I don't think my mind processed even half of what he said. My body's taken over, ruled by the sensations it's feeling as he gently kisses my neck.

"Be with me tonight," he whispers.

I shouldn't do it. It's wrong. My mind knows that, but my body doesn't care.

We leave the kitchen and go upstairs. To Steven's room. To his bed.

26

LAUREN

It's just past midnight and I've been lying here awake since Steven and Hannah got home. Hannah came into my room to check on me, but I pretended to be asleep. I had to, so she'd be available to Steven.

I knew he'd tried to seduce her, especially after I had her wear that red dress. Steven loves the color red on a woman, and that dress fit Hannah perfectly. When he saw her in it, he couldn't take his eyes off her. I knew she'd be in his bed tonight.

He thinks I don't know. He's always thought that, which is why he's been unfaithful to me for our entire marriage. That, and because it was so easy for him to hide it. He'd say he had to work late or travel for business and I—as his doting wife who's completely dependent on his income for the lifestyle I'd become accustomed to—had no choice but to be okay with him not coming home.

Sometimes I wonder how many more women like me are out there? How many wives look the other way while their husband cheats? I never thought I'd be one of them. When Steven and I got married, I thought I'd beat the odds. I'd found the one husband who was extremely handsome, highly successful, and yet still faithful to me. It's hard to believe I was ever that stupid, especially after seeing my mother's mistakes with men.

At least I had enough sense to include that clause in the prenup that said if Steven was ever unfaithful, the prenup would no longer be valid. I didn't want to believe he'd cheat on me, but I had enough evidence of him being flirtatious with other women that I thought I better be safe than sorry.

Steven insisted on the prenup to protect his premarital assets, which were surprisingly substantial for someone his age. He'd received a big inheritance when his parents died, and with his uncle's investment help, he grew that money to a very large sum. He considered that his money, not mine. He didn't want me getting even a penny of it if we ever divorced.

When he gave me the prenup, I didn't want to sign it. Steven assured me I'd still come out ahead financially if we divorced, saying I'd get half of whatever money he made during our marriage. But what if our marriage only lasted a couple years? I'd get almost nothing. So I insisted on adding that clause. Steven fought me over it, to the point I thought he'd call off the wedding. But then one day, without explanation, he agreed to it.

It's time for that clause to finally pay off. If I was ever going to catch Steven cheating, it's now. I invited a beautiful young woman into our home who looks strikingly similar to me at that age. I dressed her up in a way Steven would like. And I let them spend time together. I even encouraged it.

As for Hannah, I made her question if I'm a good enough wife for Steven, lowering her resistance to him. I let her live in my beautiful house, drive my expensive car, wear my designer clothes—all leading her to fantasize about taking my place.

I set Steven and Hannah up and they took the bait, much sooner than I thought they would. As soon as they met, I watched how Steven looked at her. I listened to how he spoke to her. It was clear he wanted her, but I wasn't sure Hannah was ready for that. So last Friday night, I tested them. I went to bed early and told Hannah to have dinner with him. I thought Steven might try to kiss her. I didn't think it'd go farther than that.

But then I heard the crackling of the fire. The clinking of the wine glasses. Steven was setting the stage and Hannah fell for it. I heard the whimpers, the moaning. It made me sick to my stomach knowing they were doing this just a few feet away from me, but I wasn't surprised. Steven loves the thrill of knowing he could be caught at any moment.

When I heard their footsteps going up the stairs, I wondered what was going through Hannah's mind. Was she worried I'd find out? Or was she thinking I deserved this for being a terrible wife to Steven? I've given her plenty of evidence to think that. If Steven says he loves me, I don't say it back, and when he goes to kiss me, I turn away. I make sure Hannah sees this, of course, knowing it will make her feel sorry for Steven and want to be with him all the more.

I also change up my personality to make Hannah unsure if she should like me or hate me. Sometimes I'm kind to her and other times I'm harsh and demanding. I hate to play games like this, but I need Hannah to see me as unstable, and an unsuitable wife for Steven. Clearly, it's worked because she's upstairs with him right now.

I'm sure Steven's done his part as well to lure her to his side, although not for the same reasons as me. He just wants her in his bed, so he's poisoned her thoughts with tales of how I'm neglectful and demanding and frigid. It's the same lies every cheating husband tells his new love interest to convince her he's done everything possible to create a happy marriage, but his evil witch of a wife just doesn't appreciate him.

I really don't care what Steven told her about me, or if he

even believes it. I'm past caring what Steven thinks of me or what he tells others. After experiencing true and honest love from a man who I'm convinced was my soulmate, I see Steven as a sad, unhappy man who will never know love and never realize what he's missing.

I've wasted too much of my life with that miserable man. I want out of this marriage, but not without getting the money I deserve for putting up with him all these years. I've set the plan in motion. Now all I have to do is collect evidence of Steven cheating, which will be easy since it's happening in my own house.

Poor Hannah. She's going to have her heart broken, but that's the price you pay being with Steven. He takes hearts, then breaks them into pieces, and doesn't feel a thing. In a way, I admire him for that. It's hard not to feel some guilt when you watch someone being destroyed by your actions. Believe me, I've tried. I know what lies ahead for Hannah, and I feel bad for her, but that feeling goes away when I remind myself that she's sleeping with my husband. Lying to my face. Pretending we're friends when she's betraying me. Then again, I'm betraying her too, so maybe that makes us even.

On the bright side, Hannah's young. She'll find love again, hopefully with a man who loves her back. Just look at me. I didn't think I'd ever find true love, but I did. It just ended far too soon.

"I wish I could've been there tonight," I whisper into the darkness, hoping David can hear me. I've never been religious, but I want to believe David is somehow still with me, watching over me, helping me get through this. He wouldn't approve of what I'm doing, but he was a better person than me, and a much better man than Steven.

Even back in college, I knew David was the better man, but I picked the man who would give me a beautiful house, a nice car, and financial security. Steven seemed like the safe choice, while David seemed like a risk. It turned out I was wrong.

If I could go back and relive that time of my life, I'd choose David.

27

SOPHOMORE YEAR OF COLLEGE

LAUREN

"Come out with us Saturday," David says as I come into his dorm room. "We're going to dinner to celebrate being back. I guess that's not something to celebrate, but you know me." He laughs. "I'll find any reason to celebrate."

It's our first day back at college after summer break, and even though I just saw David last week, I missed him. David's from Maine, but he worked in Boston for the summer. Since I was there too, we hung out all the time and became really good friends.

Audrey introduced me to David last spring. She had Freshman English with him and sometimes he'd come to our room to study. As soon as I met David, I instantly liked him. He was funny and he smiled a lot.

David's smile is his most attractive feature. The rest of him is just okay. He's average height and kind of skinny and his light brown hair is always a mess because he scratches his head a lot. Audrey kids him about it, saying he has fleas. But I've noticed it's something he does when he's thinking, like all that scratching's going to wake up his brain.

"I can't," I say, turning down his invite. "I promised Audrey I'd go out with her."

"Bring her with. I'd love to hear about her summer."

Audrey spent the summer in Chicago interning at a public relations firm. She wanted to intern in New York but couldn't afford to live there. She has an aunt in Chicago so she was able to stay there for free. I've really missed her. We lived together last year and got to be best friends.

"I'll ask her," I say, getting out my phone. I call her, and when she answers, David grabs the phone from me.

"Hey, we're going out Saturday," he says.

"Who is this?" I hear her say.

"The man you've been pining over all summer." He smiles at me. "Don't even try to deny it. Lauren told me how much you love me."

"David!" she squeals. It's so loud he backs away from the phone, which makes me laugh.

David's always making me laugh. He's the funniest person I know, and the kindest and most generous. Last summer when I was late paying rent and almost got evicted, I got a note from my landlord saying my rent was paid up through August. David paid it, but he never told me. I found out when I asked the landlord to see the check.

David wasn't rich, but he made more money than I did at his summer job and didn't think twice about paying my rent. And sometimes he'd ask to borrow my car just so he could fill it with gas.

"We're all going to dinner Saturday night," he says to Audrey, putting the phone on speaker. "It's on me, which means it can't be one of those fancy places you like."

"I'd love to, but I already have plans with Lauren this weekend," Audrey says. "Speaking of her, why do you have her phone?"

"She's right here. I took her phone so I could convince you to go to dinner with us. You're on speaker."

"Hey, Audrey," I say. "I'm open to going on Saturday if you are."

"Is anyone else going?" she asks.

"Steven," David says.

Audrey doesn't say anything.

"My roommate?" David laughs. "You know Steven. You saw him all the time last year when you'd come over."

"Yes, of course I know Steven. So is this a double date?" Audrey asks in a teasing tone.

"I don't know." David smiles at me. "What do you think, Lauren?"

David and I have never been anything more than friends. I haven't let our relationship go beyond that because I value our friendship and don't want it to change. Plus, I'm not sure David's the right guy for me. I love him to pieces, but he's kind of flaky. He changed majors twice last year and still has no clue what he wants to do with his life. He's not someone who plans for the future. He just assumes everything will work out. But that's not how life works. Things don't always work out. I don't want to spend the rest of my life worrying about tomorrow or the next day. I want certainty. I want security. Those are things I grew up without, but I want them now. I want a nice house and a reliable car and enough money that I can buy what I want without worrying about how I'll pay for it.

I don't think David could give me that kind of life. He'd be a loving partner. There's no question about that. But I need more. I need a loving partner who can also provide a good life for me.

"I think you have your answer," Audrey jokes when I don't respond.

"It's not a date," I say. "We're just friends having dinner. Hey, what time will you be home? I was thinking we could go to the bookstore together."

"I'm almost there. I'm walking to our dorm. Where are

you?"

"In David's room. I stopped over on my way back from the gym."

She sighs. "Would you stop working out? You're already too skinny. You make me look like a cow."

I've always been thin. I've tried to gain weight so I'd have curvier hips or a bigger bust, but no matter what I ate, the number on the scale didn't move. I thought lifting weights might add some muscle so I wouldn't look so waif-like. That's why I went to the gym, but today was my first day and I already don't like it.

"How about six on Saturday?" David says. "We'll meet here and go in Steven's car."

"Works for me," Audrey says. "Lauren, when do you want to go to the bookstore?"

"Maybe around two? I'll head back to our room in a few minutes."

"Okay, see you soon."

We end the call and David walks up to me, handing me my phone. "So no double date, huh?"

"I don't know why she said that," I say with a laugh. "She knows we're just friends."

"Yeah," David says, looking down, then back up at me. "So what kind of guy are you looking for? You've never really said."

I shrug. "I don't know. Someone that makes me feel secure, I guess."

"You mean safe?"

"Not just safe, but secure financially. I want someone with a good job. Someone who's stable and dependable."

"Sounds boring," David jokes.

"Maybe, but I'd rather have that than the life I had growing up. It's not like my life was terrible, but it was unpredictable, which is scary as a kid. I never knew what was coming next. My mom would go out with whatever guy would buy us stuff and let us live with him. Then she'd break up with the guy and we'd have to move. Everything was always changing and I hated it. I wanted some stability in my life."

"What's more important?" David asks. "Security or love?"

"I want both." I smile at him. "Is that too much to ask?"

"Not at all. I'm sure that guy is out there." He looks into my eyes. "Just waiting to be with you."

"David, promise me that whatever happens to us in the future, I won't lose you as a friend."

He gives me that smile of his I love so much. "You'll never lose me. I'll always be here for you. For as long as you let me."

"Always." I wrap my arms around him and rest my head on his chest.

He hugs me back and I notice how safe and secure I feel in his arms. I wish I felt that way about a future with him.

A few minutes later, I head to the door to leave when his roommate walks in. We both stop abruptly before running into each other.

"Pardon me," the guy says as he gently grasps my arm. "Are you okay?"

"I'm fine," I say, hearing the breathiness in my voice. My heart took off the moment I saw the guy. He's almost too handsome for words. Dark silky hair. Gorgeous blue eyes. Strong angular jaw. Extremely white teeth. And he's wearing a dress shirt and tie. He's only in college and already looks successful.

"Steven, this is Lauren," David says, coming up beside me. "Audrey's roommate. She's the girl I told you about."

Steven's eyes haven't left me since he walked in the room. He's staring at me in a way that makes me kind of nervous, but in a good way. I like the attention, especially from a guy like this. Just his presence changed the energy in the room. It's hard to explain, but I felt a shift the moment he walked through the door.

"It's very nice to meet you," he says, shaking my hand.

"It's nice to meet you too."

"David talks about you constantly," Steven says, taking his eyes off me long enough to glance at David.

"He's exaggerating," David says. "I only talk about you a few hours a day."

I laugh. "I hope it's not that much. For your sake," I say to Steven.

"Lauren and Audrey are coming to dinner with us Saturday night," David says to Steven. "I was hoping you could drive us in your Beemer."

"You have a BMW?" I ask Steven.

"I bought it last summer. One of my investments paid off so I rewarded myself with a new car."

"Steven's an investment nerd," David kids. "He's always on his laptop, making spreadsheets and watching the market."

"Call me what you want," Steven says, going past me to his desk. "But only one of us made six figures last year."

My eyes get huge as I turn to Steven. "You made that much? While going to college?"

"It's just a hobby for now," he says, taking his laptop out of his bag. "My uncle works on Wall Street. He taught me everything I know."

"Steven lived with his uncle growing up," David explains.

"My parents died when I was a child," Steven says, walking back to David and me. "I don't really remember them."

"My parents are gone too," I say.

"Sounds like we have a lot in common," Steven says, giving me a slight smile. It's very alluring, and so is he. He's clearly very smart and good with money. What college sophomore generates that kind of income from a hobby? I can already tell he's going to be very successful someday. I can only imagine how wealthy he'll be in 10 years.

I'm staring at Steven and he's staring back. I can't take my eyes off him. He's so good-looking.

David clears his throat. "You should probably get going," he says to me. "Audrey's waiting for you."

"Yeah." I force my gaze off Steven and back to David. "I'll see you later."

"I'll walk you out," he says.

When we're in the parking lot, David stops and looks at me. "Do you like him?"

"Who?"

"Steven."

"No. What gave you that idea?"

"You couldn't take your eyes off him."

"He's good looking. I'm sure a lot of girls look at him that way." We continue to my car, which is rusty, dented, and has a broken windshield. "Did he really make that much money last year?"

"Probably. The guy's some kind of stock market whiz. He said he's been investing since he was 12. God only knows how much money he's made over all those years. I'm sure he's lost some too, but I'm guessing he wins more than he loses. Steven hates to lose. He's the most competitive guy I know."

We reach my car and David opens the door for me. It makes a loud screeching noise.

"Remind me to oil that," he says, and once again I'm reminded how much I love him. As a friend.

"Bye." I give him a hug, then let him go. "See you soon!"

As I drive off, my phone rings. I don't recognize the number.

"Hello?"

"Lauren, it's Steven."

I smile. "David's roommate Steven?"

"The one and only."

"How'd you get this number?"

"Audrey. I called her and asked her for it. I hope that's

okay."

"It's fine. So, um, why are you calling?"

"I know we just met, but I'd love to take you to dinner tonight and get to know you better. Are you available?"

"Yes!" I say, my heart beating like crazy. I can't believe he's asking me out. A guy like him must get constant attention from girls. He could have anyone he wants, but he chose me! I need to calm down. I don't want to seem overly eager to go out with him. Some guys find that a turnoff. "So what time were you thinking?" I casually ask.

"Seven. I'll pick you up."

"Great! You know where I live, right?"

"Yes. Same room as Audrey."

"That's right," I say with a nervous laugh. "I keep forgetting you two are friends."

"I wouldn't say we're friends, but yes, I know her because of David."

"Okay, well, I guess I'll see you in a few hours."

"I'm looking forward to it. Goodbye, Lauren."

We end the call and I'm so excited about our date that I almost drive right through a stop sign. I take a deep breath, trying to calm down. It's just a first date. It doesn't mean anything. Tonight could be our only date if things don't go well.

Or it could be the start of a relationship with my future husband.

The rest of the way to my dorm, I imagine myself with Steven. I imagine what our life would be like. What our house would look like. Maybe we'd have more than one. What kind of car would I drive? Would we go to fancy high-society events and belong to a country club? What would my wardrobe look like? Would I have expensive gowns and cashmere sweaters and jackets made of real leather?

If only I could have that life.

28

PRESENT DAY

LAUREN

"I'm so sorry I'm late," Hannah says, racing into my room. It's after eight. Hannah is usually in my room by seven to check if I need to use the bathroom. "I overslept, but I promise it won't happen again."

As she frantically wheels my chair next to the bed, I try to hold back my smile. I'm secretly loving this, the way she's trying so desperately to hide what she did last night. She's doing a terrible job. Even if I didn't know, I'd suspect something was up by her jittery movements and fast speech.

"I was starting to worry," I tell her as she helps me into the wheelchair. "I thought something might have happened to you."

"I just forgot to set my alarm." She wheels me to the bathroom. "But it won't happen again. I've already set the alarm for tomorrow."

After I use the bathroom, Hannah helps me back into bed.

"I'll go make breakfast," she says. "Then we'll do your shower."

I usually shower before breakfast, but now our schedule is messed up and I need to eat or I get lightheaded. I have low blood sugar and it's always worse in the morning.

"Don't worry about breakfast," I tell her. "I texted Audrey and asked her to bring me something. I wasn't sure what time you'd be up."

Hannah sighs, her face covered with guilt. "I'm so sorry."

"Yes, you said that." I give her a slight smile. "Was it a late night? Is that why you forgot to set your alarm?"

"No. We were home by 10."

"Sit down," I say, motioning to the chair next to the bed. "I'd like to hear about the event."

She sits on the edge of the chair, her back straight, her hands fidgeting in her lap. She's a terrible liar. She needs to learn to calm down.

"What do you want to know?" she asks, avoiding eye contact. She keeps looking down at her hands, then back at me, then back at her hands.

"Were you able to enjoy any of the event, or were you stuck in the kitchen all night?"

"I didn't have to clean up, so yes, I was able to join everyone in the ballroom."

"And? Were you able to meet some people?"

"Um, yeah, I met David's uncle."

"Gus." I smile, remembering him. "He was David's favorite uncle and like a second father to him. They'd go on a fishing trip together every summer. I always liked Gus. Did you tell him who you were?"

"Yes, I said I was your nurse." She pauses. "And then he said something kind of strange."

I cock my head. "What did he say?"

"Nothing. Forget it." Hannah shakes her head really fast. "I'm sure it didn't mean anything."

"Hannah." I wait until she looks at me. "Tell me what he said. Was it about David?"

"Kind of." She looks down at her hands.

"What about him?"

She hesitates, chewing on her bottom lip.

"Hannah, please. Just tell me what he said."

"He, um... he said David was a really good driver and that he'd never had an accident before."

"Yes. That's true. But why was he telling you that?"

"He said he couldn't believe David ran into a tree." Hannah glances up at me before looking back at her hands. "Like he didn't believe that's what happened."

"Are you saying Gus doesn't think it was an accident?" I say it with a hint of humor, like the very idea is comical, but part of me is panicking right now, wondering if there's even a shred of truth in Gus' comment.

"I kind of got that idea," Hannah says. "But I'm sure it's just his way of coping. People come up with crazy things to explain why tragedies happen. I learned that in my college psych class."

Gus wouldn't say that unless he really believed it. But why would he think the crash wasn't an accident? Is it just because of David's flawless driving record up until that night? I agree it's odd David lost control like that, but there's no other explanation.

I wish I remembered more about that night, but I hit my head when we crashed and can't recall the moments leading up to it. I remember David and I talking in the car, then next thing I know I'm waking up in an ambulance. What happened in between those moments is gone. The doctor told me that's common for traumatic experiences, explaining that the brain will sometimes forget the most horrific part of it to save ourselves from the pain of reliving it. He said that, combined with hitting my head, is why I don't remember the actual crash.

"What else did Gus say?" I ask.

"Not much. He was bartending. He made me a Rob Roy. He told me he's the one who got David to like them."

"Yes, David loved them," I say, an image forming in my head of David sitting in his favorite chair—a brown leather recliner he'd had since college—and drinking a Rob Roy. "He tried to get me to like them, but I don't enjoy hard liquor. I'm more of a wine girl."

"It was good, but really strong. I didn't even finish it."

So Hannah wasn't drunk last night, which means she willingly spent the night with Steven. I assumed that was the case, given how guilty she's acting this morning. If she'd been drunk, she might've convinced herself the alcohol made her do it.

"Did you talk to anyone else last night?"

"Audrey." Hannah looks up at me. "She really hates me, doesn't she?"

"She doesn't hate you. She's just protective of me. She's always been that way. Back in college, she tried to convince me to end things with Steven." I smile a little, thinking back to how Audrey used to tease me about Steven, saying I'd be bored to tears if I ended up with him. But boredom wasn't the issue. It was disappointment. The Steven I dated, who was loving and affectionate, wasn't even close to the one I married. The day after our wedding, he became cold and distant, the old Steven only showing up when other people were around. That's the only time he'd hold my hand or put his arm around me or even notice me. I began craving those moments, purposely planning dinners with friends or filling our calendar with parties and events so that I'd get back the Steven I fell in love with, even if it was just for a couple hours.

"Audrey didn't like Steven?" Hannah asks.

"She didn't back then. She didn't think he was good enough for me. She was constantly telling me I could do better."

"But why? He's smart, successful, handsome." Hannah quickly looks away, as if she regrets saying that last part.

"You think Steven is handsome?" I ask with a slight smile.

"I mean, for an older man? Sure."

"He's in his thirties. He's not that old."

"So why didn't Audrey think he was good enough?" Hannah says, trying to get off the topic of Steven being handsome.

"He was just so serious back then. He still is, but not nearly like he was. He rarely smiled, except around me. And he rarely laughed. David's the only person who could make him laugh and that was only because David could be so ridiculous sometimes that you couldn't help but laugh. He wasn't afraid of embarrassing himself." I pause. "David was one of a kind." I choke on the words as I hold back the urge to cry.

I miss him so much. I don't know how I'll go on without him.

"Do you want some water?" Hannah asks as I clear my throat.

"Yes, please." I wait as she goes to get it, then watch her hurry back into the room with my glass. "I needed some water last night," I say, taking the glass from her. "You must not have seen my text."

"You texted me?" Hannah gets her phone out. "Oh, Lauren, I'm so sorry. I didn't see this. You sent it last night?"

"Yes, around 10:30," I say, knowing that's when she was with Steven.

"I thought you were asleep." Hannah sits down on the chair, her foot nervously tapping the floor. "I checked on you when I got home."

"Yes, I fell asleep around nine, but woke up when I heard a noise. It must've been you and Steven getting home. I thought I heard talking, but I wasn't fully awake. I dozed off, then woke up and needed a drink of water."

"I should've refilled your glass when I came in to check on you," Hannah says with regret. "I'm so sorry."

"Why didn't you?"

She looks at me, confused. "What?"

"Why didn't you check my glass?"

"I, um..." She clears her throat. "I was just tired, I guess. It'd been a long night and I must've just forgot."

I keep my eyes on her. "What about Steven? Did he check on me?"

"No." Hannah shakes her head. "He went straight to bed."

"Huh. That's odd."

"What's odd?"

"He usually has a drink before bed. He says it helps him sleep."

"Oh, um, yeah, I think he did. I wasn't really paying attention."

"Hannah, is there something you're not telling me?"

"No," she blurts out. "Why—why do you ask?" she stutters.

She is such a bad liar.

"Steven didn't kiss me goodbye this morning," I say. "He didn't even come into my room. I thought maybe something happened last night that you don't want me to know about."

I wish I could take a photo of her face right now. It's pure panic. Her eyes are darting around. Her lip's twitching. And there are faint patches of red forming on her neck. I almost want to put her out of her misery and tell her I know what she did. But it's not time. Not yet.

"I don't know what you mean," Hannah says. "Steven seemed okay to me."

"You didn't see him talking to anyone at the party?" I ask. "Someone who might've upset him?"

Her body relaxes as she realizes the question wasn't referring to what she did with Steven, but what happened at the event.

"I saw him talking to some people," she says. "But they didn't seem to be arguing."

"That's good," I say, taking another sip of water. I set the glass down. "Hannah, are you sure you're okay? You seem kind of nervous."

She forces out a smile. "I'm fine. I just feel bad that I overslept."

Her voice had more confidence that time. Maybe her lying skills are starting to improve.

29

LAUREN

"I'll get it," Hannah says as the doorbell rings. She races off to the door. "Good morning, Audrey!"

Audrey says nothing back. I hear her high heels clicking on the wood floor as she makes her way to my room.

"How's the patient today?" she asks, smiling as she brings me my latte. She sets the sack from the local bagel shop on the nightstand. I've been craving an egg sandwich from that place. It's only a block from Audrey's condo so she was happy to stop there on her way over.

"I didn't sleep well," I say. "I'm tired, but this should help." I take a sip of the latte.

Audrey sits down and picks up the bagel sack. "You'll need a plate for this. Hannah!" she yells to Hannah, who's in the other room. "Bring Lauren a plate!"

"Audrey," I say.

"What?" She opens the sack.

"You can't order Hannah around like that. She doesn't work for you."

Hannah rushes in with a dinner plate and a napkin. "Is this okay?"

"It's fine. Thank you." I take the plate and the napkin.

Hannah stands there, like she's waiting for direction.

"Please, leave," Audrey says to her. "I'd like to talk to my friend."

Hannah hurries out of the room.

"You did it again," I say to Audrey.

"She was standing there like an idiot. She needed to go. And at least I was nice this time. I said please." She puts the bagel on my plate. "You need to watch that girl."

"Why?"

"She has her eyes on Steven."

I laugh. "That's ridiculous. He's way too old for her, and far too serious. She's not interested in him."

"If you'd seen her last night, you wouldn't be saying that."

"Why? What happened?"

"She kept looking for him in the ballroom, and when she saw him, she got this dreamy look in her eyes, like a high school girl with a crush."

"Maybe that's all it is. She has a crush on him. A lot of women do. He's a very handsome man."

"Yes, but other women aren't living in the same house as him. Hannah is, and as much as I don't like her, I have to admit she's pretty. She almost looks like you did at that age, but of course, you were much prettier."

I smile at her compliment. "I think you're worrying about nothing. Even if Hannah had a crush on Steven, it wouldn't go anywhere. He wouldn't be unfaithful to me."

"You don't think it's possible?"

"Anything's possible. Our marriage certainly isn't perfect, but I can't imagine him cheating, especially with someone Hannah's age."

"Are you kidding? Guys his age love having affairs with young girls. Look at her face. There's not a single wrinkle, and I bet there's no cellulite on those skinny legs."

"Even if Steven wanted to cheat, he doesn't have time. He works constantly."

"Yes, but Hannah is here, in your house. Steven doesn't have to go anywhere. And you can't get out of bed. They could be going at it upstairs and you'd be none the wiser. They could be—"

"Okay, I've heard enough. Let's talk about something else."

She sighs, frustrated that I'm not taking her concerns about Hannah seriously. She doesn't understand, but she will. Soon.

I pick up the bagel sandwich and take a bite.

"I hope it's still hot," Audrey says. "It took me forever to get here. There was an accident a few miles from downtown and they set up a detour."

"Was it serious? The accident?"

"It didn't look like it, but there was glass on the road so they had cones up and were redirecting traffic." She leans back in the chair and sips her coffee.

"Why didn't you get a sandwich? They're really good." I take a bite, savoring the fluffy scrambled eggs, crisp bacon, and chewy bagel.

"Are you kidding? Those things are like a thousand calories. I could have a whole bottle of wine for that."

"You could have both. Splurge a little."

"And weigh 500 pounds? I don't think so. I choose my calories wisely. Not everyone can eat what they want and stay skinny like you."

Audrey's always been envious of my figure. She's much curvier than me and has to practically starve herself to maintain her weight.

"So tell me about last night," I say, taking another bite of my sandwich.

"It was very David," she says, smiling. "His dad read some of David's jokes. You know the ones that weren't really funny but used to make us laugh because of the way David said them?"

"Yes, he was quite the performer." My voice is light but my heart is heavy, remembering David and the way he'd tell those silly jokes. Just seeing his smile would make me laugh. He was always able to cheer me up. There were so many wonderful things about him. I'd never met anyone like him, and never will again.

"The band played all his favorite songs, even that one David wrote about the blue canary." Audrey laughs. "People were singing along. It was horrible, but David would've loved it."

David would scribble down song ideas whenever they popped in his head. He kept a small notebook with him because he preferred to write them on paper rather than type them into his phone. They were ridiculous songs, but very funny. I used to imagine David as a father, singing those silly songs to his kids. He would've been a wonderful father.

"Oh, that guy didn't show," Audrey says. "The one you tried to set me up with?"

"Mark. Yes, he said he wasn't sure if he could make it. He was closing on a house yesterday and said it might run late. Sorry, I forgot to tell you."

"I'm happy he didn't show up. I was able to mingle." She sips her coffee.

"Does that mean you met someone?"

"Maybe. I want to see how it goes before I say anything."

"Is it anyone I know?"

"It could be." She sips her coffee again.

"Audrey, you can't keep a secret like that. Who is it?"

She smiles. "That new developer. The one who's building those houses outside of town? He's only living here until his project is done so I figured he'd be good for a short fling."

"Or maybe it could turn into something. You never know."

"I'm not looking for that. I'm technically still married, although we're getting close to a final agreement. My lawyer said if Barry cooperates, I could have the papers to sign in a couple weeks."

"That's great."

"It is. I'm going to celebrate when it's over. Maybe you'll be able to go out by then and we can go to that martini bar we love."

"I doubt I'll be able to go out that soon, and definitely not to Boston."

"Why? It's not that far. It'd be good for you to get out for a few hours."

I put my sandwich down. "I'm not ready."

"You will be in a few weeks. Look how well you're doing. You're sitting up, moving around more."

"I don't mean physically. I mean I'm not ready to drive by there again. The place it happened."

"Oh." She sets her coffee down. "I wasn't thinking about that."

The accident happened just a few miles from the martini bar she's talking about. It was one of our favorite places to go. It's outside of the city in an old brick building that's over a hundred years old. The inside is dark and moody. The ceilings are short and have chandeliers hanging from them. Long velvet drapes hide the windows. Going there feels like you're stepping back in time, which is why Audrey and I liked it. I'd love to go back, but not if it means passing by the crash site.

"We'll go somewhere else," Audrey says. "Some place around here. Or we could stay in. I'll bring champagne and we'll live it up in your room."

I give her a half-hearted smile. "Yeah, that'll be fun."

She leans over to me and puts her hand on my arm. "I didn't mean to upset you. I know you're still grieving him."

But she doesn't know how much, or why. Someday I'll tell her, but not now.

"Audrey, I need to ask you something."

"Of course." She sits back in the chair. "What is it?"

"Hannah was talking to Gus last night. David's uncle?"

"The guy he went on those fishing trips with?"

"Yeah, that's him. He was bartending last night."

"Was he? I didn't recognize him."

"Did you talk to him?"

"No, they had wine on the table so I didn't go over to the bar. But I saw an older man there making drinks. He's aged a lot since I last saw him."

"Hannah said he made a comment about the crash."

"What about it?"

"He implied that maybe it wasn't an accident."

"What do you mean? What did he say?"

"That David was an excellent driver and had never had an accident, which is true. He was always cautious, even more so if he had someone else in the car with him."

"So Gus is basing his theory on David being a good driver?" She picks up her coffee. "He doesn't think good drivers can have accidents? That's ridiculous. Why would he even say something like that? He must be getting senile." She takes a drink of her coffee.

"It *is* kind of strange that he'd drive off the road like that. The weather was good. The roads were clear. He hadn't been drinking."

"Lauren, think about what you're saying. You really think David didn't do this?"

"I don't know," I say, my voice trailing off.

"What do you think happened? Someone pushed him off the road?"

"No. We were the only car around when it happened. I

remember making a comment to David about how we had the road to ourselves."

"It's because of the detour. They'd just reopened that road after doing construction and people didn't realize it was open. It's a lot busier now."

"Do you think the construction had something to do with it? Like maybe they left something on the road that David didn't see and he swerved to avoid it?"

"If he did, it would've been there when the police got there."

"Yeah, you're right. What about an animal? David might've swerved to avoid it and by the time the police got there, it was gone. It ran off."

Audrey lets out a long sigh. "Lauren, you've got to stop this. I know you want a better explanation for why this happened, but there isn't one. David just made a mistake."

I nod, knowing she's right, but not wanting it to be true.

David could be silly and irresponsible at times, but he wasn't careless, especially with me. He would've done anything to protect me from harm. Gus knows that, which is why he's questioning if it really was an accident.

But it had to be. The police said it was. They investigated the crash site. They ruled it an accident. *Driver error*, it said on the police report.

David just made a mistake. A mistake with a tragic end.

30

HANNAH

"Steven just texted," Lauren says, tossing her phone on the bed. "He's going to be late again."

It's Friday night and Steven's been late every night this week except Tuesday, the night of the celebration of life.

"Did he say what time he'd be home?" I ask.

"He said after seven, which isn't at all helpful." She reaches for her blanket at the end of the bed.

I get it for her and pull it over her. "It's okay if he's late. I can keep dinner warm."

"You're far too forgiving. It isn't right for him to make us wait. He's late almost every night," she huffs. "As if he thinks our lives revolve around him."

"We could eat without him."

"He doesn't like eating dinner alone. Breakfast or lunch, yes, but not dinner. It's one of his quirks."

"Then we'll wait. Or I'll eat now and you can eat when he gets home."

"I can't wait. I can already feel my blood sugar dropping."

"I'll go get your dinner, but what about Mr. Bishop?"

"Would you mind waiting and having dinner with him? I know it's a lot to ask but—"

"I don't mind. I'm not that hungry. I can wait."

"Thank you." She sighs. "I'm sorry to have to ask. Steven's just very demanding and wants things a certain way."

I don't think he's demanding. He just knows what he likes and what he wants. I appreciate that in a man. It's a sign of maturity. Younger guys have no idea what they want. They say they do, but then change their mind. They jump from one job to the next and can't commit to a relationship. It's frustrating, and the reason I gave up on dating.

"Do you know if he took my car for an oil change?" Lauren asks as I'm folding the sheets I took off her bed this morning.

"I don't know. He didn't mention it."

"I'm sure he forgot," she says, rolling her eyes. "He has no problem remembering to do maintenance on his own car but neglects mine."

"He's been really busy at work. And you're not really driving your car right now."

"Yes, but you are, and it needs an oil change. Steven should've done it."

"I could bring it in for an oil change. Just tell me where to go."

"That's not your job," she says, picking up her phone.

She's been really angry at Steven this week. I haven't heard them fighting, so I don't think that's the reason. I think she's just been in a bad mood, although she's been okay with me.

"He was supposed to order me this." She shows me her phone. There's a photo of a diamond necklace on it.

"It's beautiful."

"It'd be more beautiful if I was wearing it," she says, sounding annoyed. She throws her phone down beside her.

What is wrong with her? She's acting like a spoiled child and has been this way all week. Is this the real Lauren? A wealthy housewife who throws tantrums when her husband doesn't do what she wants?

Maybe she's been putting on an act this whole time and now I'm seeing the real Lauren. Maybe the locals knew she was like this and that's why people kept asking how I was getting along with her.

Poor Steven. He works all those hours, gives Lauren this wonderful life, and then she complains about him. I see why he doesn't love her. How could he? She's so ungrateful, and no matter what Steven does, it's never good enough.

Steven said Lauren didn't come from money, so how did she get this way? She should be thrilled that she escaped her old life and got this one, a life of luxury. If that happened to me, I'd never take it for granted. I'd be beyond grateful. I wouldn't be pouting when my husband had to work late or mad at him for not getting me diamond jewelry I don't even need.

"Steven better spend time with me tomorrow," Lauren says. "He said he would, but I'm not counting on it."

"What are you two planning to do?"

"I'd rather not share that with you. You're still going into town tomorrow, right?"

"Probably, if the weather's okay."

Tomorrow is my day off. I'll have to get Lauren ready in the morning and ready for bed at night, but the rest of the day is mine. I'm planning to go downtown to do some shopping. It was Lauren's idea. She said I needed to get out of the house. She gave me the names of some stores to check out and a recommendation for lunch. I thought she was just being nice, but now I'm thinking she's just trying to get rid of me so she can be alone with Steven. I'm a little concerned she wouldn't tell me what they're doing. Why is it a secret? Is she planning to be intimate with him? She can't. Not in her condition. I guess they could find ways to pleasure each other, but would Steven want that? After being with me?

"The weather shouldn't be an issue," Lauren says. "We're

only getting a few inches of snow and you can take my SUV. You'll be perfectly safe on the roads."

"Then yes, I'll plan to go out."

"Please don't be back before three. I need time alone with my husband."

The husband she constantly complains about? I don't understand her. Why doesn't she just end it with Steven and go find someone else?

I go to the kitchen to get her dinner, then sit with her while she eats and watches another episode of her housewives show.

"Get rid of this," she says, pointing to her half-eaten plate of food. "Then help me get ready for bed."

"You're going to bed this early?"

"It's after seven and I'm tired. And I don't like you telling me when I'm allowed to go to sleep."

"I wasn't telling you anything. I'm just concerned. Fatigue can be a sign something's wrong, like you have an infection."

"I don't have an infection," she snaps. "It's simply been a long day and I'm tired. Now would you hurry up?"

Taking the tray from her, I race out of her room and bring the tray to the kitchen. I'll clean it up later. I don't want to get yelled at for taking too long.

I help her change clothes, then bring her to the bathroom so she can take off her makeup and brush her teeth. While she's doing that, I go back to the kitchen and fill her glass with water.

"Hello, Hannah," Steven says, coming into the kitchen from the garage.

My heart takes off seeing him there, looking so handsome in his suit and black wool dress coat.

"Hi!" I smile at him. "I didn't even hear the garage door open."

"Sorry I'm late," he says, taking his coat off. "One of my

clients had to reschedule a meeting and, of course, he couldn't meet until five."

"Don't worry about it. I kept your dinner in the oven so it'd be ready when you got home."

"I hope you'll be joining us," he says.

"I will, but it's just you and me. Lauren already ate."

"Hannah!" she yells. "I need help getting back to bed!"

"I'm coming," I say, racing back to Lauren. She's coming out of the bathroom, trying to wheel herself back to the bed.

"You're not supposed to do that," I tell her. "You could hit your leg on the doorframe."

"Yes, well, my nurse disappeared," she says, glaring at me. "I couldn't stay in the bathroom all night."

"Sorry." I wheel her back to her bed.

"Can I help?" Steven asks, appearing in Lauren's room.

"Steven," Lauren says, glancing at him. "You finally made it home."

"I'm sorry, sweetheart," he says, coming over to her. "I know I promised you I'd be home on time tonight." He looks at me as I lock the wheels of the chair. "Can I do it?"

"You want to move her?"

"Yes." He smiles a little. "Do you think I'm not qualified?"

"No, it's fine. Go ahead. Just go slow. And make sure you support her upper body as well as her leg."

Lauren watches as he leans down to pick her up. "Steven, why don't you let Hannah do it?"

"I've got you, sweetheart," he says, as he carefully transfers her from the chair to the bed. He pulls the blanket over her and kisses her forehead.

I'm swimming in jealousy, wishing I had a husband like that. He doesn't even love her, but he still wants to take care of her. He has such a good heart.

"How'd I do?" he asks Lauren.

"Fine," she says in a cold, angry tone. "But that doesn't make up for you being late."

"We'll spend tomorrow together. I promise."

"I won't count on it," she mutters.

"I'll let you get some rest." He leans down and kisses her forehead again, then leaves the room.

Lauren looks back at the nightstand. "Hannah, where's my water?"

"Oh, I left it in the kitchen." I run back to get it, then place it exactly where she likes it on the nightstand. "Do you need anything else?"

"Please close the door on your way out. I don't want to hear dishes clanking."

"Okay." I leave, shutting the door behind me.

I'm finally done with her for the day. Now I can relax and enjoy my evening.

It's Friday night and I'm spending it with Steven, just like last Friday. But will we end up in his room again? I know it's wrong, but I'm hoping the answer is yes.

31

HANNAH

"Dinner is wonderful," Steven says, smiling at me from across the table. He changed out of his suit and is wearing a light blue cashmere sweater that brings out the blue in his eyes.

"I'm not great at cooking," I say, "But I'm getting better."

"This is far better than anything we'd get in town. I wish someone would open a decent restaurant here." He picks up his glass of wine and takes a long drink of it before setting it down. "It feels good to have a nice, quiet dinner. A glass of wine. I needed this. This week has been very stressful."

"At least you have a few days off now." I set my fork down, deciding I've had enough to eat. I only ate a few bites, but I'm not hungry. I'm too focused on what might happen later tonight. "So what are you and Lauren doing tomorrow?"

"I'm not sure yet. We can't do a lot with her stuck in bed. Perhaps I'll get her out to the living room. Make a fire. She'd like that." He cuts into his steak and takes a bite.

"It's sweet of you to do so much for her. I mean, given your situation."

He looks at me. "And what situation is that?"

"You know. The situation with you and Lauren."

"I don't know what you're getting at."

"What you said last week, about how your marriage isn't real."

He laughs a little. "Of course it's real. I have the marriage certificate to prove it."

I feel a knot forming in my stomach. Why is he pretending he doesn't know what I'm talking about?

"You said you didn't love her. You said you were going to divorce her."

His brows draw together. "I don't recall saying I planned to divorce her."

"Why would you stay with her if you don't love her?"

"Marriage is complicated. You'll see that once you're married yourself."

I get up and take my plate to the sink, not caring that it made a loud clanking noise that probably woke up Lauren.

"Hannah." Steven comes up behind me. "I didn't mean to upset you. Come sit down. Let's finish dinner."

"That is not what you said."

"What are you talking about?"

"You said it was over with her. You said your marriage was a sham."

He puts his hands on my shoulders and leans down to my ear. "Give me time. I have obligations."

What is he saying? Is he divorcing her or not?

I turn to face him. "What does that mean?"

"It means you need to be patient." He cups my face and leans down to kiss me. It's what I was hoping for, but I want more. I want him to pick me up and carry me upstairs and show me how he really feels about me.

But instead, he pulls away. "Let's go finish dinner."

We return to the table and he takes out his phone and texts someone. Then he puts his phone down and pours himself more wine.

"We're getting low on groceries," he says. "Would you mind going to the store tomorrow?"

It's my day off, but I say, "Sure, I can go."

"Thank you. Oh, and the maid called and said she can't make it tomorrow. She slipped on some ice and injured her knee. She won't be able to clean for several weeks. I called around but couldn't find a replacement. I hate to ask this, but would you mind cleaning the house? I'd pay you extra."

"Sure, I can do it," I say, showing him how agreeable I am. I want him to see how much better I am than Lauren. I bet she's never cleaned their house, not even when they were first married.

"I need to remember to pick up my dry cleaning," Steven says.

"I can do it," I tell him. "I'm going into town tomorrow anyway."

He smiles. "Thank you. I appreciate it."

"I'm happy to help." I smile back. "Would you like dessert? We have chocolate cake."

"That's one of my favorites. I'd love some."

I know it's his favorite because Lauren told me. She told me his favorite meal, his favorite dessert, his favorite color. She's told me a lot about him and I made sure to remember it all.

"I got it at the bakery," I say as I get up to serve the cake. "I would've made it myself, but I still need to work on my baking skills."

We have the cake, then I ask Steven if he'd like to take our wine to the living room. I'm assuming he'll agree to it, knowing where it will lead.

"Not tonight," he says. "I need to get to bed. I haven't slept much this week."

"Oh, okay." I get up. "I'll clean up dinner."

"It was wonderful. Thank you for making it."

I nod as I gather up the plates from the table.

"Goodnight, Hannah," he says as he leaves.

"Goodnight, Mr. Bishop."

I don't understand. What happened? Why did he leave?

He kissed me by the sink. Talked in my ear. Put his hands on my shoulders. He was definitely flirting. I didn't just imagine it. But when we returned to the table, he went back to being my employer. There was no flirtatious smile. No seducing looks across the table. He was all business. And then he just left and went upstairs.

Did I do something wrong? Is he no longer interested in me?

I don't like this. This isn't how tonight was supposed to end. Instead of being with Steven right now, I'm alone in the kitchen feeling empty, rejected, and confused.

This is all Lauren's fault. Steven wants me, but he feels an obligation to Lauren. She's his wife and she's injured, so he doesn't feel right leaving her. That's why he acted that way tonight. I'm sure of it. It's not about me. Steven's made it clear he wants me. He just needs Lauren out of his life.

32

HANNAH

When I left to go into town this morning, Steven was in Lauren's room and the door was closed. I don't know what they were doing in there, but I could hear Lauren and she sounded angry.

I feel sorry for Steven, having to spend the day with her. She's so mean to him. When I was helping her get ready this morning, she was complaining that Steven wasn't up yet, despite knowing how hard he worked this week and how much he needed the rest. Then she told me not to make her breakfast or clean up her bathroom because she wanted Steven to do it. She said she's tired of him not helping out. I didn't bother reminding her that I was hired to do those things. Steven already has a job and works very long hours, and then he drives all the way here to be with her at night. He commutes more than two hours a day just to be with Lauren, and then she complains about him and says he's not doing enough.

She doesn't deserve him. Maybe at some point in their marriage she was a good wife, but she's not now. I don't know why Steven stays with her. He could divorce her and just pay someone to care for her. It wouldn't be me, since I'd be with Steven, caring for him the way his wife should have.

"Can I help you?" a woman asks as I walk into the clothing store that Lauren suggested. She said it's where a lot of younger women in town go to shop because the clothes are trendy and modern, more like what you'd see in big city stores.

"I'm just looking around," I say.

"I'm Jane," she says, smiling at me. "Just let me know if you need any help."

Jane's Boutique is the name of the store so I guess she's the owner. She looks like she's my age. How'd she get the money to open a store? She had to lease the space, probably had to renovate it, then buy all the inventory. Maybe she has a rich husband. I glance at her hand as she rearranges a shelf of jeans and see the huge diamond ring on her finger. Just as I thought, she married a guy with money.

What would I be doing if I married a rich guy? Would I spend my days shopping and going out to lunch like Lauren did before her accident? Or would I be more like Jane and do something I liked that made money but didn't feel like a job?

"How long have you had this place?" I ask as I look through a rack of sweaters.

"Almost two years." She walks over to me. "Are you new here? I don't think I've seen you before."

"I've only been here a few weeks," I say, but it feels much longer than that. I feel like I've been here for months. "I'm a nurse. I'm helping a woman who's recovering from an accident."

"Lauren Bishop?" she asks.

"Yeah, that's her."

Of course she knows her. Everyone knows everyone in this town. I'm still not used to that.

"How's she doing?" Jane asks.

"Okay. She had multiple fractures in her leg so that'll take a long time to heal, but her cuts and bruises are mostly gone and the swelling around her ribcage is way down."

I shouldn't have said that. Lauren doesn't want me telling people about her health. She's told me that more than once, saying her health is nobody's business. Oh, well, too late now.

"It's such a shame what happened," Jane says. "David was such a nice man. And they were so good together. Lauren must be devastated."

"Yeah, it sounded like they were really good friends."

"Friends?" Jane pauses, looking confused. Then she turns to the rack of sweaters and pulls one out. "This just came in. It'd look great on you! You should try it on."

"Wait—what were you saying about Lauren?"

"Nothing." She shakes her head. "I thought you knew. But never mind."

"Knew what?"

"I really shouldn't say." She walks to the dressing room, which is just a black curtain hung between two wooden panels. "I'll put this in here," she says, holding up the sweater. "In case you want to try it on."

I walk over to her. "Are you saying there was something going on with Lauren and David? That they were more than friends?"

She glances around the store like she's making sure we're alone. We are. The store just opened and I'm the first and only person here.

"They'd come into the store sometimes," she says. "Lauren has great taste in clothes so I was flattered that she shopped here. She usually came alone, but sometimes she brought David. She'd hold up clothes and ask him if he thought she'd look good in them. I thought it was kind of odd that she'd bring some guy in here to get his opinion on her clothes, given that she's married and all. But then I thought maybe David's one of those guys who has a good eye for fashion, although I always thought Steven was a way better dresser than David."

"So why do you think David and Lauren were involved? Other than them shopping together?"

She leans toward me and lowers her voice as if someone might be listening in, even though nobody's around. "I saw them holding hands. Here in the store."

I shrug. "That's not a big deal. I've held hands with guys who are just friends."

"Yes, but it's also the way they looked at each other. It was that look you have when you're really in love and can't seem to take your eyes off the person. They thought I didn't see them. I was back by the register and they were over there." She points to a rack of clothes near the front of the store. "But I could see what was going on."

"I can't imagine Lauren risking her marriage like that. She's got it made with Steven. He gives her whatever she wants."

And yet she still complains about him. She's so ungrateful.

"I know what I saw," Jane says. "Those two definitely had feelings for each other. Oh, and then there was the dressing room thing."

"What dressing room thing?"

"It was a Wednesday morning and I'd just opened. I was going to go to the bank next door to drop off a deposit, but then Lauren and David came in. I told them I had to leave for a few minutes but to go ahead and look around."

"Yeah? And what happened?"

"He was in the dressing room with her," she whispers.

I don't know why she's whispering. We're still the only two people here.

"She probably just tried something on and asked him to go in the dressing room to look at it," I say, still not believing there was anything going on with David and Lauren. The way people gossip around here and make up stories about each other, I've learned not to believe everything I hear.

"She wasn't trying something on," Jane says. "She didn't even bring anything into the dressing room. When they left, I checked. There was nothing in there."

"So what are you saying?"

"When I got back from the bank, they must've heard me coming into the store because I heard laughing and then saw David coming out of the dressing room. His hair was a mess, his shirt was untucked from his pants, and his belt was undone. He said something about the weather, like he was trying to distract me from whatever I thought was going on, but then I glanced down at the dressing room floor and saw Lauren reaching down to pick up a pair of black silk panties."

I gasp, no longer doubting her story. Lauren and David had sex in the dressing room. There's no other way to explain what Jane saw. Or maybe they almost had sex and Jane caught them before they could. Either way, Lauren was definitely cheating on Steven. With his best friend!

"I didn't actually see them together," Jane says. "But the evidence makes it pretty clear what happened, or what was about to."

"Yeah, I think you're right."

"Please don't tell anyone I told you this," she says. "I assumed you already knew since you're Lauren's nurse and living in her house."

"How would I know? David's gone. It's not like I'd see them together."

"I thought Lauren might've told you, or Steven."

My eyes widen. "Steven knows?"

She shrugs. "I don't know how he couldn't. The rumor around town was that David and Lauren were seeing each other."

"Steven doesn't listen to rumors. He said they're just stories made up by people who are bored with their lives. And he rarely comes into town. I doubt he heard whatever rumors people were spreading."

"So what's the latest? Is Steven planning to stay with her?"

"I don't know," I say, not wanting to add to the gossip mill. "Steven isn't around much, but when he is, he's very loving to Lauren."

But he doesn't actually love her. I'm not telling Jane that, but I want her to know that Steven's a good man who takes care of his wife, despite Lauren being a spoiled, ungrateful woman who cheated on him with his best friend.

I wish Steven knew about that. If he did, he'd leave her. He'd have to. How could he stay with her after finding out she was having an affair with his best friend?

Now that I know this, any guilt I felt for sleeping with Steven is gone. In fact, I'm now determined to make him mine. I would be such a good wife to him. I wouldn't lie to him or cheat on him or yell at him for having to work late. I'd appreciate all his hard work and reward him for it by being caring and loving and supportive.

"I think I'll try on that sweater," I say to Jane, deciding I need something new to wear, something Steven would like, something that will make him take notice of me. I know he wants me, but he's trying to resist me because of Lauren. Forget her. She deserves to be cheated on after what she did. When Steven sees me tonight, he won't be able to resist me. I'll make sure of it.

"That looks great on you!" Jane squeals as I walk out of the dressing room.

The sweater I tried on is dark red and clings to my body in a way that will definitely get Steven's attention. And the neckline is cut low enough to show some cleavage, which I don't currently have with the bra I'm wearing, but I have another bra that'll work.

"I'll take it," I say to Jane.

"Great!" Her face lights up. I like her energy. She's very upbeat. "You want to try on some more?"

"This is enough for now." I'd like to buy more, but I just got paid and I can't use all my money on clothes. I need to save up for a place to live when I leave the Bishop house, unless Steven offers to get me a place. If we were a couple, I could totally see him doing that. He's very generous.

I just realized I sound like my mom. *He's very generous*. She'd say that to people when they'd comment on her fancy jewelry or expensive clothes. She'd say they were gifts from her boyfriend and follow it up with 'he's very generous'.

My mom only dated guys with money. She said all men are basically the same so why not choose a rich one? She decided this after my dad killed himself. She never loved any of her boyfriends, but she loved my dad, even though he wasn't rich, drank too much, and was abusive.

Before she died, she told me to find a man that made enough that I'd never have to worry about money. She said it was easier to find a man with money than to find love, and that if I found both, it'd be like winning the lottery.

At the time, I didn't like her jaded outlook on life, but after years of struggling to pay my bills and working jobs I hated that paid next to nothing, I've started to see the wisdom in her words. I thought I'd have to settle for a guy I didn't love in order to have financial security, but I don't.

Steven is everything I could ever want or need, and I'm falling in love with him. I know he'll eventually feel the same way about me. I just need to get him there.

33

HANNAH

Just after three, I get back to the house. Lauren's asleep in her room and Steven's in his office with the door closed. I go up to my room, take a long hot shower, then cover myself in scented body lotion since I don't have money for expensive perfume like Lauren wears.

At five, I go down to her room to check on her. She's awake and watching a crime documentary on TV.

"How was your day?" I ask, going into her room.

"It was fine," she says, in a tone that tells me it wasn't fine. Her eyes remain on the TV. "How was yours?"

"Good! I really liked that store you recommended. I bought a sweater there."

I'm finding it hard to be nice to her now that I know what she did, but I don't have a choice. I need this job.

Lauren doesn't comment about the sweater, her attention still on the TV. I look over at it and see a bloody stump of an arm that was chopped off at the elbow. It's gross, and I'm a nurse. I'm used to blood. Lauren's not, yet she doesn't seem bothered by it, her eyes glued to the screen.

"Do you like these shows?" I ask.

"If I didn't, I wouldn't be watching it."

She's in one of her moods, one I don't like. I need to leave her alone. If she needs something from me, she'll tell me.

"I'm going to go," I say, walking to the door.

"Hannah, wait."

I turn back and see her turning the TV off. "I need to talk to you."

"About what?"

"Shut the door and come over here."

This can't be good. Why do I need to shut the door? So she can yell at me without Steven hearing?

I shut the door and walk back to her bed.

"Sit down," she orders.

I take a seat on the chair.

"Not there. Here." She pats the bed. "It's too hard to look at you when you're in the chair. It strains my neck."

"I could move it."

"Would you sit down on the bed, please?" she says, sounding frustrated with me.

I sit down, facing her. "What do you want to talk about?"

"I've seen how you look at him," she says in a serious tone. "I know you want him."

My throat goes dry and my heart slams against my chest.

She knows. But how? Did Steven tell her? Is that what happened today? Steven told her about us?

"I heard you with him," she says. "You thought I was sleeping, but I wasn't. I was awake, listening to you two by the fire. I heard you talking. The wine glasses clinking. The soft moans coming from your lips."

"Mrs. Bishop, I—"

"Didn't mean to sleep with my husband?" She smiles at me, but it's an angry, sinister smile that sends a chill down my spine. "Yes, I suppose you didn't. Steven's a powerful man and very persuasive. And you're young and impressionable. How could you possibly resist him?" She says it sarcastically.

She wants me to admit what I did, and maybe I should. Maybe she'd respect me for it and reward me by giving me a day or two to find a place to live.

"Okay, yes," I say. "I did something I shouldn't have. I drank way too much wine that night. I wasn't thinking. I'm so sorry, Mrs. Bishop. I know what I did was wrong. I—"

"How many times?" she asks.

"What... what do you mean?"

"How many times did you sleep with my husband?"

I pause, not sure what to tell her, knowing whatever I say won't make this better.

"Be honest with me, Hannah."

"Just a few times. Maybe three? I don't remember."

"You do." She looks me in the eye. "You just don't want to tell me."

I hesitate, then just blurt it out. "Four. Four times."

"Was this four different nights?"

"No. Two nights."

"I see." She takes a slow, even breath and lets it out.

It's over. She's firing me, and there's no way she's letting me stay here tonight.

I get up. "I'll go pack my things."

"Sit down," she says.

"Mrs. Bishop, I already know I'm fired, and I get it. I'll just—"

"Sit down," she says, more forcefully.

I do as she asks and wait for her to continue.

"I'm not angry at you for what you did."

Wait—what? Did she just say she's not angry that I slept with her husband?

"I'm angry that you didn't tell me," she says. "If you had, I would've given you my blessing."

What is going on? There's no way this is happening. Lauren did not just say that.

"You're telling me if I told you I wanted to be with your husband," I say, my heart still pounding so hard I'm breathless, "that you would've been okay with it?"

"I don't have a choice." She points to herself. "Look at me. I'm confined to this bed. Even if I wanted to be with Steven, how would that work? He can't be near me with this metal contraption on my leg. I've got pins holding the bones in place. Just moving it causes me extreme pain. Can you imagine how much pain I'd be in trying to make love?"

"You could do other things."

"We're not in high school, Hannah. We're a married couple. There are expectations that come with that. And right now, I'm unable to meet those expectations."

"So what are you saying?"

"Steven needs a companion. Someone who can take care of his needs. I'm not able to do that, so he needs someone else."

"And you want that to be..." I wait for her to finish that statement.

"I wanted it to be you, but knowing you lied to me, I'm not sure I can trust you anymore."

"When were you planning to tell me this?"

"A week or two after you started, but then I heard you two together and waited to see if you'd tell me. When you didn't, I considered finding someone else. I need someone I can trust."

"I still don't get why you're doing this. Mr. Bishop is your husband. You've been together for years. How can you be okay with him being with another woman?"

She pauses for several beats, then sighs. "Our marriage is ending."

"You're divorcing him?" I try to hide any hint of excitement, but inside I'm jumping for joy. Steven will soon be single, and all mine!

"It's a mutual decision," she says. "We've talked about it for years, but it's time now. Our marriage can't be saved."

"When is this happening?"

"Not until I'm healed. I'll have to create a whole new life for myself and I can't do that until I'm able to walk on my own."

"I understand," I say, but I'm disappointed. Her recovery's going to take months, maybe longer. She has to have more surgery done on her leg, then more recovery time, and then physical therapy.

"I'm willing to forgive you for lying to me if you promise to never do it again."

"Are you saying I still have a job?"

"Yes, with the understanding that you will take care of Steven's needs. I don't want him sneaking around behind my back with some woman I don't know."

I can't believe she's asking me to do this, and that I'm about to agree to it. This is insane. But hey, I'm already sleeping with Steven. The only difference is that now I have his wife's approval.

"I'll do it," I say.

Her lips slide up to a satisfied smile. "Excellent. But there's a caveat."

Of course there is. I knew there was a catch. There's always a catch.

34

HANNAH

"Steven can't know," Lauren says. "He'd never go along with this if he knew I was aware of it. Even though our marriage is ending, Steven still feels the need to protect my feelings. He'd assume this arrangement would be painful to me, even if I told him otherwise. He wouldn't be with you if I told him I knew about it."

I could see that being true. He's always worrying about her.

"You're really okay with this," I say, confirming it because it seems completely ludicrous.

"I am, if you agree to keep quiet about our arrangement."

"And you're okay with this going on here, in the house?" I ask.

"Yes. It'll make it better for Steven. He loves when risk is involved. It's why he loves investing. Being here with him at the house, he risks being caught." She laughs a little. "It'll be much more exciting for him than if he did it with some woman at the office."

This is so strange. I can't believe we're having this conversation. I thought I was going to be fired, but instead, Lauren tells me to sleep with her husband. This is completely messed up, and yet I'm still on board with it. I don't even feel guilty about it now that she told me she's ending her marriage.

"Oh, and don't tell anyone about the divorce," Lauren says. "That needs to remain private."

"Who else knows?"

"Just you, me, and Steven."

"Audrey doesn't know?"

"No, and I'm not telling her. I don't want her worrying about me. She worries enough as it is."

"Why would she be worried if it's what you want?"

"Even if divorce is the best option, it's still stressful and emotionally draining. Audrey's going through a divorce herself right now and it's been very hard on her. She barely sleeps. She wouldn't want me having that kind of stress when I'm trying to recover."

"But you said you weren't getting divorced until you were better."

"Hannah, please don't argue with me about this. I don't want Audrey to know. I'll tell her when I'm ready."

I nod. "Okay."

"I'm going to watch TV. Why don't you go start dinner? I want to eat early. I don't want to be up late tonight."

She turns the TV on to that crime show she was watching. I leave her room, shutting the door behind me. As I walk to the kitchen, I feel a mix of emotions. I'm relieved she didn't fire me, but I feel bad that she knows about Steven and me. She says she's okay with it, but it still feels wrong. It's strange, but for some reason it felt less wrong when she didn't know about it. I should be happy I get to be with Steven without getting in trouble, but I don't feel happy. I feel sick to my stomach.

Maybe I just need some time to let this sink in. I need to remind myself that Lauren doesn't want him anymore. She's divorcing him. Steven is practically single. Well, not really, but their marriage is basically over. They just need to file the paperwork.

"You're home," Steven says, coming into the kitchen, a big smile on his handsome face. "How was your day in town?"

"Good. I did some shopping, then had lunch, got some groceries." I notice the sacks sitting on the counter and start unloading them.

Steven helps, unloading the one next to mine. "I'll make sure you get paid for the grocery shopping. That shouldn't have been done on your time off."

I don't argue with him because he's right. I should've got paid for the time I spent at the store. I didn't mind doing it, but I want to get paid for my time. I need the money.

"What are we having tonight?" Steven asks as he takes a jar of marinara sauce and a can of tomatoes from the sack.

"Chicken cacciatore. Lauren said it's your favorite meal."

He stops unpacking the groceries and looks at me. "Is that why you're making it?"

"Yes." I look back at him, giving him a flirtatious smile. "I thought you deserved it after working so hard this week."

"That's very nice of you." He goes back to putting the groceries away.

He didn't flirt back. What's going on with him? Lauren made it sound like she and Steven talked about their divorce today, so why isn't he pursuing me? He was so aggressive earlier in the week and now... nothing.

"I got a really nice sweater at one of the stores I went to today," I say as I put the chicken in the fridge. "I was going to wear it tonight for dinner."

"What does it look like?" he asks, handing me the green peppers to put in the fridge.

"I'll show you. Oh, I left it in the car. I'll go get it."

"You can show me later. I need to get back to work." He wipes his hands on the kitchen towel. "What time is dinner?"

"I'm planning on six. Does that work?"

"It's perfect. I'll be in my office."

He leaves and I gather up the empty grocery sacks and take them to the garage, tossing them in the recycle bin. I go over to Lauren's SUV and get the bag with my sweater from the back seat. Seeing Jane's name on the bag reminds me of our conversation this morning. Lauren cheated on Steven. With his best friend. So why would I feel even the slightest bit guilty about being with him? Lauren doesn't want him. I do, and if I don't make that clear, he might find someone else. Like Lauren said, Steven has needs, and if she can't meet them, he'll find someone who will. I need to make sure that someone is me.

Taking the sweater inside, I race up to my room and put it on. I'll change out of it when I'm cooking, but I want Steven to see it now, to get a taste of what's to come. I put on my push-up bra, adjusting it to get more cleavage, then I put on the sweater. I smile as I look at myself in the mirror. This will definitely get his attention.

Going back downstairs, I quietly walk past Lauren's room and down the hall to Steven's office. The door's open so I walk in, not bothering to knock.

"What do you think?" I say, but Steven's not there. Maybe he's in the bathroom. I'll just wait for him. I go behind his desk and sit down on his leather office chair. His laptop is on the desk but it's closed. I thought he was working, but maybe he decided he's done for the day.

I swivel around in the chair and my leg bumps into something. It's the bottom drawer of the desk. It's not fully closed. I reach down to shut it and notice something in the drawer. I open it more and see a gun. It's not in a case or a holder. It's just sitting there. My pulse races as my mind tries to come up with reasons why Steven would need a gun.

The smart thing to do would be to close the drawer and pretend I didn't see it, but instead, I pick it up. My curiosity made me do it. I've never held a gun. I've never been this close to one.

"What are you doing in here?"

I hear Steven's voice and get up from his chair, the gun still in my hand.

"I was, um... waiting for you."

He stalks over to me and points to the gun. "What are you doing with that?"

"I... I saw it in the drawer. I've never held one. I wanted to see how heavy it was."

He takes it from me. "You are not to come in here. I've told you that."

"Yes, I know, but the door was open and I thought you were coming right back."

He walks around the desk, puts the gun in the drawer, and closes it.

"Why do you have a gun?" I ask.

He looks at me, seeming confused.

"The gun," I repeat. "Why do you have it?"

He smiles a little. "That's not the reaction I was expecting."

"What were you expecting?"

He steps closer to me. "A lot of people would be afraid, finding that in my drawer."

"Afraid of what?" I ask, but I know what he's implying. He assumes I think he's dangerous, maybe even a murderer. The thought did cross my mind, but I don't think Steven could kill someone. Then again, I didn't think I could either and look what happened.

"You fascinate me," he says, his eyes locked on mine.

"Why is that?" I ask, my heart beating faster.

"I never know what to expect with you."

"And that's a good thing?"

"Very good. Predictable is boring."

"You never answered my question. About the gun."

"It's for protection. You can't live in a remote area like this and not have a gun. It'd take the police forever to get here. By the time they made it, it'd be too late."

"So if someone broke in, you'd shoot them?"

"If I had to, yes."

"I can't imagine you shooting someone."

"There are a lot of things you don't know about me." He glances down at my sweater, at my cleavage, which I have to say looks amazing in this bra.

"Do you like the sweater?" I ask.

"I do," he says, his eyes rising back to mine. "I've never seen you wear it before."

"It's new. It's the one I was telling you about. I came in here to show it to you."

He steps up to me, so close we're almost touching. "I told you not to come in here. And you did it anyway."

"Sorry," I say, wondering if he's going to yell at me. "I'll go. Let you get back to work."

"That would be impossible now." He glances down at my sweater. "I'm too distracted."

"By what?" I ask in a teasing tone.

He wraps his hands around my face and kisses me as he backs me up to the desk. Finally! This is the Steven I was hoping would show up again. I knew this sweater would do the job.

"This is what you get for not obeying the rules," he says over my lips.

"Then I'll be breaking the rules a lot more."

He shoves his laptop aside and lifts me up on his desk. I was planning to do this after dinner, but if he's ready now, I'm all for it.

I got him back. Steven wants me. He's all mine now. And I couldn't be happier.

35

LAUREN

"Are you still coming over?" I ask Audrey. She was supposed to be here at noon and it's twelve-thirty.

"Yes, sorry. My meeting ran long. I'm on my way. Did you eat? I can stop and get lunch."

"Forget lunch. I need you to hurry. I want to talk to you before Hannah gets home."

"Where is she?"

"I sent her into town to run some errands, but she'll probably be back within the hour."

"Okay, I'm on my way."

Everything's coming together perfectly. Getting Hannah to be with Steven was even easier than I imagined. I thought she'd have at least a little hesitation when I asked her to "entertain" my husband. Most people would think the very idea of it is crazy. I think Hannah questioned it for a moment, but then she was all in.

I figured she would be. She'd already been with Steven several times, so it's not like I was proposing she do something she hadn't already done. The look on her face when I told her I knew about her and Steven was priceless. I'll never forget it.

She thought for sure I was going to fire her. But instead I gave her my blessing, and she ran with it.

The two of them were at it all weekend. I heard them in the living room, the kitchen, Steven's office. They thought I was asleep. I asked Hannah for a sleeping pill, but I didn't take it. I just wanted her to think I did.

I'm curious if Steven will make it home on time this week now that he has something to come home to. Throughout most of our marriage, he's come home late to either avoid spending time with me or to be with one of his many mistresses. He started cheating on me a few months after our wedding. I could never prove it and he'd never admit it. Even when I found panties under the seat of his car, he wouldn't admit they belonged to another woman. He claimed they were mine, as if I don't know what my own underwear looks like. But for a moment he had me thinking that maybe it was an old pair that I'd forgotten about.

Steven's an expert at making you question yourself. He's so convincing that during our first few years of marriage, I thought I might be going crazy. Steven would vehemently deny something that I knew was true. Looking back now, I swear he did it to make me think I was losing my mind. Even something as simple as taking out the garbage could make me question myself. I'd ask Steven to do it, he'd promise he would, and then it'd still be there a day later. He'd ask why I didn't take it out, as if it was my job, not his, and when I told him he promised he'd do it, he'd look at me with concern and say I might need to see someone. He acted like I was crazy. He did this so many times with so many things that I really thought I was going insane.

David's the one who saved me from admitting myself to a mental hospital. Steven and I hadn't seen David much after our wedding. We all lived in Boston but didn't make time to get together. Then one day, when Steven was out of town, I asked David to come over. He'd known me for years so I thought he'd be the best person to tell me if I was losing it.

He laughed when I told him. He said I was one of the sanest people he knew. Then he told me to just ignore Steven and that what he was doing was something he'd always done. He said Steven did it to mess with people, mostly girls he dated. He tried doing it with David, but David didn't put up with it. He said I needed to do the same. So I did, but it didn't make being with Steven any better.

I felt like I was married to two different people. The Steven I knew at home was cold and aloof and wanted nothing to do with me. We slept in separate bedrooms. Didn't eat meals together. Didn't have date nights. We sometimes made love, but it was only out of obligation. Steven wasn't into it, and I only did it because I craved affection, even just crumbs of it.

The other Steven, the one he presented in public, was a warm and caring husband who opened doors for me, held my hand, kissed my forehead, and said he loved me, but only when he knew people would hear him. Women would tell me how lucky I am to have him. My friends called him a dream husband. They'd tell me how jealous they were of me, asking how I found such a wonderful man.

I could've divorced Steven years ago, but I didn't, because of that clause in the prenup. After everything I've put up with, I want him to pay up and give me part of the fortune he acquired before we got married. I know I don't need it. I'd be a wealthy woman even without that money. Steven's made a lot in the years we've been married. Even half of that is enough to live comfortably. But it's not just about the money. I want people to know Steven's not as wonderful as they think. I want the details of our divorce to go public with proof that he cheated. He'll be furious when people find out he's not as perfect as he pretends to be. He doesn't want even a speck of dirt on his shiny reputation.

"It's me!" Audrey yells as she comes in the front door. I hear her heels clicking on the wood floor as she walks to my room.

"Thanks for coming," I say, noticing she's out of breath. "Did you run here?"

"Only to the front door. I saw some kind of critter by your driveway and didn't want it getting near me." She takes a moment to catch her breath. "I don't know how you can live out here with all this wildlife."

"I like the wildlife, as long as it stays outside."

She takes off her coat and sits down on the chair. "So what's going on? Why did I have to rush over here?"

"It's Hannah."

"What about her?" Audrey asks, taking off her gloves.

"You were right. About her and Steven."

Audrey sets her gloves on the nightstand and looks at me. "What do you mean? Did something happen?"

I nod and grab a tissue to dab the fake tears from my eyes. "I heard them together in the living room."

Audrey gasps. "When?"

"Last weekend. I think I heard them in the kitchen too." A tear slides down my face. "I don't know what to do."

"Divorce him! Kick his ass to the curb."

"You know I can't do that."

"Why? He's cheating on you. Why would you stay with him?"

"Because I love him," I say, another tear sliding down my cheek. "And I can't really blame him for doing this."

"Of course you can! What are you talking about?"

"He has needs, Audrey. All men do. You know that. And right now, I can't be with him that way."

"That doesn't give him the right to cheat on you."

"Maybe you're right." I let out a heavy sigh. "I'm torn. I want to save my marriage, but if I can't, I want proof that he did this. It's the only way Steven will even consider giving me a divorce."

"You don't need his permission to divorce him."

"No, but he could make it very difficult for me. Or he could refuse to sign the paperwork. But if he knows I'm aware that he has someone else, he'll be more open to the divorce, especially if I threaten to go public with proof of his infidelity."

"How are you going to get proof?"

"That's where you come in. Remember those cameras you installed when you thought Barry was cheating?"

"You want me to install cameras?"

"Would you?"

"Of course. Whatever you want. But I think you should divorce Steven no matter what. You can't trust him, and what's a marriage without trust?"

"It's not that simple. Audrey, I know it doesn't make sense to you, but I need you to do this for me. I need you to get the cameras and install them for me as soon as possible."

She gets her phone out and scrolls through the screen. "I could do it tomorrow morning. Can you get rid of Hannah for an hour or two?"

"Yes, I'll send her out to do some more errands." I reach for Audrey's hand and hold it in mine. "Thank you for doing this."

"I'm just sorry it's happening. This is the last thing you need when you're already going through so much."

I check the clock by the bed. "Hannah will be back soon. You should go."

She gets up. "What time do you want me here tomorrow? I have a meeting at ten. Could I come early, like at eight?"

"Yes, I can make that work. Thanks again, Audrey."

Even though she's my best friend, Audrey doesn't know my history with Steven. He made me swear to never talk about our marriage to anyone, even Audrey. And I knew if I told her, she'd tell me to divorce him. But I wasn't ready to get divorced. I held out hope that things would get better. When they didn't, I told myself to be grateful for what I had. My marriage was a sham, but at least I had two beautiful homes and gorgeous clothes and enough money to buy whatever I wanted.

It wasn't until I started spending more time with David that I realized I couldn't keep living this way. David was so different than Steven. I felt alive when I was with him, in a way I hadn't felt in years. With Steven, I felt lonely. Trapped. Dead inside. I didn't know who I was anymore outside of being Steven's wife. I spent my days shopping and going out to lunch. I had some friends, but nobody I could confide in. Until David showed up.

And then, finally, I came back to life.

36

A MONTH BEFORE THE ACCIDENT

LAUREN

"We can't keep meeting like this," I say to David as we lie in bed in the hotel room he got us a half hour outside of Boston.

"I had to see you." David wraps me in his arms and smiles at me. I love his smile. It's so genuine. He couldn't put on a fake smile even if he tried. He can't hide how he's feeling. I can look at his face and instantly know if he's stressed or sad or bursting with happiness. Right now, he's happy, because we're together.

I feel the same way. I always feel that way with him, like I can't contain my happiness, like it's bursting out for everyone to see. That's why I have to be careful around Steven. I make sure to shut down my emotions when I'm with him. He'd be very suspicious if he saw me this happy. He hasn't seen me this way since college, when I was young and in love and had no idea what a life with him would be like.

"I wanted to see you too," I say, "but I'm worried Steven's going to find out. I'm worried he already has."

"Then let's end this."

I pull away from David, feeling panicked and confused. "You... you want us to stop seeing each other?"

"No," he says, like he can't believe that's where my mind

went. But after spending years with a man who didn't want me, I assume no man will, at least not longterm. "I'm talking about us hiding. Sneaking around." He brings me back into his arms. "I don't want to keep doing this. I love you, Lauren, more than you'll ever know. I want us to be together for real." He kisses me, then looks into my eyes. "I want to marry you and wake up to you every morning and sleep beside you every night."

"I want that too, but it's not the right time."

"Lauren, come on." He falls back on the bed and stares up at the ceiling. "You've been saying that for three years. We could've been married by now. We could have had a child."

My heart aches hearing him say that, the part about having a child. I've wanted a baby since my first year of marriage, but Steven said we should wait. Another year went by, then another, until Steven finally told me he didn't want a child. He just said he did because it's what I wanted to hear.

I was furious, but then decided I could change his mind. I put all my efforts into convincing him he'd like being a father. I appealed to his ego, saying how the child would be his legacy and carry on his name. He eventually warmed up to the idea and we began trying. I was thrilled, and for the first time in a long time, I had hope that our marriage could turn around.

Five years went by without a baby. I begged Steven to go to a fertility clinic, but he wouldn't do it. So I went without him. The doctors ran tests but couldn't find anything wrong with me. They thought Steven might be the issue. I was almost certain he wouldn't go in for testing, but I couldn't just give up. So I told him I went to a fertility clinic and what I found out. I knew Steven would be furious I did this behind his back, but I was willing to deal with his anger if it meant finding an answer to our fertility problems.

To my surprise, Steven didn't get angry, but his response was far worse than anger. We were sitting across from each other at the dining room table we never used and I'd just fessed up about going to the fertility clinic. I told Steven the doctors wanted him to come in to be tested. Steven was silent a moment, then slowly smiled. I didn't know what was happening. He rarely smiled, and this was not something to be smiling about, unless he was about to tell me he'd be happy to get tested so we could finally have the child we always wanted.

But that's not why he was smiling.

"Do you really think I'm that stupid, Lauren?" he said.

"I don't know what you're talking about. What do you mean?"

"I told you I didn't want children. I told you that years ago."

"Yes, but you changed your mind."

"No. I got tired of listening to you go on and on about wanting a child, so I agreed to it to shut you up. But when have you ever known me to agree to something I didn't want?"

My heart was pounding and I was finding it hard to breathe. "You're saying you've been lying to me the past five years?"

Steven didn't answer. He just stared at me across the table, a slight smile on his face.

"I... I don't understand," I sputtered, trying to wrap my mind around this. "We didn't use protection. I wasn't on birth control. Why did you have sex with me when you knew I could get pregnant?"

He laughed a little.

"What's so funny?" I asked, angry that he found this to be even the slightest bit humorous.

"I had a vasectomy when I was 19, before some woman could trap me with a child."

"Nineteen?" I felt faint, like my world was spinning out of control. "That's how old we were when we started dating. Are you saying—"

"I did it right after we met. Remember when I told you I

had the flu and needed to spend the weekend getting better? I didn't have the flu. I was recovering from the procedure."

"But that's not possible. No doctor would do that on someone that young."

"They will if you pay them enough." Steven leaned back in his chair and rubbed his hand along his jaw. "I love taking risks, but I wasn't going to risk having a child. I wasn't going to ruin my life with that kind of obligation, and I certainly wasn't going to let some woman gain control over me, financial or otherwise, by tricking me into fatherhood."

"Steven, you knew I wanted children, at least one. How could you not tell me this before we got married? How could you lie to me like that?" I slammed my hands on the table and screamed. "What kind of sick person does something like that?"

"I was taking control of my life," he calmly said. "It's as simple as that."

He didn't think what he did was wrong. In fact, he seemed proud of himself for doing it. I didn't want to believe it was true. But knowing Steven and his obsession with control, it made sense.

"What about the girls you were with before me?" I asked, wanting to prove he wasn't as clever as he thought. "One of them could've gotten pregnant. Maybe they did and you're a father and don't even know it."

"Didn't you know?" he asked, in that eerily calm tone.

"Know what?"

"You were my first. Before you, I didn't have much interest in girls. I went out with them and we'd fool around, but I'd end it before we had sex. I didn't want a girlfriend. I was focused on studying the stock market, finding patterns, learning how to time it just right to increase my gains and cut my losses. Girls were nothing but a distraction. But you were different. I wanted you as soon as I met you."

"I don't believe you. There's no way I was your first."

"Ask David. He used to give me a hard time for waiting so long. He finally shut up when I told him what we'd done."

"You told David?" I asked, shocked because Steven's a very private person. David's his best friend and yet Steven tells him very little about his personal life.

Steven got up from the table and walked over to me. He yanked my chair back and got in front of me, then grabbed my chin and lifted my face up to his. "You were the first woman I gave myself to. Do you know what that means?"

"No," I whispered.

"It means you're mine. For as long as I want you." He leaned down to my ear. "I'll decide when I'm done with you. Or maybe I'll keep you forever. You'll just have to wait and see."

"No!" I shoved him away and stood up. "It's over, Steven! I'm done! I can't do this anymore. This isn't a real marriage. You don't even like me. We don't spend time together. We don't talk. We don't even sleep in the same bedroom!"

He waited a moment, looking at me like I was a deranged lunatic. "Are you done now?"

"I don't know what else to say other than I want a divorce."

He grabbed my arm, squeezing his hand around it so tightly I thought he might break a bone.

"Steven, stop it! You're hurting me."

He didn't let go of my arm, or even acknowledge I was in pain. He looked into my eyes and very calmly said, "I'm the one in charge here. Even when you think I'm not, I am. You have no idea what I'm capable of, and pushing me to the point of having to prove what I'm capable of will end poorly for you. Do you understand?"

"Yes, you're threatening to kill me," I said sarcastically. I didn't think he actually would. In fact, I knew he wouldn't. I'd watched enough of those true crime shows to know that whenever a woman was killed, the police always went after the husband. Being investigated for murder would destroy Steven's life, his reputation, his business. Even if he was found innocent, enough damage would be done to destroy all that he'd worked for.

So I didn't think he'd kill me, but I knew he could hurt me. I didn't know what to do, but I knew filing for divorce would only make things worse for me. I wasn't sure how, but I didn't want to find out.

I'd seen a whole new side of Steven that night. A dangerous, deranged side that scared me into keeping quiet. I went back to playing the role of the happy housewife with the perfect husband who had everything she could possibly want.

"Lauren, what's wrong?" David asks, bringing me back to the present. "Why are you so quiet? Was it something I said?"

"A child." I smile at him. "I want that. I've wanted it for years."

"I know." He runs his hand softly down my arm. "And I want to give that to you. We'll have all the babies you want. But we can't keep waiting. We need to start living our lives."

"I'm just... I'm afraid."

"Afraid of what?"

"Steven." I haven't told David my fears about Steven. I wasn't sure he'd believe me. Steven only shows that side of himself to me. "He's not well."

"What do you mean?" David moved back a little, concern on his face. "Steven's sick?"

"Not physically. He's... unhinged. Deranged. He keeps saying I'm his and that the only way I can leave is if he lets me."

David sighs. "Ignore him. He's been saying weird shit for as long as I've known him. Honestly, I think he just says it to get a reaction."

"No, David, I'm serious." I sit up. "He's not just saying it.

He means it. Just last week, he said if he ever found me with someone else, another man, he'd end it. I didn't know exactly what he meant, but it almost sounded like he was saying he'd kill him."

"Steven? Kill someone?" David shakes his head. "No. It's too messy. Takes too much planning. And there'd be too many loose ends to tie up to make sure whatever he did didn't lead back to him."

"So then why did he say it?"

"To scare you into staying with him." David takes my hand and pulls me back down beside him. "Trust me, Steven's all talk. He's not going to do anything. He knows he can scare you by saying those things, so that's why he does it." He pauses. "Maybe I should talk to him."

"No. Absolutely not. I'm not going to risk something happening to you."

"Nothing's going to happen. Steven and I have been friends for years. And I know he wants out of this marriage as much as you do. He just wants to be the one who decides when it happens. He has to be in control. He's always been like that."

"If he wants out of the marriage, why isn't he doing anything? What's he waiting for?"

"I don't know, but I'm not going to keep waiting for Steven to make up his mind. You need to end this, Lauren. Yes, Steven will be upset, but I can handle him."

"He'll go nuts when he finds out about us. I'm telling you, David, he's not well. I really am worried he'll come after you."

"Yeah, so let him try. I'm not a scrawny college kid anymore. I'm bigger than him. One punch and I'd knock him out before he even had a chance to take a swing at me."

"He wouldn't use his fist." I pause. "He has a gun."

"He's not going to shoot me. He's not going to risk going to prison for the rest of his life."

"Can I just have a little more time to think about this?"

He sighs. "Okay, but it's not going to be another year. I've waited long enough." He looks down, then back up at me. "Since college."

"College?" I laugh a little. "What are you talking about? We were just friends back then."

"But I wanted us to be more."

I assume he's kidding, but he's not smiling. He looks serious.

How is it possible he liked me back then? He never once made a move on me. I assumed I wasn't his type or that he had his eyes on someone else.

"David, why didn't you tell me?"

"I was going to. But Steven got to you first."

37

SOPHOMORE YEAR OF COLLEGE

DAVID

"I'm going to tell her tonight," I say, lying on my bed, staring up at the ceiling. I've spent all day thinking about Lauren and what I'm going to say to her tonight. I want to tell her I love her, but I think it's too soon for that. Even though we spent the whole summer hanging out, we pretended to just be friends. She didn't know how I really felt about her.

Tonight she will. She might not feel the same way, but I'm going to tell her anyway. I don't want to go my whole life regretting not telling her how I feel and wondering if we'd be together if I did.

"I don't think that's a good idea," Steven says as he sits at his desk, tapping away on his laptop. He's on that thing night and day, studying the financial markets, making spreadsheets, coming up with formulas. He's such a nerd, but he's good-looking so girls flock to him. He also knows how to turn on the charm. He opens doors. Showers girls with compliments. Buys them flowers and gifts. And then he dumps them. He says he doesn't want to get serious with a girl, so if he senses she wants something more than a casual relationship, he ends it.

I was shocked when he told me he was a virgin. Last year,

he was with one girl after another. He had plenty of chances to have sex. What's he waiting for?

"What's not a good idea?" I ask.

"Talking to Lauren tonight." Steven continues to type on his laptop.

"Why? I can't keep putting it off. She's gorgeous. If I don't make a move, some other guy's going to ask her out."

"Maybe one already has."

"What's that supposed to mean?" I look over at him. "Did you see her on campus with someone?"

He stops typing and turns to me. "I don't know how to tell you this." He looks down, shaking his head. "I should probably just say it."

"Say what?"

He looks back at me. "I asked her out."

"You WHAT?" I jump up from my bed and storm over to Steven. "You better be joking right now."

"Hey." He stands up, reminding me how much bigger he is than me. We're similar in height, but he's filled out more and has more muscle. I still have the body of a teenager. "I didn't expect to feel anything for her, but then I saw her and there was an instant connection between us. She felt it too. She told me when I saw her last night."

My hands ball into fists. "Last night? You're saying you already went out with her?"

"We went and got something to eat. It wasn't a big deal."

"Are you serious? You really don't see a problem with this?" I wait for him to say something, to apologize, or at least explain how he could possibly think this was okay. But instead he just looks at me, a slight smile on his face, like he somehow finds this amusing. "I can't believe you did this. You knew how much I liked her. You knew I was going to tell her tonight. So you beat me to it. Before I had a chance. You purposely stole her from me!"

"I didn't steal her. If she wanted you, she wouldn't have been with me last night."

"She went out with you," I say through gritted teeth, "because she thought I only saw her as a friend. If she knew the truth, she would've told you no."

"You're wrong." He folds his arms over his chest. "Lauren doesn't see you that way. She told me last night."

"You asked her about me?"

"I asked if there was anything going on with you two, and she said no, that she only sees you as a friend, nothing more."

I walk back to my bed, slumping down on it and feeling defeated. I really thought Lauren loved me the way I loved her. But apparently I was wrong. Either that or Steven is lying. He's a good liar. It's possible he's making this up.

I have to talk to her. I'm not giving up the girl I love based on what my roommate told me. Steven and I are friends, but I don't always trust him.

"I'll see you later," I say, getting up and grabbing my room key from the hook on the wall.

"Where are you going?" Steven asks as I'm leaving.

I don't answer him. I shut the door behind me, then hurry across campus to Lauren's dorm. The door to her room is open and she's on her bed, studying.

"David!" She jumps up when she sees me and runs over to give me a hug.

"Hey." I hug her back. "Do you need to study? I can come back."

"No, I can do it later." She smiles at me, making my heart swell. She has the best smile. It's one of the many things I love about her. "So what's up?"

"I was just talking to Steven."

Her eyes light up. "And? What did he say?"

Why does she care? And why does she look so excited? It was one date. It couldn't have been that great.

"He said you two went out last night."

She lets out a dreamy sigh. "He took me to that new restaurant. The really expensive one? Dinner was over a hundred dollars and he acted like that was nothing."

Is that why she likes him? Because he's rich? I don't know what else it could be. He's not at all her type. He's too serious. The guy never even smiles.

She grabs hold of my arm. "So what did he say about me? Does he like me?"

"Do you want him to?" I ask, but I already know the answer.

"Well, yeah, of course. He's really hot. And smart. Rich. Oh, and he kept opening doors for me. He's such a gentleman."

"So you like him," I say, getting a sinking feeling in my gut.

"I really do. I felt something the moment we met."

"You met him yesterday. When did he ask you out?"

"Right after I left your room. He called when I was driving back here. I'm hoping he'll ask me out again. Did he say he would?"

"No. He didn't say."

Her phone rings and she races over to her desk to check it. "It's him!" She answers the call. "Hey, Steven." She smiles as he talks, looking more excited by the second. "I'd love to! See you then!" She ends the call and runs over to me. "He asked me out for tonight."

Tonight. The night he knew I was going to tell her I love her.

I can't believe he did this. I guess I shouldn't be surprised. When Steven wants something, he gets it, even if it means stealing it from his best friend.

38

PRESENT DAY

HANNAH

"It'll be about a half hour," Johnny says. He's the mechanic doing Lauren's oil change. He's also the guy who checked me in and the guy I'll pay when he's done. He seems to be the only person who works here, but in a town this size, he probably doesn't get a lot of business. He told me his dad owns the garage but recently retired and now Johnny runs it.

He's not bad looking for a guy who's probably around 40. He's tall and really muscular, with dark hair and greenish-blue eyes. He greeted me with a smile when I walked in, but as soon as I said I was there to get an oil change for Lauren's SUV, his smile went away and he got all serious. He must not like Lauren. Not many people do, including me. She's so moody and demanding. And I don't trust her. I always feel like she's up to something.

She keeps sending me to town to run errands. I don't mind doing them. It gets me out of the house, but that's what concerns me. Why does she want me out of the house? When I first started working for her, she didn't want me to leave, and now she keeps telling me to go to town.

I'm not going to worry about it. I only have a month left at this job and then I'll probably never see Lauren again. But I'm hoping I'll still see Steven. I'm sure I will. We're in a relationship now, and I know he'd rather be with me than with Lauren.

Maybe after I'm done here, he'd let me live in his house in Boston. I looked it up online and it was gorgeous, much nicer than the house here. I'm going to ask Steven if he'd consider it. If he didn't want his neighbors knowing about us, he could just tell them I'm housesitting.

I look around the small waiting area for something to read. I should have brought one of Lauren's magazines. She has tons of them. She doesn't even read them. She just flips through them, then tells me to put them in the recycle bin. Instead, I've been keeping them in my room, looking at them when I'm up there with nothing to do. I never got the TV I was promised, but I really don't need it since I spend every night with Steven.

He's such a wonderful man. I don't know why Lauren can't see that, or why she's willing to give him up. What woman would ever want to give up a smart, successful, incredibly handsome man?

Almost an hour later, Johnny returns to the waiting area, wiping his hands on a greasy rag.

"It's ready," he says. "It's out front."

I meet him at the register and hand him Lauren's credit card.

"Tell her she's about ready for new tires," he says, swiping her card. "Other than that, everything looked good." He hands me the credit card and key fob. "I just need to print a receipt." He clicks on the computer behind the desk and gets the printer going. It's sitting next to the register and looks really old.

"How well do you know Lauren?" I ask, wondering if he'll give me dirt on her.

"Never met her," he says, staring at the computer. "I've

heard her name. I know who she is. I've just never actually met her."

"How is that possible? This town isn't very big."

He shrugs. "She never came in here. She's from Boston, right?"

"Yeah. Why?"

"Big city people think small town mechanics don't know what they're doing. That's why I was surprised when you said you were bringing in her car. I'm guessing she usually takes it to some place in the city and ends up paying ten times what she'd pay here, but I guarantee that place won't do as good a job."

"Maybe you should charge more."

"I can't. The people around here aren't rich. Except for the people you work for." He checks the printer, which is still printing the receipt. It's really slow. I think it's time to get a new printer.

Johnny leans back against the wall behind him, folding his arms over his chest. "So what's your job? You their maid or something?"

"I'm Lauren's nurse. I help her get ready in the morning, make her meals, make sure she doesn't fall. Stuff like that."

He nods, his eyes on the insanely slow printer. "How's she doing? She gonna be okay?"

"She's getting better, but her leg's still in bad shape. It was fractured in several places. It's going to take awhile to heal."

I shouldn't have told him that. I keep forgetting I'm not supposed to talk about Lauren's health.

"Did you know that guy?" I ask, changing topics. "The one who was killed in the accident?"

Johnny looks down, rubbing his jaw. "Yeah, David grew up here. Really nice guy."

"I didn't know him, but I volunteered at the fundraiser

they had for him. Well, for the library, but it was in his honor. Were you there?"

Johnny shakes his head.

The printer finally stops and he moves up behind the desk, grabs the receipt, and hands it to me. "Good luck."

I laugh a little. "Why do I need luck?"

The door swings open and a woman walks in. It's Audrey. What's she doing here? This doesn't seem like a place she'd go for car maintenance. She seems like someone who'd take her car to the dealership.

She sees me and storms up to me. "Why are you still here? Lauren said you should've been home over an hour ago!"

"When did you talk to Lauren?"

"I just left her house. She needs help getting to the bathroom. I tried to help, but almost dropped her. Now hurry up and get back there!"

I check my phone and see a text from Lauren, asking when I'll be home. She sent it a half hour ago. I didn't see it. I didn't even hear a notification go off. I text Lauren that I'm on my way.

"As long as I'm here," Audrey says to Johnny. "I need you to check my headlights."

I race out of there, wondering how it got to be so late. I left at eight and it's after ten. I only had to go three places but they all took forever. There was a long wait at the post office, then the dry cleaner couldn't find Steven's shirts, and the oil change took almost an hour.

"I'm really sorry," I say to Lauren, racing into her room and moving her wheelchair next to the bed. "Everything took forever."

"You should've let me know. I didn't think you'd be gone that long."

"Let's get you in there."

"Where?" she asks, seeming confused.

"The bathroom. Don't you have to go?"

"Oh. Yes." She puts her arm around me as I lean down to transfer her to the chair. Audrey made it sound like Lauren desperately needed to go, but Lauren isn't acting like it's any kind of emergency. Maybe the feeling passed.

When she's done in the bathroom, I get her back into bed. "Do you want to watch TV?"

"No, I'm going to rest," she says. "My leg's bothering me today."

"How? What do you mean?"

"It's just painful. Is that normal? Maybe I should call the doctor."

"It's normal for the pain to come and go as it heals, but if you'd feel better calling a doctor, we can. Or I can give you a pain pill."

"I'll just rest for now."

"I'm going to do some dusting," I tell her. "I'll stay downstairs in case you need me."

Her eyes are already shut so I leave her room and close the door.

I get to work cleaning, something I normally hate doing, but I'll do it for an extra five hundred a week, which is what Steven's paying me. It's what they pay their maid, so he said it was only fair he pay me the same amount.

It's easy money. The house isn't even that dirty. I was already being paid extra to keep it picked up, so all I really have to do is some dusting and vacuuming. I start with the living room, and as I'm dusting, I keep thinking of what Johnny said, how he wished me good luck. I've heard at least three people tell me that since I moved here. Either good luck or be careful. Why would they say that?

I feel like they're warning me, but about what? What do they think's going to happen?

39

LAUREN

"What time are we meeting them?" David asks as I get into his car.

"The reservation's in an hour."

"So we have time." He leans across the seat to kiss me.

I pull back, smiling. "We don't have time. Traffic's going to be bad and we need to try to get there early. You know how Steven gets if I'm even one minute late."

David lets out a frustrated sigh as he backs out of the driveway. "I'm done catering to Steven. You're divorcing him. What Steven wants no longer matters."

"I love the sound of that." I take a breath, noticing how free I feel. I haven't even filed for divorce yet, but knowing I'm going to makes me feel like I'm about to get parole after a very long prison sentence. "Say it again."

David laughs. "What Steven wants no longer matters."

"Yes! Go to hell, Steven!"

David reaches over to hold my hand. "I love you. We're going to have a great life."

I look at him. "I wish I'd chosen you all those years ago instead of him."

"I wish he hadn't stolen you from me before I even had a chance with you."

David told me that story a few months ago, about how Steven asked me out the night before David was going to tell me he loved me. I was furious Steven did that, but not surprised. When Steven wants something, he takes it, and if someone else wants it too, Steven turns it into a competition and doesn't stop until he wins.

I didn't know it at the time, but I was the prize. Steven and David both wanted me and Steven won. If I'd picked David over him, Steven would've found a way to steal me back. He wouldn't have given up. He'd rather die than see David win.

Steven was determined to make me his wife from the moment we met. But it wasn't because he liked me. It's because I had the look he wanted in a wife. Tall, thin, blond hair, blue eyes, fair skin. I know this because I found a picture of a girl that looked just like me in his goal folder. It was an expandable folder with several pockets, each dedicated to a different part of his life; personal goals, financial goals, health goals. The photo of the girl was in his personal goals section. I found it when I was in his room one day, waiting for him to get back from class. The girl looked just like me. For a moment, I thought it *was* me, but it was just some model who looked eerily similar to me. Steven wrote 'wife' on the back of it and it was dated freshman year, before he even knew me.

That should've freaked me out, but it didn't. I'd been dating Steven for two years by then and I loved him. So, as many people do when they're in love, I ignored that feeling in my gut telling me something wasn't right and continued on as though I'd never seen that photo. But looking back now, I realize why Steven was so intent on making me his wife. He knew what he wanted and I fit the mold perfectly. There was no way he was letting David have me.

It all makes so much sense now, why Steven changed right

after we got married. Everything before then was an act, and it worked. I thought I'd found the perfect man. Then, after the wedding, he became someone else. He lost interest in me. He'd won the prize, achieved his goal for a wife, and no longer had to give attention to me or our marriage.

Even if David had told me he had feelings for me back in college, I still would've ended up with Steven. He knew how to play me and I fell for it. I was young and stupid and desperate for a life better than the one I'd had growing up. Steven knew that and used it to his advantage. David never stood a chance.

"Something doesn't feel right," David says as he drives around a corner.

"What do you mean?"

"The brakes feel soft." He glances at the dash. "But there aren't any warning lights on."

"Then I'm sure they're fine."

"Yeah, probably, although I've been having issues with those warning lights. They keep flashing on and off. Last week the low gas light went on after I'd just filled the tank."

"When's the last time you had the car serviced?"

"A couple months ago. They said everything was good."

"Then I'm sure it is." My phone rings. It's Audrey. "Hey, what time are you meeting us at the restaurant?"

"I'm here now. I'm waiting at the bar." She lowers her voice. "There's this really hot guy three seats down. I'm hoping he'll buy me a drink."

I smile. "You're not even divorced yet. Maybe you should wait before picking up a guy at a bar."

"Yeah, you're probably right. Did you and Steven leave the house yet?"

"Steven's meeting us there. He had to work late. David picked me up. We're on our way to the restaurant."

"Okay. I'll see you guys soon." She ends the call.

"Was that Audrey?" David asks.

243

"Yeah, she's at the restaurant. She's waiting in the bar."

We're all going to dinner because tonight would've been Audrey's tenth wedding anniversary and we didn't want her sitting home alone, feeling sad about her marriage ending.

"You haven't told her yet, have you?" David asks.

"That I'm leaving Steven? No. I have to tell Steven first."

"Are you sure he doesn't know?" David rounds a curve, going a little too fast. He's a very safe driver, so I'm not worried. I just wish he'd slow down.

"If Steven knew, he would've told me. Then he would've kicked me out of the house. It's okay for him to cheat, but I'm not allowed to even look at another man."

"It's just that he said something the other day. Something that made me think he knew."

My heart thumps harder. "What did he say?"

David glances at me. "Game on."

"Game on? What does that mean?"

"It's what he'd say in college when we'd compete for something, like who would get the highest score on a test, or who would win at golf. He said it to me when we were fighting over you. I told him I wasn't giving up, that I was going to try to get you back, and he smiled and said 'game on'."

"What does that have to do with now?"

David pauses. "The other day he told me he wanted to get rid of the house in Maine, but that you wouldn't agree to it. He asked me if I knew why. It's almost like he knew the reason you wanted to be there was because of me. Then he smiled and said 'game on'."

"Oh my God," I say, my heart pounding. "What if he knows?"

"Shit." David says, sounding panicked as he grips the steering wheel with both hands.

"What? What's going on?" I brace my hand against the dash as we speed down a steep hill. "David, slow down!"

"I can't! The brakes aren't working! I can't slow down!"

There's a curve up ahead. We're barreling toward it going way too fast. There aren't any cars coming toward us, but large trees line both sides of the road.

"Hold on to something!" David yells. "I'm going to try to force it to stop."

"How? What are you doing?"

He yanks on the steering wheel, turning the car perpendicular to the road. It slides sideways down the hill and slams into something.

The car comes to a dead stop. I'm disoriented for a moment, trying to process what happened.

I look over at David and see him slumped over in the seat, blood pouring from his head. "David! David, wake up!"

I try to rip off my seatbelt, but I can't move. I look down and see the car door crumpled against my leg, trapping me in my seat. The pain in my leg is so bad I'm getting lightheaded, but I can't pass out. I have to save David.

"David, please!" I grip his arm. "Please wake up!"

40

LAUREN

"David, wake up! Please! Wake up!"

"Mrs. Bishop!" I feel someone touching me. "Stop! You're going to hurt yourself."

My eyes blink open and I see Hannah above me, her hands on my shoulders, holding me down.

"What are you doing?" I ask, my heart pounding.

"You were trying to get out of bed." Hannah slowly lets go of me. "You could've fallen down. I thought you did. You were screaming so loud."

"I was screaming?"

"Yes." She sits beside me. "It scared me. I ran in here as fast as I could and saw you trying to get up. I got here just in time."

"I was having a nightmare." I swallow. "About the accident."

"I thought you didn't remember it."

"I don't." I stare at the wall in front of me, the images flashing in my head. David trying desperately to stop the car. Me screaming for him to stop.

"But you had a dream about it?" Hannah cautiously asks.

I look at her. "I think the dream really happened."

"Mrs. Bishop, dreams aren't real. It's just your mind playing a story while you sleep."

"No." I shake my head. "It really happened. I know it did. It's all coming back to me."

"What did you see?"

"The car. There was something wrong with it. The accident wasn't David's fault. I knew it wasn't. He was such a good driver."

"What was wrong with the car?"

"It was the—" I stop, realizing I shouldn't tell her this. She's sleeping with Steven. Her loyalty is to him, not to me. And he's the reason the brakes on David's car didn't work. It had to be him. He knew about David and me. He wouldn't have made that comment to David if he didn't know. *Game on.* He was challenging David, warning him, letting him know he could never have me. He'd rather have David and me dead than to see us together as a couple.

Oh, God. Steven, my own husband, tried to kill me. He killed his best friend. And I'm living with this man. A man who tried to kill me!

What if he tries again? Steven doesn't stop until he achieves his goal. He wanted me gone, but I lived, and now he needs to finish the job. In Steven's eyes, I'm damaged goods. I betrayed him. What's even worse, I gave myself to David, someone Steven claimed was his friend but was really someone Steven despised for having all the qualities he didn't.

Steven hated that David didn't worry about impressing people and yet everyone liked him. He hated that people flocked to David at parties to hear his silly jokes or funny stories. He hated that David easily made friends, without even trying.

Steven wished he could be that way, but he couldn't. It's just not his personality. He's quiet and serious and lives in his head. He's not good at relating to people or connecting with them. He's not funny. He doesn't put people at ease. He's pretty much the opposite of David.

I always thought Steven was secretly jealous of David, but I didn't think he'd do anything about it. I should've known that would change if Steven found out I was seeing David.

He killed him. Steven killed David. This whole time, he's been playing the role of the grieving friend, knowing he's the one responsible for the accident.

"Mrs. Bishop." Hannah puts her hand on my arm. "What were you going to tell me? About the car?"

"Nothing." I force out a smile. "You were probably right. It was just a nightmare. It wasn't real."

She cocks her head to the side. "Are you sure? You seemed pretty certain just a minute ago that it actually happened."

"It seemed real, but it wasn't. It was just a nightmare."

"Lauren." Steven rushes into my room and my heart nearly stops. What is he doing here? It's the middle of the day. He should be at work.

He comes to the side of the bed opposite Hannah and grips my hand as he sits down beside me. "What happened? I heard screaming. Is it your leg? Are you okay?"

"I'm fine." I want to pull my hand away, but don't. I can't give him any indication that I know what he did. It'll just make him want to get rid of me faster. I'm safer pretending I remember nothing about the accident. "What are you doing here?"

"There's a storm coming," Steven says. "I decided to come home and work here so I don't get stuck in Boston for the night."

"I think you should consider staying there more," I say. "It'll save you time from having to drive back here every night, and it would be safer." I fake a concerned look. "I worry about you driving in bad weather."

He rubs my arm. "You don't need to worry about me,

sweetheart. You know I'd rather be here with you than by myself."

It's such a lie. He'd rather be here because of the hot young nurse who spends every night in his bed. Steven used to find any excuse he could not to come home to me. Sometimes he wouldn't get home until midnight. And yet now, with Hannah here, he's managed to be home every night before seven.

"I better head out," Hannah says, getting up.

"Head out?" My eyes shoot over to her. "You're leaving?"

"I need to get a few groceries before it starts snowing."

"No!" I yell, then lower my voice. "You shouldn't go out if a storm is coming."

"It's not starting until later this afternoon," Steven says. "She'll be fine."

I don't want Hannah to leave. Knowing what Steven did, I don't want to be alone with him.

"I thought you got groceries this morning," I say to Hannah.

"I didn't have time. I just need a few things for dinner. I'll be back soon." She smiles at Steven. "Mr. Bishop can take care of you while I'm gone."

She leaves before I can stop her.

"How's the leg today?" Steven asks, his tone devoid of any care or concern now that Hannah's gone. He doesn't need to put on the perfect husband act around her, but he's so used to doing it when others are around that it's become habit now.

"Fine," I say, clearing my throat and looking away from him.

"Is something wrong?"

"No. Everything's fine." I look back at him and smile.

He stares at me a moment, then gets up from the bed and heads to the door.

"Where are you going?" I call after him.

249

"Hannah!" I hear him yell. "Can I talk to you before you go?"

"Sure," she says.

I hear them talking in the kitchen, but can't make out what they're saying.

Moments later, Steven returns, sitting on the chair and taking his phone out. He swipes through it, ignoring me as usual.

"You don't have to sit here," I tell him. "You can go in your office."

"I wanted to talk to you." He sets his phone on the nightstand.

"About what?" I ask.

"The night of the accident."

My heart pounds faster. "What about it?"

"You still don't remember anything?"

I shake my head. "No. Nothing."

He nods. "Huh. That's interesting, because Hannah just told me you had a nightmare about the accident. She said that's why you were screaming."

"It was just a silly dream," I say, laughing it off. "And I wasn't screaming. Hannah's exaggerating."

"What happened in the dream?" he asks, leaning back a little in the chair.

"I saw myself in the car on my way to meet you at the restaurant. Oh, and Audrey called me. She said she was already there, sitting at the bar. But I don't know if that really happened."

Maybe it didn't. Maybe Hannah's right and the dream wasn't a memory at all but just something my mind came up with while I was sleeping.

"Yes, she was there early," Steven says, "and sitting at the bar. I saw her there when I arrived at the restaurant."

That really happened? Then the dream was real. I didn't

make it up. It was my memory of that night coming back.

"What else did you see?" Steven asks. "In the dream?"

"That was it. I woke up."

His brows draw together. "Then why were you screaming?"

"I turned on my side when I was waking up and it hurt my leg." I sigh. "Anyway, it was nothing. I'm fine."

Steven's eyes haven't left me. They move from my face down to my hands, then back to my face.

He smiles a little. "You're lying."

"What?" I laugh. "What are you talking about?"

"You won't look me in the eye and you keep doing that thing with your hands." He points to them. "Making a fist and then letting it go, over and over. You do that when you're nervous or trying to hide something. You've done it since I met you. You didn't know that?"

I knew, but I didn't think I was doing it. I look down at my hands and see they're both fisted. I slowly relax them and rest them on my lap.

Steven moves to the bed, sitting beside me and taking my hand. "What did you see, Lauren? In the dream?"

"Steven, stop it." I yank my hand back. "You know how it upsets me to talk about that night."

"Deal with it," he says in a harsh tone. "I'm tired of pretending."

"Pretending what?" I ask, my throat going dry.

"That I didn't know."

I stare at the wall in front of me, my heart pounding, my breaths shallow and fast.

Steven leans down to my face and talks in my ear. "I know what you were doing with him. I know you lied to me so you could be with him. I know he's the reason you made me buy this house. I know all of it, Lauren. Every little detail."

Oh God, he's going to kill me. Right now. He's going to shoot me with his gun and dump my body in the woods. Or maybe he'll take me out back, push me off the cliff, and tell everyone it was an accident.

"Steven, please," I beg. "Please don't do this."

He backs away, a slight smile on his face. "Do what?" He looks down at my hand, which is fisted again, and picks it up, lifting it to his mouth and kissing the top of it. "You know I would never hurt you, Lauren. You're mine."

I used to love it when he said that. I found it endearing, a sign of how much he loved me. Then I wised up and realized he was telling me he owned me. Controlled me. And that I'd never be free of him.

But if that's true, if he wanted me to be chained to him for life, why did he try to kill me? He knew I was riding in the car with David that night. In fact, he suggested it after telling me he had to work late and would meet us at the restaurant.

"You should rest," he says, setting my hand down and getting up from the bed. "Do you need anything before I go?"

"No." I look out the window, at the snowflakes swirling in the air.

"I'll be in my office," Steven says.

What do I do? He's lying when he said he wouldn't hurt me. He did something to the brakes on David's car. He wanted it to crash. He wanted David and me to die. But I survived.

Steven didn't get what he wanted. He's going to try again. He has to.

Because Steven always gets what he wants.

41

LAUREN

"Audrey, I need you to get over here!" I say when she finally calls me back. I've been calling and texting her all afternoon.

"I can't. I'm stuck in Boston. Have you seen this weather?"

She's still in Boston? I was hoping she was in town. I'm scared to be alone in the house with Steven. Hannah's here, but I can't trust her now that she's sleeping with Steven.

What if she's part of this? What if the two of them are planning my murder? She's in the kitchen with him right now, making dinner. What if they try to poison me?

"You're staying there tonight?" I ask Audrey.

"I have to. The roads aren't plowed. There's already a foot of snow and it's still snowing. I got a hotel for the night. Lauren, what's wrong? You left me like 20 messages."

"I really need to talk to you."

"Go ahead."

"Not over the phone. I need to talk to you in person. It's urgent. I need you to come here as soon as you can."

"Lauren, you're scaring me. What's going on?"

"I'll tell you when you're here. When do you think you'll be able to get out of Boston?"

"It depends on when the storm ends and how fast they clear the roads."

"What about the cameras?" I ask, lowering my voice to almost a whisper. "Did you see anything?"

"Not yet."

The cameras record whenever motion's detected. The recordings are saved to a cloud server and can be accessed on an app. I had Audrey put the app on her phone instead of mine, in case Steven was somehow able to unlock my phone and see it.

"Nothing?" I ask. "Are you sure?"

"I just installed the cameras this morning. We're not going to see anything until tonight, when they're together."

"Yeah, I guess you're right. Let me know first thing tomorrow. This can't wait."

"Would you just tell me what's going on?"

I hear footsteps in the hall.

"I will, but not now. I have to go."

Hannah walks into my room, smiling. "Mr. Bishop made chicken and rice soup. He said it's your favorite. You want some?"

"I'm not hungry. I'm just going to skip dinner tonight."

Her smile falls as she walks over to me. "Are you feeling okay?"

"I'm fine. I'm just not very hungry."

"You should eat. With your low blood sugar, you'll get lightheaded if you skip dinner."

"I'll be okay. You and Steven go ahead and eat."

She nods. "I'll check on you later."

They eat dinner around six. I hear them talking and Hannah laughing at something Steven said. He's not the least bit funny, but sometimes he tries to be and fails miserably. Hannah is eager to please him so of course she laughs at his sad attempt at being humorous.

Around seven, she returns to my room to check on me.

"I'd like to get ready for bed," I tell her.

"Already? It's still early."

"I'm not going to sleep. I'll probably read or watch TV. I'd just like to get ready now."

"Okay," she says, going to my dresser to get my pajamas.

"So how was the soup?" I ask.

"We didn't have it. We ate the leftover lasagna I had in the fridge."

It was one of those frozen lasagnas from a box. Steven would never eat that unless he had to, because his only other option was poisonous soup.

"You sure you don't want the soup?" Hannah asks. "I could heat some up."

"I'm not hungry. Maybe I'll have some tomorrow."

I'm not eating that soup. I'm not eating anything Steven makes, or Hannah. I can't trust those two. I'll just go without eating until Audrey can get back here and bring me some food.

42

LAUREN

"I'm here," Audrey says, coming into my room holding a sack from the deli in town. I've never been more happy to see her.

It's noon the following day. I survived the night with Steven and Hannah. The snow stopped around ten last night, much earlier than predicted. Audrey drove here as soon as the roads were cleared. She had to cancel a meeting, which I hated to make her do, but this couldn't wait.

"Shut the door," I tell her as she hands me the deli sack.

She walks to the door and closes it, then returns to my bed. "Okay, what is going on?"

"Hold on. I'm starving." I open the sack, take out the sandwich, rip off the paper wrapping, and take a big bite.

Audrey sits on the bed, watching me. "If you were that hungry, I could've got two."

"I haven't eaten since yesterday," I say, my mouth full. I want more of the sandwich, but I'll have to eat it later. I just needed a bite to help stabilize my blood sugar. I've been lightheaded all morning.

"Why didn't you eat?"

"Because I can't trust that any of the food in this house is safe."

She laughs a little. "What are you talking about?"

"Where's Hannah?"

"I don't know. She wasn't around when I came in."

"What about Steven? Did you see him?"

"No. He must be in his office."

"Did you see anything on the cameras last night?"

"No, Steven was alone in his bed. I never saw Hannah."

"That's strange. They're together almost every night."

"Lauren, seriously, tell me what's going on. I cancelled an important meeting to be here."

I set my sandwich down. "I had a dream yesterday. It was more of a nightmare. It was about the accident."

"What about it?"

"I was in the car and we were going down a steep hill. David was driving too fast and I told him to slow down, but he couldn't. The brakes didn't work. He kept pushing on the brake pedal, but the car just kept going faster." I grab hold of her arm. "It was Steven. He tampered with the brakes. I don't know how, but it had to be him. I know it was." I pause a moment to let that sink in before I tell her more.

She's quiet, then says, "You're saying you think Steven tried to kill you. And his best friend."

"Yes."

She looks over at the pill bottles on my nightstand. "Are you taking something? A new medication?"

"I'm not on drugs, and I'm not making this up. I saw it happen."

"In a dream. You know dreams aren't real, right?"

I sigh in frustration. "It was real. And it wasn't just a dream. It was a memory. Before the crash, you called me and told me you were sitting at the bar in the restaurant, waiting for us to get there. Is that what happened?"

"Well, yes, but Lauren, what you're saying is crazy. Why would Steven do that? And how?"

"I don't know. I just know he did it."

"Steven is not a violent man. He wouldn't try to kill *anyone*, but especially not his wife and best friend."

"He would if he suspected there was something going on between David and me."

"Why would he think that? Everyone knows you two were just friends."

"Because that's what we wanted them to think."

"Wait—what are you saying?"

I look down, then back up at her. "David and I were seeing each other."

Audrey gasps and puts her hand over her mouth. "When? For how long?"

"A few years. It started with us just spending more time together. Steven was always working and I was lonely. David wasn't dating anyone so we'd make plans to go out. Movies. Dinner. Walks at the park. It was completely innocent at first. But as time went on, we developed feelings for each other. Feelings we'd been trying to deny for years. I never told you this, but that summer before sophomore year, when David was living in Boston and we were spending all our time together, I fell in love with him. But I didn't think he felt the same way. Then I met Steven and instantly knew how he felt about me. He wanted me the way I hoped David would, but David always treated me like a friend. He never even tried to kiss me. So I let David go and fell in love with Steven." I look down. "I found out later that David actually did love me back then. He was going to tell me, but then I met Steven and... he never did." I look back at Audrey. "Connecting again after all those years, David and I thought we were getting a second chance. We even talked about getting married. But then the accident happened."

Audrey gets up and walks over to the window. "We're best friends. Why didn't you tell me this before now?"

"Because I knew you'd tell me to divorce Steven and be angry with me if I didn't."

"I wouldn't be angry." She turns back to me. "But I don't understand why you'd want to stay with him if you were in love with someone else."

"I didn't know how to leave Steven. I was afraid of what would happen if I did, especially if he found out about David. And I was obviously right to worry because look what he did."

"Steven didn't mess with the car." She walks over to me. "He would never do that."

"You don't know him like I do."

"I know his career means everything to him. What if he got caught? He'd spend the rest of his life in prison. Do you really think he'd do that? Risk losing everything he's worked for?"

"Steven loves risk. He gets off on it. It's why he's sleeping with Hannah when his wife's in the next room."

Audrey shakes her head. "That's different. Cheating on your spouse and murder are two very different things." She sits down on the bed. "Are you sure he knew about you and David?"

"Yes. He told me."

"When?"

"Yesterday. I had a feeling he knew, but I wasn't sure. Now I am, which is why I'm certain he messed with the brakes." I grab her hand. "Audrey, you have to believe me. You know I'd never say this if I didn't believe it. You have to help me."

"What do you want me to do?"

"Find the car. See if you can have it towed to a garage so someone can look at the brakes. The police won't believe any of this if I don't have proof."

"The car is gone. It was totaled. Taken to a junk yard. It's nothing but scrap metal now."

She's right. I never thought about what happened to the

car until now, but of course it wasn't salvageable. It was a horrific crash. I'm sure the car was nothing but a twisted piece of metal.

"I could try to find out what junk yard they took it to," she offers. "But it's been weeks since the crash. I can't imagine—"

"No. It's gone." I collapse back on the stack of pillows behind me. "What am I going to do? I know Steven caused the crash, but I can't prove it."

She glances at the closed door, then back at me. "When is he going back to Boston?"

"Tomorrow. He has meetings all day."

"So it will just be you and Hannah here?"

"Yes. I wasn't worried about Hannah doing anything, but now I'm not sure."

"What if you stayed at my place? I have an extra bedroom. You could stay there until you figure out what to do next."

"That's sweet of you to offer, but I can't with this." I point to my broken leg. "I can't get around on my own. And the bathroom isn't big enough for my wheelchair. I wouldn't be able to use it."

"What if you got your own place and hired a new nurse?"

"Steven would never allow it. He's still pretending we have the perfect marriage. Having his wife move out wouldn't look good. Unless you can get proof that he's cheating. Once we have that, he'll have no choice but to admit our marriage had issues. People won't even question me moving out."

"But in order for people to find out, you'd have to let them know. You'd have to put the videos out on social media. Either that, or make some kind of announcement. And once this is made public, it could hurt Steven's business. Are you sure you're willing to do that?"

"I have to. And why would I care what happens to Steven's career? He tried to kill me. He deserves whatever happens to him."

There's a knock on the door. "Lauren? Can I come in?"

It's Steven.

"What do you need?"

He opens the door, looking surprised when he sees Audrey. "Audrey. I didn't know you were here."

She stands up. "I just came by to see Lauren and bring her lunch."

Steven looks at me. "I made you soup. Didn't Hannah tell you?"

"Yes, but I wasn't in the mood for soup. Did you need something?"

"I wanted to tell you I'm going into the office this afternoon. I'm leaving in a few minutes."

"Oh. When will you be home?"

"Probably not until Friday. I'm falling behind and need to stay late the next couple nights."

"So you're staying in Boston?"

"If that's okay with you."

"Of course. I'll see you on Friday."

He comes over to me and leans down to give me a kiss. "Call if you need anything."

"I'll be fine," I say, smiling at him.

He glances at Audrey. "Goodbye, Audrey."

"Bye, Steven," she says, watching him leave.

He shuts the door behind him and I hear him walking away.

"That buys you some time," Audrey says.

"Yes, but now I'm alone with Hannah."

"Are you really worried about her? If she wanted to do something, she would've done it by now."

"I suppose that's true. I've been alone with her for weeks. She's had plenty of chances to harm me."

"I'd offer to stay here with you, but I have an all day

meeting in Boston tomorrow. It starts early so I got a hotel room for tonight."

"I bet Barry would let you stay at the house if you asked."

"That's just what I want." She rolls her eyes. "To spend the night in the same house as my ex."

"It's a huge house. You wouldn't even have to see him."

"I'll stick with the hotel." She checks her phone, then texts someone.

"Do you need to go?"

"Yes. I'm supposed to be on a conference call right now. I completely forgot."

"Go. I'll check in with you later."

She leans down to hug me. "Everything's going to be okay."

"I hope you're right."

43

AUDREY

"I didn't think I'd make it back here tonight," I say, taking a sip of Chardonnay as I gaze out at the city lights. "I could tell she wanted me to stay, so I told her I had an all day meeting tomorrow." I take another sip of wine. "She thinks you caused the accident."

"Yes, I know," Steven says with a slight smile as he sets his empty wine glass on the table. "She has quite an imagination." When I don't respond, he looks at me next to him on the couch. "You don't actually believe her, do you?"

I laugh. "Of course not. I know you wouldn't risk your career like that."

"But do you think I'm capable of it? Plotting the death of my wife and closest friend?"

I look back at him, at his handsome face, his freshly trimmed brows, his dark hair that never has a single strand out of place. Steven's a perfectionist. He likes things to be neat and tidy, and unfortunately, murder is the opposite of that. It's messy and unpredictable. Even when you have what you believe to be the perfect plan, things can go wrong, leaving you with loose ends you're forced to clean up.

"No," I tell him. "I don't believe you could do it."

"And yet my own wife does. What does that say about her?"

"Lauren's always been dramatic." I swirl the wine around in my glass. "She makes up stories and believes they're true." I pause, gazing out at the city. "Now she thinks Hannah's a danger."

Steven chuckles. "That's ridiculous. Hannah's about as wholesome as they come. She wouldn't hurt anyone. She's a nurse. She chose a career in which she could save people, not harm them."

He can't possibly be that blind, can he? Hannah's as far from wholesome as I am. Beneath that fresh young face and annoying smile is a dark girl with a twisted past. I know because I hired a man to investigate her after Lauren told me she'd chosen Hannah to be her nurse. I had to know who I was dealing with and make sure she wouldn't derail my plan.

Turns out, Lauren's choice for a nurse was more perfect than I could've ever imagined. I could get rid of Lauren and let Hannah take the blame. The police would assume she did it. She had motive since she was sleeping with Steven and had to get rid of his wife so she could take her place. And Hannah's murdered before, or that's what the police will be led to believe when they look into her background.

If Lauren had done some digging into Hannah's past, she would've found out that Hannah killed her mother's boyfriend. If I were to guess, I'd say Hannah killed him because she held a grudge against him and felt he needed to be punished. Her mother had lived with this man for two years before she fell down the stairs and died. Perhaps Hannah believed the man pushed her mother down the stairs. Or maybe he'd been abusive to her. Whatever the reason, Hannah wanted him gone, so when he showed up at the hospital where Hannah was a nurse, she gave him a deadly overdose of his medication.

There was an investigation, but it was ruled an accident. It's frightening how often things like that happen. I did a quick internet search and found medication errors resulting in death are quite common in hospitals. It's one of those dirty little secrets in the medical world.

In Hannah's case, it wasn't an accident. I can't prove that, but I find it a little too much of a coincidence that her one and only error as a nurse just happened to result in the death of her mother's boyfriend. Following the investigation, Hannah resigned from her job and didn't go back to nursing. She tried waitressing, but quit after eight months and didn't work again until she got the job with Lauren.

I'm still unsure why Lauren chose her. Lauren's usually very cautious, but she hired Hannah without even looking into her background. Then again, if she had, she wouldn't have found much. Hospitals try to hide errors that result in a patient's death. That investigator I hired had to do a lot of digging to get to the truth.

Her background aside, why would Lauren hire a woman with very little experience who is also young and extremely attractive? And then she's surprised when the little vixen goes after her husband?

Lauren is beyond stupid and painfully naïve, which works in my favor because she'd never suspect that I'm the one planning to kill her. We've been best friends since college. She trusts me more than anyone else. She has no idea that I'm the reason she's now confined to bed after nearly dying in a car crash.

I can't believe that bitch didn't die. I did all that work, all that planning, to make sure she and David were out of our lives so Steven and I could finally be together, and then Lauren somehow survives.

Steven takes the wine glass from me and sets it on the table, then presses his lips to mine. He arouses so much more in me than Barry, my ex, ever did. I think it's his quiet nature. I'm never quite sure what Steven's thinking. I find him mysterious in a way that's alluring and irresistible.

"I missed you," he says, kissing my neck as he lowers me down on the couch.

"I would've been here sooner if that bitch would've stopped whining about how terrible her life has become. I wanted to strangle her just to shut her up."

"Listen to you," he says, smiling at me, "talking about your best friend that way."

"You said much harsher things about David."

Steven unbuttons the top of my blouse. "David was sleeping with my wife. I think the things I said about him were more than justified."

It's true, but to be fair, Steven was cheating on Lauren with me, so neither one of them was faithful. Steven should've filed for divorce years ago, but he kept putting it off. Then he found out David was sleeping with Lauren and was determined to stay married to her. Steven's extremely competitive. He always has been. He won Lauren from David back in college and there was no way he was letting David take her from him. He became obsessed with David and Lauren's relationship, to the point it was interfering with ours. The only way to end Steven's obsession with David and Lauren would be to get rid of them. And I knew I'd have to be the one to do it.

A car accident seemed like the easiest option, although it involved some research. Doing the research online would leave a digital trail so I went to see Johnny. He's a mechanic in town who recently took over the garage his father owned. I asked him a series of questions about how brakes go out, pretending I was concerned about it happening on my car. He showed me how to check the brake fluid, explaining that without brake fluid, the brakes will stop working. Then, as part of normal maintenance, he offered to change out my brake fluid. I agreed to it and watched as he siphoned out the old brake fluid, then replaced it with the new. It didn't look hard. In fact, it looked incredibly easy. After I left there, I went to the hardware store and bought a siphon and decided on the day and time for the crash.

After the accident, the people in town were making up all kinds of stories about what might've happened. They all loved David and knew him well. They couldn't believe he'd just drive off the road like that. But the police investigated the scene and ruled it driver error, forcing the locals to accept that the accident was David's fault. The only person who didn't accept it was Johnny.

He called me a few days after the crash and asked me to meet him at his apartment. When I got there, he was nervous and fidgety. He didn't actually come out and accuse me of messing with David's car, but the questions he asked made it clear he thought I was guilty. I laughed it off, then explained my long friendship with David and Lauren and how I'd never do them any harm.

Johnny still seemed suspicious of me, so I did what I've always done to shut men up. I had sex with him, and I kept it up until I ended our relationship last week. Johnny didn't seem upset it was over. We both knew it was a short-term fling. But just to be safe, I gave him money to keep him quiet. Of course, I didn't actually say that. I told him the money was because I cared about him and wanted to make sure he kept doing what he loved. He's great at fixing cars but terrible at managing finances. Word around town was that his business was about to go under because he wasn't paying his bills on time.

He accepted my reasoning and took the cash. Even if he still believes my interest in how brakes work and David's accident are somehow connected, he won't tell anyone. If he was going to, he wouldn't have taken the money. And if he did tell someone, he can't prove that it's true. The car is gone now. It's nothing but scrap metal.

"I have the suite until Friday," I say, undoing Steven's tie. "We'll have all week together. Just imagine all the things we can do."

We're on the top floor of a beautiful downtown hotel in our usual room. I always put it in my name, but Steven pays me for it since it's very expensive and all my money is currently going to pay for my overpriced divorce lawyer.

Steven sits up, taking off his tie and tossing it aside. "I can't commit to every night."

"Why? You already told Lauren you were staying in Boston all week."

"Yes, but given her state of mind right now, I might need to go back to Maine for a night or two."

"For what?" I huff. "She thinks you tried to kill her. She doesn't want you anywhere near her right now."

"I need to assure her that I'm not out to harm her. The last thing I need is her telling someone in town about her concerns and starting some ridiculous rumor about me."

"Lauren doesn't leave the house. Who would she tell?"

"She has a phone. She can call whoever she wants, and if she's just sitting in bed, letting her imagination create more untrue stories about me, she might be compelled to tell someone."

"She doesn't want you there. She told me that several times today. In fact, she asked me to try to persuade you to stay in Boston through the weekend."

"Because she fears me, based on stories she made up in her head. I need to go there and spend time with her. I need to show her she can trust me and that I'm not a threat."

I stare at him in disbelief. "What's going on here?"

"What do you mean?" he asks, undoing the top two buttons of his dress shirt.

"Why do you care what Lauren thinks? You're divorcing her."

He sits back on the couch, rubbing his jaw. "About that."

"About what?" I snap. "You ARE divorcing her. You said so last week."

"Yes, but I didn't say when. Now isn't a good time. Just think what people would say. Divorcing my wife when she's recovering from a car accident that almost took her life? It's not good for business."

I bolt up from the couch. "You have *got* to be kidding me!"

"Audrey, don't be like this. You know I hate when women get all dramatic about things."

"Dramatic?" I toss my hands up. "You think I'm being dramatic?" I stand over him as he sits on the couch. "You've been telling me you're going to divorce her for years. I patiently waited, and just when I thought it was about to happen, you found out about Lauren and David and decided you couldn't leave her because of your obsession with making sure David never gets her. Now David is gone, and you can finally end things with Lauren, and you're telling me it's not happening?"

"Keep your voice down," he says in a scolding tone that turns my anger up another notch. "People will hear you."

"I don't care." I turn and walk away from him. "I'm sick of this. I'm sick of you going back on your word. If you only knew the things I've done for you."

"What are you talking about?"

I turn back and see him walking toward me. "What did you do?"

"Nothing," I say, knowing if I told him the truth, he'd turn against me. He may have hated David and wanted him gone, but he wouldn't approve of me killing him, or Lauren. He likes to be in control of everything, so having me take control of this situation would anger him. But I had to. The only way he'd give up Lauren is if David no longer wanted her, and the only way that would happen is if David were dead.

"What I mean," I say, "is that I've sacrificed a lot to get to this place. I ended my marriage. Gave up my dream house. Told countless lies so I could sneak away with you."

"And soon we'll be together," he says, putting his arms around me. "But not now. I can't have my clients thinking I'm cold and heartless. They won't trust me, and trust is what keeps them investing with me."

I am not going to keep waiting. I've waited long enough. I'm not waiting another year or two for Lauren to recover. I'd already planned on killing her, but then I changed my mind when Steven said he was divorcing her. I no longer needed to kill her. In fact, I was looking forward to having her see me with Steven, living the life she had but never appreciated. I'd keep her alive for that alone. But if Steven feels obligated to stay with her, then I have to get rid of her. And having her dead means Steven won't have to give her his money, another bonus. He can use all that money on me.

His phone rings. He picks it up and sends it to voicemail.

"Was it Lauren?" I ask.

"Hannah," he says, looking at his phone. "She didn't leave a message."

"She's probably wondering why you're not with her tonight," I say in a harsh tone as I pull away from him and walk over to the window.

"Don't start with that, Audrey. You weren't exactly saving yourself for me."

I turn back to him. "You expected me to just do nothing while you spent night after night with that girl? Honestly, Steven, if you wanted some side action, you could've done better than her."

"I could say the same for you."

"Hannah's young and inexperienced. Johnny's old enough

to know what he's doing. And he's a mechanic. He's good with his hands." I smile. "Among other things."

"Enough about them," Steven says, coming up to me and wrapping me in his arms. "Tonight is about us."

I'm happy about that, but I want more. I want a life with Steven, and that will only happen if Lauren is dead.

44

AUDREY

It's Saturday morning and I'm driving back to Maine to see Lauren. I made up a work emergency to explain why I had to stay in Boston all week. The truth is, I worked during the day and spent every night with Steven. He ended up not going home to Lauren. Why would he when he could spend his nights with me?

I'm so much better than her. Steven knows this, but he can't seem to let Lauren go. So I have to help him.

As I drive through town on the way to Lauren's house, I consider when to put my condo on the market. I cannot wait to get rid of it. I hate this town. There's nothing to do here and the locals are idiots. Lauren used to feel the same way until she started sleeping with David, who grew up here and convinced her it was a quaint, small town with wonderful people. She bought a house here to be closer to him, but lied and told me it was because of the beautiful scenery.

Lauren never told me about her affair with David. She lied to me just as much as I lied to her, so I don't feel bad about killing her. We were never really friends. We just pretended to be. Back in college, she stole Steven from me and I never forgave her. She'd deny that she stole him, but that's only because she's selfish and doesn't consider how her actions affect others.

The first night she went out with Steven, he was supposed to go out with me. I'd spent all of the previous year trying to get him to notice me. I'd go over to David's room, hoping Steven would be there, but when he was, he was always on his stupid laptop. He wouldn't even look at me. Sophomore year, I decided to be bold and ask him out for coffee. He accepted the invite, then cancelled on me and went out with Lauren.

I didn't actually say the coffee invite was a date, but it was clear that's what I intended. Steven probably didn't get it, given that he's a man and men are clueless, but Lauren knew it was a date. How could she not? She knew I didn't just ask out random guys for coffee. And yet she still went out with Steven, and kept going out with him. She tried to set me up with other guys, but I didn't want someone else. I wanted Steven. He was quiet and reserved and extremely smart. He wasn't what I'd consider fun, but he was handsome, sophisticated, and wealthy, which is exactly what I wanted.

Looking back, I don't think Lauren even liked him. Before Steven, she'd always dated guys who were the opposite of him. Guys who had no ambition and weren't very bright, but could make people laugh. The life-of-the-party type of guy. That was David. She should've chosen him back then, but she chose money over happiness, knowing with Steven, she would always have money. I wonder if she regrets that now. She hasn't been happy since the day they got married. I tried to warn her. I told her over and over that they weren't a good match, but she married him anyway. Sometimes I think she just did it to make sure I couldn't have him.

I'm passing through downtown now and glance up at my condo. Maybe I'll put it up for sale next week. I could tell people I'm so distraught over Lauren's death that I can't take being in this town anymore. There are too many memories of being here with her.

Lauren thinks I bought the condo because of her, so we could spend our summers here together. The truth is, Barry bought the condo. He surprised me with it, saying he knew I'd miss Lauren when she came here every summer so he got me the condo so I could be here too. He's such a moron. He could never tell when I was lying. After being married to me for years, he should've figured out how much I despised Lauren and her perfect life. He should've noticed how jealous I was of her, spending her days shopping and getting facials while I was working my ass off to pay the mortgage on a house we couldn't afford because my husband chose to work at a free clinic instead of getting a good-paying job.

It should've been me living the life of leisure, not Lauren. Steven and I would've had a wonderful life if that bitch hadn't interfered. She knew I liked him, but she went out with him anyway. She deserves the miserable life she had with him, and she deserves what I'm about to do to her.

When I get to her house, I let myself in and quietly walk to her room. Lauren texted me earlier this morning and asked me to come over. I told her I would, but didn't know what time. She said Hannah was going to town this morning to get groceries and go to the pharmacy. Lauren saw her doctor yesterday and he thinks there might be an infection in her broken leg. To be safe, he put her on antibiotics, which is what Hannah is picking up at the pharmacy. Lauren's been complaining about pain in her leg all week. It was bad enough that she's been taking pain meds, the strong prescription opioids she was given after she left the hospital.

Taking pills is something Lauren almost never does. She's one of those all natural people who doesn't even like taking aspirin. So as soon as she told me she was taking those pain pills she was prescribed, I immediately took action. This was my chance to finally get rid of her, and it's easy—almost too easy. All I have to do is switch out Lauren's pain meds for lethal street narcotics, let Hannah give them to her when I'm gone, and it's done. Lauren dies from the drugs and Hannah gets blamed. It'll be the second time Hannah gave a patient pills that led to their death, leading the police to believe she did it intentionally. Add in my testimony that Hannah was obsessed with Steven and had fantasized about a life with him, and Hannah has motive for killing Lauren. The police will assume she was a disturbed young woman who was jealous of Lauren and wanted to get rid of her so she could steal her life.

Hannah will likely admit that she had a relationship with Steven, but he'll deny it, making her look even crazier. And there's no proof of their affair. I never turned on those cameras Lauren made me install. I didn't want her having evidence she could use to try to get more of Steven's money in the divorce. This was before I'd planned to kill her, when I thought Steven was going to file for divorce soon. I really wanted her to live so I could see her expression when I took Steven from her, but sadly, I'll never get the chance.

She's sound asleep when I go into her room. I walk over to her nightstand and pick up her prescription pain meds. I open the bottle, smiling when I see the ones I'm replacing them with are an exact match. There are eight pills in the bottle. I pour them out, stuff them in my pocket, take out the bag with the street opioids, and count out eight of them. I put them in the bottle, replace the cap, then place the bottle exactly how I found it.

I smile at Lauren as I gaze at her asleep in her bed. "Goodbye, dear friend. May you rest in peace."

I leave her room, go out the front door, and lock it behind me. I drive to the coffee shop downtown and go inside to order. The place is busy, as it always is on Saturday morning, giving me plenty of alibis should I need one.

As I'm waiting for the young girl behind the counter to make my caramel soy latte, I call Lauren. She doesn't answer so I leave a message. I tell her I'm in town, but that I have a client issue that needs immediate attention and that I'll be over as soon as I can. If the cops get into her phone after her death, they'll hear the message and know I wasn't anywhere near her when she died. I'm not at all worried the police would suspect me, but I always like to cover my bases, just in case. Lauren used to tell me about all these bizarre murder cases and how sometimes just a tiny little detail led the police to the killer. She was obsessed with those true crime podcasts. She talked about them all the time.

"Order for Audrey," the girl behind the counter says.

I smile at her as I take my drink, then look around the coffee shop for an open table. I considered going home, but thinking about those true crime podcasts has convinced me to stay here. I'm being extra cautious, making sure I'm surrounded by alibis so there's no possible way the police could connect Lauren's death back to me.

The cops might be able to trace the drugs back to the dealer, but they can't prove I was the one who bought them. If anything, they'll think Hannah got them since the guy who sold them to me was around her age and the place I met him was only a few blocks from her old apartment.

One of my clients told me about this drug dealer after his son almost died from taking just one tiny pill. He didn't want anyone knowing this, so I did some PR work to make sure people believed his son's hospital stay was because of an illness and not a street opioid that nearly killed him. The only reason he lived is because he was only two blocks away from a hospital.

Lauren's in the middle of nowhere. It'll take the ambulance at least a half hour to get to her house and another half hour to get to the hospital, maybe longer.

Poor Lauren. At least she'll be reunited with David soon.

An hour later, I get the call. It's from Steven.

"Audrey, something happened to Lauren," he says, in his usual serious tone. "She's in the ambulance on her way to the hospital."

I gasp. "What happened? Is it serious?"

The lady at the table next to mine hears this and looks at me, probably hoping to get some juicy gossip to spread around town.

"I don't know," Steven says. "Hannah just called and said she gave Lauren one of her pain meds, went to make her something to eat, then came back and Lauren was unresponsive. I'm on my way to the hospital."

"I'll meet you there." I stuff my laptop in my bag and hurry to get my coat on. "Is it the hospital outside of town or are they taking her to Boston?"

"The one near town. Boston's too far. I'll see you there."

I force back my smile, replacing it with a somber, worried look.

"Is everything okay?" the lady who was eavesdropping on me asks.

"No." I get up from my chair and gather up my purse and laptop bag. "My friend is being rushed to the hospital." I choke on my words and a tear slides down my face. "I have to go." I race out of there, knowing the lady is watching, along with everyone else in the coffee shop.

Not to brag, but it was an excellent performance. My next one will be even better, when I arrive at the hospital and respond to the news that my dearest and closest friend has passed away.

45

HANNAH

I can't believe this is happening. All I did was give Lauren a pill for her pain and now she's in the hospital fighting for her life and I'm locked up in jail.

The police arrested me an hour ago. They say I gave Lauren an illegal synthetic opioid that contains ingredients that can be deadly in amounts as small as one dose. They're street drugs, made overseas, that are being sold by dealers up and down the East Coast. I learned about street drugs in nursing school, but I've never bought them and never would. The police don't believe me. As soon as they tested the pills from the bottle on Lauren's nightstand, they assumed I tried to kill her.

I can see why they think that. I was the only person there when it happened and I'm the one who gave Lauren the pill. Plus, the police know my history. They looked into my background and found out what happened at the hospital. They don't think Hank's death was an accident. They didn't come out and say that, but I know they think I killed my mom's boyfriend by giving him the wrong pills. And they're right, I did.

But I didn't kill Lauren. I would never do that. She's not

like Hank. She didn't do anything to deserve death. Hank, on the other hand, needed to die. He lured my mother with money and gifts, then after she moved in with him, he became an abusive monster. She was covered in bruises, and when I asked her what happened, she'd lie for the jerk and say she was just clumsy and bumping into things. I know Hank's the one who pushed her down the stairs and left her there to die. My mother always took stairs slowly and held on to the railing. She would never fall on her own. Hank did it and got away with it. Until I killed him.

I should've known I'd be punished for that eventually. Having it be ruled an accident seemed too easy, and nothing ever comes easy for me. Just when I think things are turning around for me, something happens to ruin it. Like this job. I thought I'd hit the jackpot working for the Bishops. It was an easy job, the pay was good, and I got to live in a fancy house overlooking the ocean. I never in a million years thought I'd end up in jail, accused of trying to kill someone.

What am I going to do? I can't afford a lawyer. I can't afford bail. I thought Steven would help me out, but instead, he turned on me. He thinks I did this to Lauren. All the things he said to me about us being together and having a future? It was all lies. He was just using me to satisfy his physical needs since his wife couldn't. I feel used and betrayed by a man I truly thought I loved. I think part of me still does, which makes this hurt even more.

How could Steven do this to me? How could he leave me here rotting in jail and not even listen to my side of the story?

I didn't try to harm Lauren. But if I can't prove it, it's over. I'm going to prison.

46

AUDREY

She didn't die. Again!

How many lives does this woman have? That pill should've killed her. She arrived at the hospital two hours after I gave it to her. She should've died on the way there. But no, she lived.

The doctors called it a miracle. Once again, Lauren comes out ahead. And now I have to figure out what to do next. At least I got rid of Hannah. Now that she's in jail and charged with trying to kill Lauren, Steven won't have his little play toy anymore. But he'll no longer need her now that I'll be in his bed. I offered to move in while Lauren's in the hospital. I'm back to playing the role of the kind and generous best friend, and as usual, Lauren has no idea that it's all an act.

"Don't worry," I told her when I went to visit her at the hospital. "I'll take care of everything at home. You just focus on getting better."

"I'm so lucky to have you," she said, her big blue eyes looking at me with genuine gratitude. I almost felt sorry for her, but then I remembered how she took Steven from me all those years ago and I was back to hating her.

Maybe while I'm living with Steven this week I can convince him to divorce her. I'll have him all to myself, every night, for as long as Lauren's in the hospital. The doctors discovered her leg infection was worse than they thought so she'll likely be staying there for the next couple weeks. That should be plenty of time for me to show Steven what a better wife I would be than Lauren.

The phone rings as I'm pouring myself a glass of champagne. I smile when I see Steven's name on the screen.

"I was just thinking of you," I say. "I was going to start packing up some things to bring over, but if you can't take another second without me, I could come over right now."

"That won't be necessary," he says in a cold, brusque tone.

"What are you talking about?" I say with a laugh, assuming he's joking.

"You won't be coming here. It's over, Audrey."

"Over?" I laugh again, but his serious tone is concerning me. "Steven, stop this. You know I don't like games."

"I'm not playing games. I know what you did. And I never want to see you again."

"Steven," I say, my heart pounding. "What in the world are you talking about?"

"I thought I knew you, Audrey. All those years we were friends, I never once imagined you were capable of this. To think I was planning a future with you... it makes me sick to my stomach. I've never been so wrong about someone."

"Steven, I don't know what's going on, but I didn't—"

A loud knock on the door stops me.

"Audrey Lancaster?" a man says. "Can you open the door? It's Detective Myles. I need to speak to you."

Detective Myles? What does he want? I've already told him all about Hannah and how it didn't surprise me at all that she tried to kill Lauren. I have nothing else to say, and I shouldn't need to. The police have all the evidence they need to prove Hannah did it.

"Goodbye, Audrey," Steven says.

I look down at the phone and see he ended the call.

There's another knock on the door. "Ms. Lancaster, we know you're in there. Please open the door."

I walk over to it and open it. Detective Myles is standing there, a serious look on his face.

"Hello, again," I say, smiling at him. "How can I help you?"

My smile drops when I see the police officer behind him, holding a pair of handcuffs.

"Audrey Lancaster, you are under arrest for the murder of David Jenson and the attempted murder of Lauren Bishop."

47

LAUREN

When Detective Myles came into my room yesterday to tell me they'd made an arrest, I was certain it was Steven. I'd already told him Steven did this to me when Detective Myles questioned me the first time. I assumed he took that information, found whatever evidence was needed for an arrest, and that Steven was now in jail.

It had to be Steven who did this. He wanted out of the marriage, but didn't want to divorce me and part with his precious money. So he tried to kill me. Besides that, on almost every true crime podcast I listen to, it's always the husband or boyfriend behind the murder, or attempted murder in my case. Sometimes it's the mistress, and yes, Hannah had motive to get rid of me so she could take my place, but I know her and I know she wouldn't do it, at least not intentionally. I assumed Steven set her up, filling that bottle with toxic pills, knowing she'd give them to me and be blamed for it.

"Is Steven in jail?" I asked Detective Myles when he told me they'd made an arrest. "Or is he out on bail?"

I couldn't imagine Steven staying in jail for one second longer than he had to. I pictured him sitting on our Italian leather couch, sipping expensive bourbon, while contemplating how to get out of the mess he'd created.

"Mrs. Bishop," Detective Myles said, "Your husband wasn't who we arrested."

"Then who was it? Hannah?"

"We had her in custody, but we released her. She was only in jail a few hours when the new evidence came in."

"What new evidence?"

"Your husband provided us with a recording from the camera in your room."

"There wasn't a camera in my room."

"There was. Your husband placed it there to make sure you were getting proper care from your nurse. He said he wasn't involved in the hiring process and was concerned that Hannah wasn't vetted by a home health care agency like the ones he encouraged you to use."

That's just like Steven to pretend to care about me and convince others that it's true. Concern about my care is not why he put a camera up, so what's the real reason? Did he do it because I had Audrey put that camera in his room to catch him cheating? Was that his way of telling me he knew about it? I'm sure he found it, along with the other ones in the house.

"So what was on the camera?" I ask.

"We saw someone switch out the pills before Hannah got home."

"I don't understand. That's not possible. The doors were locked. Only Steven and Hannah have a key, and if you didn't arrest them, then—" I stop as I remember the other person who has a key to the house. But there's no way it could be her. It's not possible.

"We arrested Audrey Lancaster," Detective Myles says.

My heart sinks. I feel sick to my stomach. Lightheaded. Like I can't breathe.

It can't be Audrey. She's my best friend. She worries about

me like an overprotective mother. She'd never hurt me. Never in a million years.

"That can't be right," I say, my voice shaking. "Audrey's my best friend. We've been friends since college."

Detective Myles sighs. "I understand this comes as quite a shock, but sometimes the people closest to us are the ones we can't trust. The video clearly shows her switching out the pills."

"There must be some mistake. Maybe the woman you saw was someone else."

"There was no sign of forced entry. The woman who entered your house had a key. Your husband told us only you, him, Hannah, and Ms. Lancaster have a key to your house. Is that correct?"

"Yes, but—it can't be true. It just can't be." I'm feeling dizzy. I rest my head on the stack of pillows behind me and close my eyes as I take a deep breath.

"Mrs. Bishop, are you okay?" I hear the detective ask. "Would you like me to get a nurse?"

"No." I open my eyes and look at him. "Why did she do it? Did she say?"

"She's still denying she had any involvement, but the evidence is there on the recording. The evidence in the other case is less clear, but that'll be up for the courts to decide."

"What other case?"

"Ms. Lancaster is believed to be involved in the car crash that killed David Jenson and resulted in you being injured."

I shake my head, not wanting to believe what he's saying is true. "No. Audrey had nothing to do with that. She couldn't have."

"We believe she intentionally tampered with the brakes to cause the crash."

"How?" I look at the detective. "How do you know this?"

"A local mechanic came forward and described how Audrey

had come into his garage a few days before the accident, asking what would cause brakes to go out. She told him she was asking out of concern for her own safety. He offered to change her brake fluid and she insisted on watching him do it. Later that day, the owner of the hardware store in town confirmed that Audrey had bought a siphon there. We believe she used it to siphon the brake fluid out of Mr. Jenson's car sometime before the crash. We wouldn't have even suspected that if it weren't for the mechanic coming forward with the information about Ms. Lancaster."

"Why is this coming out now? The crash was over a month ago. Why did this man wait so long to tell the police?"

"He and Ms. Lancaster had a brief relationship. He didn't want to believe she was involved in causing the crash. But when she offered him money, which she claimed was to help him stay in business, he knew she was paying him to keep quiet. As of now, we can't prove Ms. Lancaster tampered with the brakes but it certainly seems possible given the evidence."

"I... I can't believe this. Why? Why would she do this?"

"Ms. Bishop, were you aware that Ms. Lancaster had been staying at a hotel suite downtown Boston?"

"Well, yes, she had to get a hotel because her ex-husband took their house in the divorce."

"She'd been booking that hotel suite on and off for years."

"What are you saying? Are you telling me she was having an affair?"

"We believe so. We looked at the camera footage from the hotel and, well..." He looks down, then to the side.

I'm about to ask him to finish his thought, but then it hits me. It's Steven. He was at the hotel with Audrey. They were having an affair.

"I understand," I say, swallowing past the lump in my throat. "It makes sense now. Why Audrey did this."

"We can't prove anything," Detective Myles says, as if that

makes this any better. "All I'm saying is the two of them were seen together many times at that hotel."

"Detective Myles, if we're done here, I'd like to be alone."

He nods. "Of course. If you have any questions or any information to share, just give me a call." He turns and walks out of my room.

Audrey did this. She's the reason I'm in the hospital. The reason I almost died. Twice. She betrayed me. Made me think she was the only person I could trust, the only person who truly cared about me. But the whole time, she was plotting against me.

There's a knock on the door, then it opens and Steven walks in. He's wearing a suit and looking handsome as ever.

"Hello, sweetheart," he says. "I have some news to share."

He never calls me sweetheart without other people around to witness it. He's only doing it now to make me forgive him for being with Audrey, a dirty little secret he can no longer hide.

"I already know," I tell him, sitting up more. I wait until he's beside me, then I look him in the eye. "I know about you and Audrey. I know you don't love me. And I know you never did."

"Lauren, how could you say that? Of course I love you." He reaches for my hand, but I pull it away.

"I'm giving you what you want, Steven. You wanted a way out of this marriage and I'm giving it to you. But I'm not doing it for you. I'm doing it for me. I want my life back. I want to be happy again. I want to know what it feels like to be with a man who truly loves me and values me... the way David did."

Steven huffs. "You're finally admitting you were in a relationship with him?"

"I'm not going to discuss this. There's no reason to. It's over, Steven. I want a divorce."

48

ONE YEAR LATER

LAUREN

The sun warms my skin as I walk out of the yoga studio on Santa Monica Boulevard, heading to the smoothie bar down the street.

It's my daily routine. Wake up, go to yoga class, get a smoothie, then sit on the deck of my apartment, gazing out at the ocean. What I do after that depends on the day. I might stroll through the farmer's market, take a leisurely walk through the park, or just sit outside and read.

My life is simple and maybe a tad boring, but I'd rather have that than what I left behind. I'm no longer spending my days searching for just the right outfit to please Steven and impress the people in our social circle. I'm no longer spending my nights waiting for my husband to come home, wondering if he's really working late or if he's out with another woman. I'm no longer worrying about what tomorrow will bring because after two close encounters with death, I've learned that tomorrow may not come. It's best to just enjoy today.

I moved to California six months ago, after my leg was healed enough for me to get around. It's still not completely back to normal, but I'm building strength in it with my daily walks and morning yoga.

I live in a small, one-bedroom apartment that looks out at the beach. I'm renting for now. I'm not sure if I'll stay here or go somewhere else, but I know I'm not going back to Boston, or anywhere on the East Coast. I wanted a new life, which meant being far away from my old one.

"I'll have the açaí, pineapple power fusion," I say to the girl behind the counter at the smoothie bar.

"Mixing it up today?" she says, knowing I usually order the strawberry-banana smoothie.

"I thought I'd try something different." I pay her for the drink, then go sit at a table. I get out my phone and open the photos app. I smile as I look at a photo of David and me. All my photos are of him or me or the two of us. I deleted the ones with Audrey and Steven.

Audrey is now in prison for trying to kill me with those pills and for her role in causing the crash that killed David. More evidence was found to link her to the crash, but I don't know what it was. I decided not to follow all the news stories about the case or the trial. Knowing what Audrey did was bad enough. I didn't need details of how she betrayed me.

As for Steven, I made the divorce as simple as possible for him. I didn't fight him on a single thing. All I wanted was my freedom. The money didn't matter anymore, but I still ended up a very wealthy woman, even without getting a share of Steven's premarital assets. The prenup remained in place since I couldn't actually prove that Steven cheated. A video showing him at the same hotel as Audrey wasn't enough to prove he did anything with her. I could've been angry about that, but I chose to let it go. I didn't need the extra money. What I received from the divorce settlement was more than enough for my new, much simpler life.

I gave Steven the house in Boston and the one in Maine. I didn't want either of them. There were too many bad memories. I didn't even want the furniture. I wanted nothing that would remind me of that life. The only part of the past that I wanted to remember was David, which is why I still have photos of him on my phone.

"Mind if I join you?" a woman asks, standing next to my table. She's tall and thin with long dark hair and has a yoga mat slung over her shoulder.

"I'm not staying," I tell her, putting my phone away. "I'm just waiting for my drink. You can have the table."

She points to my yoga mat, which is sitting on the chair next to me. "Do you go to the place down the street?"

"Yes. I just left there."

She smiles. "You must be an early riser. I can't make it there before ten."

"Order for Lauren," the girl behind the counter says.

"That's me." I get up and go to the counter to get my drink. I return to the table and grab my yoga mat, slinging it over my shoulder. "Have a good class," I tell the woman who's now sitting at my table.

"You sure you can't join me? Class isn't for 30 minutes."

If I hadn't been through hell and back with Audrey, I'd tell her yes, I'd love to stay and chat. Since moving to California, I haven't made a single friend. This woman is close to my age and seems very nice. But I don't trust her. I don't trust anyone anymore.

Maybe someday, after more time has passed, I'll be able to accept an invite to sit down with a stranger and be open to that stranger becoming a friend. But not now. It's too soon.

"I'm sorry, but I need to run," I tell her.

"Oh," she says, sounding disappointed. "Well, maybe I'll see you here again, when you have more time."

"Yeah, maybe."

I turn to leave, then hear her talking.

"Lauren, right?"

I turn back. "Yeah."

She smiles at me. "I'm Audrey."

You've got to be kidding me.

"Audrey," I say, feeling sick to my stomach. "Got it."

Sorry Audrey, but we will definitely not be friends.

I hurry out of there, then get out my phone to find a new smoothie shop.

I won't be going back there again.

49

HANNAH

"What do you think?" the apartment manager asks.

"It's great!" I say. "I'll take it."

"Let's go to the office and fill out the paperwork."

My new apartment is in Naples, Florida. I've been living in Sarasota the past few months and working at a clothing store, but I got a job in Naples that pays more. I'll be assisting an elderly woman in her home. It's not a nursing job. I'll just be cleaning the lady's house, making her meals, and driving her around since her eyesight's too bad for her to drive. The lady has a lot of health issues so when she found out I'd been a nurse, she hired me on the spot.

She was so thrilled that I took the job that she didn't bother doing a background check or even a quick internet search. If she had, she would've seen the articles online about my arrest for trying to poison the lady I worked for in Maine. The police let me go, admitting the arrest was a mistake, but still, having those articles online hasn't made it easy to get a job.

Luckily, I had enough money to cover my expenses when I wasn't working. I was even able to buy a better car. The money I made working for the Bishops ran out soon after I moved back to Boston. Almost all of it went to pay for my new apartment. I had no idea how I was going to pay for food and other expenses.

Then a package arrived in the mail. I opened it up and inside was a diamond necklace and several pairs of diamond earrings. They reminded me of the ones I'd seen at Lauren's house. She had so many beautiful pieces of jewelry. I couldn't imagine how she could ever wear them all.

The package had no return address so I had no idea who sent it. Who would send me jewelry? Was it real? It couldn't be. That many diamonds would be worth thousands of dollars.

For a moment, I thought Steven might have sent them. I still had feelings for him, even though he hadn't spoken to me since he fired me. It happened the day I was arrested. When the cops let me go, I didn't have my car. I had no way to get home. Steven showed up and drove me back to his house. He said nothing on the way there. I asked him questions, first about Lauren, then about us, but he wouldn't answer me. He wouldn't say one word.

We got back to the house and he finally spoke. He told me to pack up my things and leave, that my services were no longer needed. He acted as though nothing had ever happened between us, like we'd never even shared a kiss.

I was furious, but also hurt. Steven and I had a relationship. I'd spent night after night in his bed. I took care of his house, ran his errands, made his favorite meals. He told me he wanted a future with me. He said I was like no woman he'd ever met and that his feelings for me were deeper than what he'd ever felt for Lauren.

How could he say all that and then just tell me to leave? Did he think I really did try to kill Lauren? Even after the police told him I didn't?

I tried to talk to him, but he wouldn't listen. He told me to be gone in an hour, then went into his office and shut the door.

Twenty minutes later, I'd packed up my room and took everything to my car. Then, right before I left, Steven appeared again. He came out to the driveway and ordered me to give him my key to the house. I did, and then he told me to never contact him or Lauren again.

Driving off, I was heartbroken. Tears were streaming down my face. I'd not only lost my job, but also the man I loved. How could he just toss me aside like that?

Flashback to the day I got the package. I felt a glimmer of hope that Steven had changed his mind about us and wanted me back. Thinking about it now, I was stupid to want him back. He's a horrible human being who used me, then threw me out on the street. But back then, I still wanted him. I was willing to forgive him.

Turns out the package wasn't from him. It was from Lauren. She called me later that day and told me to take the jewelry, sell it, and use the money to start a new life. She said she couldn't send me a check or Steven might find out, given that they were still married at the time. She didn't want him knowing she'd helped me.

I was shocked. I didn't think I'd ever hear from Lauren again. I assumed she'd think I really did try to kill her but that the cops just couldn't prove it. I'd heard the news about Audrey and how there was a video showing her switching out the pills, but I assumed Lauren thought I was in on the plan. But she didn't. When she called, she was really nice. She even apologized for all that had happened.

We didn't talk long. It was probably only a few minutes. After explaining why she sent me the package, she gave me the name of a store in Boston that would give me the best price for the jewelry, then wished me luck and that was it. I haven't heard from her since.

"I think that's it," the apartment manager says as I sign the last page of the lease. She's not much older than me and really tan. She must spend hours a day at the beach.

There's a knock on the office door, which is open. I look back and see a man in a dark gray suit with jet black hair and tan skin. He's probably close to 40 and very good looking.

"Andrew." The apartment manager pops up from her chair. "I was just finishing up." She hurries over to him, her eyes lit up, a huge grin on her face. "I just need a couple more minutes."

"Of course," he says, his arm going around her as he leans down to give her a kiss. "I'll wait outside."

She watches him leave, then races behind her desk. "Okay, so here's your copy of everything." She stuffs the paperwork in a folder and shoves it at me. "When you're back next week to move in, just come here to the office and I'll give you your keys."

"Great!" I get up from the chair and watch as she hurries to shut her computer down. "So was that your boyfriend?"

"Yes." She glances at me, that huge grin appearing again. "Isn't he gorgeous?"

"How old is he?"

"Forty, but he doesn't look it. When I met him, I thought he was maybe 34 or 35." She's done at the computer and walks over to me, still grinning. "He's rich. He's always buying me things. Like this." She holds out the chain around her neck, showing me the large diamond pendant hanging from it. "Isn't it beautiful? And it's real! It's the first real diamond I've ever owned. Andrew is so sweet and generous."

I got a bad feeling from that guy. It was the same feeling I got when I first met Steven, but at the time I mistook that feeling for attraction.

"It's hard to believe a guy like that is single," I say as we leave her office.

"Oh, he's not," she whispers as she closes and locks the door. "But he's getting divorced, or he will be."

He's never getting divorced. He probably has a beautiful wife like Lauren who's sitting alone in her beautiful home, wearing her beautiful clothes, thinking her husband is at the office right now, making money to pay for all her beautiful things. But instead, he's taking his very young mistress to lunch, or more likely, to a fancy hotel.

I've been there, done that, and just like this girl, I imagined a future with a man like Andrew. I could warn her about what's to come, but she wouldn't believe me. I was the same way. I was convinced Steven loved me, just like she's convinced Andrew loves her.

"Have a nice lunch!" I tell her.

"Thanks!" She races out of the building and gets into a shiny silver Mercedes.

She's making a huge mistake, but there's nothing I can do about it. All I can do is look out for myself and make sure I never again fall for a man like Steven.

50

STEVEN

I love women. I don't mean in a romantic sense. I mean I love how reactive they are. I love how they let their emotions get the best of them. I love how they so easily believe words that have no truth behind them. And most of all, I love how they allow themselves to be played against each other.

Let's start with Lauren. I never loved her, but she looked exactly like the wife I imagined having when I was starting out and establishing myself and my career. I even had a picture of a girl who looked just like her in my goals file. It's an expandable file where I keep detailed descriptions of my goals for various parts of my life. When I saw Lauren, she was immediately on my list as a possible wife. Then when David told me how much he wanted her for himself, that was it. I had to have her.

I've always been competitive with David. Even though I was better than him in many ways, it bothered me that people liked him better than me, especially women. So when he told me how much he wanted Lauren, I was determined to take her for myself. It was an easy win. She found me handsome and charming and she liked that I had money and freely spent it on her. David told me Lauren grew up in an unstable household with a mother who went from man to man, giving herself to whatever man had the most money and was willing to spend it on her.

Looking back, Lauren was the perfect starter wife. Her mother had taught her that money equated to happiness, so as her husband, simply providing her with money was all I had to do. I'd given her happiness through money, so if she wasn't happy, that was her own fault, not mine. It relieved me from having to do things normally expected in a relationship, like listening to her drone on about mundane things or showering her with affection. But I made sure to do those things in public so other women would see how wonderful I was and tell Lauren, reinforcing that her unhappiness was her own fault, not mine.

For most of our marriage, Lauren was willing to sacrifice her own needs and wants for mine, another characteristic of a good starter wife. She was desperate to please me and would do most anything I asked. She wanted to help me achieve my dreams, even if it meant ignoring her own. She knew my success would lead to me making more money, money she could spend to buy more things, things she hoped would make her happy.

I'm the primary reason for my success, but I must admit Lauren did help me achieve more than if I'd been single. She took care of the house, ran my errands, made my meals—all things that would've taken time away from my career if I'd had to do them myself. And she filled our social calendar with various events so I was always out meeting people, many of whom became clients.

Lauren was truly an asset in the early days of our marriage, but as with many assets, she became less valuable over time. As my success grew, my goals changed, including my goals for a wife. Lauren was no longer useful to me. She had no ambition or drive. Her social skills were waning. At a time when I was rising in my career, networking with men who had wives who were equally successful as them, Lauren was making me look bad. All she did was shop and meet her friends for lunch. When I took her to events with my colleagues and their wives, Lauren had nothing interesting to say. She was beautiful to look at, but there was nothing behind the beauty. She was an embarrassment. We were no longer a good match.

I had to get rid of her. But I didn't want her getting my money.

That's where Audrey comes in. Audrey has had her eyes on me since college. We met freshman year. She had class with David and would come over to our dorm room, hoping I'd be there. When I was, I ignored her. With her dark hair and curvy body, she wasn't my type. She looked nothing like the picture in my goals folder.

But what I liked about Audrey was her persistence. She kept trying to get me to notice her, and when I didn't, she took matters into her own hands and asked me out. We were sophomores by then, and I'd already met Lauren and decided she'd be my wife, leaving poor Audrey to find someone else.

But Audrey's obsession with me didn't end. Even when she married Barry, she still wanted me. Whenever the four of us would go out for dinner, Audrey would try to sit next to me. She'd lean in close when she'd talk and brush her leg against mine under the table. And when no one was looking, she'd give me a smile that said she was mine if I wanted her.

I took her up on the offer when I decided Lauren needed to go. My affair with Audrey moved quickly, which is what I had planned. I needed her to believe I'd wanted her all along. I even told her I married the wrong woman. That it should have been her, not Lauren. Audrey devoured my words, the very words she wanted to hear. But they weren't enough. She was hungry for more, so I fed her with words like 'I love you' and 'you're mine'. I made promises I never planned to keep. I complained about Lauren, told Audrey how unhappy I was in my marriage and how I needed a way out.

It was all just words, but the right words said to the right person at the right time can be very powerful. I could see the wheels in Audrey's twisted mind turning, scheming a plan to get rid of the dear friend she secretly couldn't stand.

It was during this time that I learned about David and Lauren. I was furious. I wanted to kill David with my bare hands. But I knew better. The whole point of my plan was to keep myself out of it. Instead of doing the dirty work myself, I orchestrated others to do it for me, with Audrey playing the starring role.

When I told Audrey about David and Lauren, I made it clear that I couldn't let David win. I'd have to stay married to Lauren just to make sure David couldn't have her.

Audrey wouldn't hear of it. She'd finally gotten her hooks into me and wasn't letting go. She wanted me to divorce Lauren, but the only way I'd do it was if David was no longer an issue. She had to get rid of him.

She didn't tell me she tampered with David's car, but I assumed she did. David was an excellent driver. It made no sense for him to just drive off the road. When Audrey and I talked about the crash, she never even hinted at her involvement. Perhaps she thought I'd think less of her for going to such extreme measures, which just goes to show how much she wanted my approval. I used that to my advantage, showering her with attention when she pleased me and ignoring her when she didn't. This system of punishment and reward kept her clamoring to find new ways to please me. She knew getting Lauren out of my life would please me, but her attempt to do that failed. She'd have to try again.

In the meantime, Hannah came into our lives. At first, I

wasn't sure how I would use her. I needed to know how loyal she was to Lauren so I tested her. I gave her attention, complimented her, touched her shoulder, her arm, her back. It was all perfectly innocent, but she assumed I was flirting with her. And she liked it. She wanted more. And when I gave her more, she didn't tell Lauren. The first night I was with Hannah, I purposely remained downstairs to see if Hannah would be with me when Lauren was just steps away. She hesitated at first, but then went along with it, and she wasn't quiet. It's almost as if she didn't care if Lauren heard us.

It's then that I knew Hannah's loyalty was to me, not Lauren. I watched her around Lauren. I saw the jealousy in her eyes. Hannah wanted this life. The life Lauren had. So I told her she could have it. I led Hannah to believe we could have a future, just like I did with Audrey. Hannah became my backup plan. If Audrey couldn't get rid of Lauren, I could get Hannah to do it. I just had to keep telling her the words she wanted to hear, making promises for the future. A future that would only happen if Lauren weren't around.

It's almost comical that Lauren hired a girl who would so easily turn against her. Lauren thought she was so clever hiring Hannah, as if I wouldn't know why she chose her. But it was painfully obvious. Inviting a beautiful young woman to live at our house, her bedroom just steps away from mine? Lauren was setting me up to be unfaithful and hoping to catch me in the act, nullifying our prenup so she'd get half of my premarital assets. She was right about me being unfaithful, but she never caught me. I saw the cameras Audrey put around the house and immediately took them down. I was a little disturbed that Audrey didn't tell me she'd done it, but perhaps she wanted to see for herself if I was doing things with Hannah or if Lauren was simply imagining it. Or maybe the cameras were never turned on. Either way, Audrey should've told me about them.

After discovering the cameras, I got an idea. I decided to

put one of them in Lauren's room so I could watch my three favorite ladies interact. I did it for entertainment. I never dreamed the camera would catch Audrey trying to kill Lauren.

Sometimes it's hard to believe my good fortune. The whole thing couldn't have worked out better. I'd been trying to come up with a way to get Audrey out of my life when all this was over, but I wasn't sure how to do it. My goal was to have the police find out what she'd done to David's car, but I had no way to prove it. I decided I'd have to wait for her next attempt to kill Lauren and try to catch her somehow. But then, like a gift being dropped in my lap, that camera I put up caught Audrey switching out Lauren's pills. It was exactly what I needed. Audrey was charged with the crime while I played the role of a concerned husband looking out for his wife, who unexpectedly caught her best friend trying to kill her.

Unfortunately, my plan didn't end the way I wanted. Lauren was still alive, but after all that she'd been through, she was desperate to get me out of her life. She didn't argue about a single thing during the divorce and left the prenup alone, even though she knew I'd been unfaithful for our entire marriage. Audrey and Hannah were just some of the women I'd enjoyed over the years. There were many more.

That brings us to today. Since ending my marriage, I sold the house in Maine and the one here in Boston and purchased a penthouse apartment overlooking the city. I've spent the last year building my investment firm and obtaining new clients. I'm projected to earn thirty percent more this year than last, which far exceeds my goal.

Despite my long hours at work, I've still managed to maintain a social life, going to charity events, art exhibits, dinner parties. I have my assistant coordinate my social calendar since I no longer have a wife to do it. She finds the events for me, then I pick and choose what I'll attend based on what will benefit me the most, specifically who will be there and if they're of any use to me. I've met many beautiful women at these events, but unfortunately, none of them fit the profile.

"Good evening," the bartender says as I take a seat at the bar. I'm at the hotel down the street from my office, the same hotel Audrey and I went to for our private meet-ups. It's been a long day and I need a drink before heading home.

"Your best bourbon," I say to the bartender. "Neat."

He takes a bottle from the top shelf. "Just so you know, this costs—"

"I don't care what it costs. I'll take it."

He nods and goes to pour the drink.

"A man who knows what he wants," a woman says, sitting beside me.

I look over at her, noticing her dark brown hair, how it just barely brushes her shoulders, the way it's parted on the side. I notice her olive-toned skin, her deep brown eyes, thick eyelashes, and the matte red color on her lips. It matches her dress, a form-fitting wrap dress that clings to her slim waistline and ample chest.

"Steven Bishop," I say, turning toward the woman.

"Sloane Kaswell." She glances at me, then looks at the bartender as he sets down my drink. "I'll have the same."

"Are you sure? It's our most expensive bourbon. It's—"

"I said I'll have the same," she says, cutting him off. She glances at me. "And put his on my tab."

The bartender takes off to get her drink.

"I'm more than capable of paying for my own drink," I say to the woman.

"Maybe I wanted you to owe me," she says, checking her reflection in the mirror behind the bar. She sits up straighter and adjusts the scarf around her neck. I love scarves. Lauren never wore them but Audrey did. We used them in the bedroom, in many different ways. I will say that's one thing I miss about Audrey. She didn't hold back in the bedroom.

"I could think of many ways in which I could repay you," I say. "But perhaps we should start with dinner."

She smiles at that and turns to face me. Her eyes drop down to my suit, like she's assessing my worth, but I don't think it's because she's interested in my money. From the designer dress she's wearing, her very expensive handbag, the way she carries herself, and her offer to pay for my drink, she clearly has enough money of her own.

I smile to myself, wondering how I possibly got this lucky. And to think I almost didn't stop here tonight.

"If I agree to dinner," she says. "I pick the place."

"Of course. Whatever you'd like." As she sips her bourbon, I notice the watch on her wrist. It's a very expensive watch and hard to find in the States. She must travel overseas. "I'm curious what you do. From your excellent taste in clothes, I'm going to guess something in fashion?"

"That's very perceptive." She sets her drink down. "I own a line of women's formal wear. I started the business five years ago and it's taken off better than I ever imagined."

My mind goes to my checklist, the one in my goals folder. Under personal goals, I have a folder marked 'second wife' and in it I have a list of attributes.

Successful entrepreneur. Dresses well. Confident enough to talk to a stranger. Able to carry on an engaging conversation. Intriguing. A challenge.

So far, so good.

I imagine the picture I printed out and added to the file. The woman has dark, shoulder-length hair, parted on the side. She has brown eyes, thick dark lashes, and wears red lipstick with no shine. Shiny lips look cheap to me. I prefer a matte finish.

"You got quiet," Sloane says. "Was it something I said?"

And there it is, the cherry on top. She's a successful woman, but still has a hint of insecurity, which is all I need to make her mine to play with. A pawn in my game. It's been all work and no play for nearly a year now. It's time to play again.

"Not at all," I tell her. "In fact, you're perfect." I smile at her. "Absolutely perfect."

56896336R00189